Wicked Transcendence

Pandora Bluett

Copyright © 2021 Cheyenne Bluett

All rights reserved. No part of this publication may be reproduced, stored in a retrieval system, or transmitted, in any form or in any means – by electronic, mechanical, photocopying, recording or otherwise – without prior written permission, except as permitted by U.S. copyright law.

ISBN-13: 978-1-7358649-2-1

Dedication

To twelve-year-old Pandora, who came up with this story idea and waited till she was twenty-one to actually write it. You did it, baby! You are a published author!

To my fellow writers. You have a story that you need to tell. Don't let fear stop you from writing and publishing that idea that is stuck inside your head. I believe in you!

Content Warning

Wicked Transcendence has a few scenes that may be sensitive to some readers. Please note that this book has a scene with a suicide ideation, but no actual attempt is done. There is also a chapter that talks about a character that had been raped in the past.

As much as I would love you to keep reading, please take care of yourself first.

Chapter I

If I knew my afterlife would've been this bad, I wouldn't've pulled the trigger so quickly, Damon Jones thinks as he walks up to a small townhouse on the skirts of Chicago. He knocks on the redwood door. The neighborhood is quiet—peaceful. Hidden away from the busy city just a few short miles up the road. The sun bears down on him and sweat prickles his brow. After a few moments of silence, he knocks again. Nothing. No footsteps behind the door.

He sighs and rolls his eyes to the sky. *Not today.*

Without a second thought, he takes a step forward, and when his foot connects with the ground again, he is standing in the house's living room, thankful for teleportation—one gift he was awarded when promoted.

"Missy?" he calls through the house, annoyance seeping through the word. She knew he was coming this morning—it was her idea.

A sound comes from the kitchen, and he pivots that way. When he walks into the yellow-painted kitchen, Missy is in a fighting stance behind the tall kitchen island, a frying pan grasped in her hands. It looks large and out of place next to her petite frame.

"I didn't invite you in," she spits through gritted teeth.

Damon chuckles and rolls his eyes. "I'm not a vampire."

"I know. You're worse."

He shrugs, walking to the kitchen table and dragging out a chair. The chair squeaks as his heavy body settles in. "What's wrong? I figured you invited me to come by because you were planning to apologize. Not be even madder."

Her chocolate brown eyes narrow at him, not amused. She is trying to appear scary, but it isn't taking. With her slender face, big eyes, and copper ringlets cascading down her neck, she is cute more than anything.

He raises his eyebrows, waiting.

The clock on the wall ticks as they stare at each other in silence. Finally, Missy looks away and sets down the pan with a clank. She doesn't move closer, however. "I'm just pissed off."

"Well, I gathered that." He snorts, but his voice softens. "What's going on?"

She looks down at her purple fingernails. "I originally wanted to apologize for last night," she admits, "then I remembered the entire conversation, which pissed me off all over again."

"Ah," Damon says. "I'm sorry for upsetting you so much."

Her head snaps up. "You didn't think I'd be upset?"

"Well, I thought you would, a little. Not enough to forbid me from your home."

"It didn't work anyway," she mutters.

He doesn't retort—it won't help the situation. Instead, Damon leans forward in his chair, resting his elbows on his knees. "Do you want to talk about it?"

"I mean, not really. The whole situation is pretty fucked up."

Damon's mouth forms in a tight line, and he nods in agreement.

She sighs and comes around the island to the small table where Damon sits. When she pulls out the chair, the feet scrape across the ground. "I don't know what to make of it. The Devil wants me to be his wife? High school didn't prepare me for this."

That comment makes Damon's stomach tighten. Missy is in college—only a few years younger than he. He doesn't want to think about an ageless god picking basically a baby to wed.

Before he can say anything, she continues. "Sure, marrying The Devil and becoming a semi-powerful goddess that rules the underworld with him doesn't seem so bad. You had me at that part. But then the whole, *You have to sacrifice yourself on Halloween night using a sacrificial knife that was forged in the fiery pits of Hell*," she mimics in his deep voice, "really rubbed me the wrong way."

He nods again. "I'm not here to pressure you. Ultimately, it is your choice. I'm just here to be a friend through it all."

Now it's she who snorts. "Friend—guide—convincer, same thing."

Damon picks at his nails, his face emotionless. "You

still have two months to decide. Think it over. Death isn't as scary as you think it is." *It's quick—painless ... the actual pain is living afterwards, being forced to do a job you hate.* He grimaces.

She doesn't answer for a while. They listen to a sparrow singing outside the window. "I'll think about it," she finally says, meeting his gaze.

Damon reaches over to touch her hand but doesn't linger for long. "Good."

Missy's stomach grumbles, and she stands, turning around and heading for the fridge. "Would you like to stay for lunch?"

"As long as that frying pan doesn't leave that stove," Damon jokes. She sets down a carton of eggs and bread and laughs.

Chapter 2

Damon lights another cigarette as he waits for Chloe. An ashtray full of cigarette butts sits on the coffee table in front of him. Music blares from his television, but he isn't paying attention to anything but his own thoughts.

The first Monday of every month, The Devil holds a meeting for all his demons where he passes out new assignments, checks on long-term missions, and makes them sweat. Damon Jones has been a demon going on two years now. He died when he was 23 and thought he was good enough on Earth to end up in a better place—Heaven, Nirvana, whatever they call it—but he sadly missed the mark and went down.

After he arrived, The Devil himself called him into his office and offered him a job he would've been an idiot to refuse—become a demon and get to do whatever he wanted as long as he did his job. Damon hated the whole idea of being a demon and what they did, but he couldn't pass up the opportunity to leave Hell and roam Earth, living another life when he was off the clock. Plus, when he thought of the other option—burning in literal flames for the rest of his life—he reminded himself to suck it up. It could've been so much worse.

People in their actual lives did things they didn't enjoy—and so did people in the afterlife.

Now, in the present, Damon racks his brain, planning what he will say when he updates The Boss on the mission he was given a month ago. Halloween is quickly approaching, and if he doesn't convince Missy to do what he needs … it won't end well for him. He shudders when he thinks about failing and the consequences.

I have plenty of time, he reassures himself, although anxiety rocks him. He was always fine and confident until The Devil was staring him down. He sucks out the rest of his cigarette and shoves the butt in the ashtray, tempted to light another.

Suddenly the door swings open, and Chloe appears in the doorway. Her beautiful ebony skin glistens like silk as she walks into the room. Chloe is the most beautiful demoness out of the entire group, and she knows it. Her perfect hourglass body makes even the most famous models envy her, and she loves to make them hate her. She loves to change up her hairstyles, and today, it is up in a deep red ponytail, slicked back and straightened down to her waist. Red is her favorite color because of its power, and she knows it radiates off her. Besides being the prettiest, she is the most ruthless and evil—she was born to become a demon.

"Hello, handsome." She winks at Damon.

He grins at her. "Chloe. You're early."

She responds by straddling his lap and crushing her lips to his. Damon kisses her back for a few moments but then pushes her back, his eyebrows raised. "What was that for?"

"I just missed you," she replies innocently, curling a finger through a strand of raven hair at the base of his neck. "How was your night? I noticed you didn't come home."

That's why she kissed me like that, Damon realizes. "I was just at a friend's house," he says, keeping his whereabouts tight. *Friend, booty call, whatever.*

She sighs, sliding off his lap and whipping out her phone, defeated.

Chloe and Damon have an unconventional relationship. She really wants to be exclusive with him, but he always says no. Romantic relationships aren't something that demons are known for. Damon thinks the whole dating thing is ridiculous—were they going to get married over the fiery chasm where all the humans burned, The Devil officiating it? Would they have little demon babies and train them how to wreak havoc on the world? No, thank you.

Not only that, but they can't ever be totally exclusive because they both have to sleep with humans as part of their duties. The Devil uses Chloe's drop-dead gorgeous body for many missions—Damon not as much, but it's always a possibility. Demons can feel normal human emotions, but most of the time, they have this nagging emptiness inside of them. Like there is always a hole in their heart, a feeling of missing something. No matter how much alcohol they drink, or how many people they kill or sleep with, or how happy they may seem, they are never fully satisfied. So, they cope in many ways—having sex with humans is one of them. Since he can teleport anywhere he wants, whenever he wants, Damon sees thousands upon thousands of gorgeous women from all around the world. He won't give that up to be exclusive with someone who will never totally be exclusive for him.

Chloe really cares about Damon, however, and that is the problem. She immediately took him under her wing when he first arrived. Damon really appreciated that, and they had a budding friendship until one night when they drunkenly slept together. That night started an addiction. The sex they had was nothing like Damon had ever experienced on Earth. It was dark and hot and powerful. They tried stopping it multiple times, reminding each other it wasn't good mixing business with pleasure. Their abstinence from each other didn't last long. Neither did it last the second through sixth times they broke it off. As much as Damon would try to stay away from her, after a few nights, somehow, he always ended up back in her bed.

He knows he is being unfair to her … but he can't help it. He craves the distraction she is always giving him—and she is damn good at doing so.

As if she knew what he was thinking about, Chloe gently sets her phone down on the couch next to her and runs her hand up Damon's thigh, stopping only a few inches away from his waistband.

He refocuses and meets her flirty gaze.

She motions to the bedroom, biting down on her perfectly plump lip. "I came early for a reason …"

Not a good idea, Damon's subconscious warns him.

But after the soft human woman last night, Damon

knows he can use some dark, love-hate sex right about now. "Let's go."

Chloe and Damon meet up with the group of demons right in front of The Boss's towering office building twenty minutes later.

"You two are a little late," Jeremy, the head demon, points out sternly. A group of men behind him snickers, and a few girls roll their eyes.

Chloe straightens the firetruck red midi dress she is wearing. "But we made it." She gives the boys a hard scowl, and they all quickly compose themselves.

Damon says nothing as he takes his place in line by William.

"How are you doing today, my friend?" William grins at him.

"Living the dream." Damon chuckles quietly as the line starts walking inside.

"Some dream, eh?" William shakes his head, ginger curls swaying.

The large group of demons files into the tall, soot-covered, brick building. There are enough windows to see the flames right outside, licking up from deep inside the chasm that surrounds their plateau of land. The building is old and creaky with ten floors, and the demons climb the stairs in silence to the very top level, where The Devil keeps it pristine and perfect, totally different from the rest of the structure. As if it were a penthouse in the heart of the city, not the tenth floor in a run-down, ugly schoolhouse.

Once they are all on the top floor, they wait in the sitting room for The Devil to welcome them in. A ten-foot demon is standing in front of the door to his private office, his arms crossed and glare harder than steel.

"Drake." Jeremy nods to the giant.

"Jeremy." He returns the nod, giving them all a once-over. "Is everyone here?"

"Everyone's here," Jeremy promises.

Drake nods once before knocking three times on the door he is guarding. "You ready, Boss?"

"Yes!" a deep, hair-raising voice booms from inside the door. Drake steps back and opens the door, allowing the demons to step inside.

"Ahh, come in!" The voice booms again as the demons file inside and stand at attention. The voice came from a man standing behind a long glass desk. A human skull, tall stack of envelopes, and expensive bottle of whiskey and glasses are the only objects decorating the glass.

The man flashes an impeccable smile. Bright white and framed between thin lips—teeth that can tear even the toughest metals apart. Sharp, high cheekbones frame his face. His small eyes are cunning, ruthless, and somehow darker than all the demons' eyes combined. Darker than night, darker than the scariest, loneliest part of the mind. His pale skin is stark white against the greased-back black hair that hangs to his shoulders. He wears a black button-down shirt rolled up to his elbows and matching black slacks. Even as he stands there, looking over all the demons in the room, the power radiating off of him is undeniable. He is handsome—terrifyingly handsome in an unnatural, inhumane way. He makes himself look that way so it will lure anyone into him, making them give in to their deepest desires and most disturbing wishes. Behind him, the large, fire-filled chasm is on full display, the blood-curdling screaming echoing throughout the room.

The Devil himself.

"How are we today, everyone?" he asks, placing his hands on the desk, leaning forward ever so slightly.

Jeremy answers for the group because of his position. The head demon answers for all unless a demon is specifically spoken to. "Fine today, sir."

"Wonderful." The Devil grins, striding lazily to the front of his desk. Leaning against the glass, he winks at Chloe. "Wow, Chloe. You are a knockout."

She unfreezes in line to curtsey. "Thank you, sir."

Another reason Damon can't be with Chloe exclusively—she is The Devil's favorite subordinate. They spend a lot of time together outside of work hours, a lot of it back at his mansion. He can never trust her completely because of it.

The Devil nods at a few other demons, saying hello to his favorites, Damon included, and compliments some more females before clasping his hands together. "Are you all ready for your new assignments?"

The demons consent. The Devil motions for Jeremy to pick up the enormous stack of envelopes. Once Jeremy is holding the stack, they turn to the group and read the names one by one. Those who he calls come to grab their folders and bow to The Boss before stepping back in line.

They finally call Damon. He walks up to Jeremy and The Boss.

"Ah, Damon," The Devil says, drawing his name out.

Damon bows low to the ground. "My lord."

"How is the mission with my beloved going?" He cocks his head to the side.

"It's progressing, sir. I've been in contact with her multiple times since you assigned her to me. She is finally opening up to the idea."

"Hm? She hasn't agreed yet?"

Damon straightens even taller. "Well, no, sir. She is still contemplating."

Anger flashes in The Devil's eyes. "I assigned you to this incredibly important mission because I thought you could handle it."

Damon's eyes tint red also. "Sir, it's been three weeks, and we still have two months. You can't expect me or her to just—"

In one quick motion, The Devil grabs Damon's forearm and squeezes tight, his skin burning like fire. "You do not have any right to tell me what I can and can't do, Jones."

Damon grimaces from the pain but tries not to make a sound as the smell of his own burning flesh stings his nostrils. "I didn't mean it like that, sir. I just wanted to remind you that these things take time."

Wrong answer. "I do not need a cocky, undisciplined

demon to tell *me* that. I am your master. You respect me, or I will end your existence. Do I make myself clear?"

The pure evil on The Devil's face makes Damon's stomach pucker in fear. "Yes, sir," he chokes out.

"Can I trust you to see this mission out? Or should I just end your pathetic afterlife now?" An evil grin slides up The Devil's face.

"I promise I will not let you down," Damon says, sweat dripping down his face. His legs are dangerously close to giving out from the pain.

The Devil glowers at him for a few more seconds before finally letting go. The burning subsides as soon as he withdraws his hand, but his handprint is seared into Damon's forearm.

"Good." The Devil motions for Damon's envelope. "Your primary focus is still on Missy, but I need you to handle Ouija duty tomorrow through Thursday."

Damon holds in a groan. Ouija duty is the worst job that demons have. If a human is playing with a Ouija board, it is their job to answer before an angel or wandering spirit does and mark the house for future possessions or missions. It usually only takes five to ten minutes unless the demon is in the mood to mess with the caller. The Devil usually reserves this job for the demons who get on his bad side, so Damon knows that this is his punishment for being disrespectful. Thankful that it isn't worse, he bows and walks away.

While walking back to his place in line, he glances down at his new, semi-permanent tattoo. The burn should heal eventually, but there is more where that came from if he fails.

Chloe shoots him a worried glance, but he ignores her. He resumes the position of attention with the other demons as the rest of the folders are dispersed.

After all the demons are back in line, Jeremy whispers a few things to The Devil before bowing and stepping back into his place.

"Now, get out of here and do not disappoint me," The Devil says and waves them off.

They all file out the door and down the stairs, silently and quickly. Once they are all back outside, Jeremy looks over the group. "Have a good week. Don't forget your weekly paperwork is due Fridays at eight o'clock sharp. Questions or concerns, you know where to find me. See you all next month."

They all nod and disperse. Chloe finds Damon. "Drinks at Gaia's while we read? A bunch of us are going."

"I'll be there," Damon says, shoving his jacket sleeve down to cover his burned arm, ready to drink all his worries away.

Chapter 3

Damon surveys the large room until he finds Chloe at a table in the back with their usual, close-knit circle of friends. She is leaning over the table talking to Ben, her breasts all but spilling out of her shirt. He rolls his eyes and continues walking through Gaia's Bar & Grill, focused on the bar rail and the many beers waiting for him. Gaia's only place on Earth where spiritual beings can lounge without the annoyance of humans interrupting. Even though it sits on Earth, the exact location is hidden from living creatures—people have to be dead and able to teleport to access it.

Teleporting is something that all spiritual beings can do. Damon doesn't know the exact science behind teleporting, besides that he's in one place one moment and then another the next. It comes in handy a lot, and it makes traveling lightning fast.

Gaia's is run by none other than Mother Nature herself. And, of course, she is a hippie. The bar is sixties themed with lava lamps, bright and colorful decorations, and beads everywhere. The staff members are sprites, who have been on the Earth since Mother Nature created it all those years ago. They, too, look human-like, except their skin has a slight green tint to it. Just as the demons all share black eyes, the sprites' eyes are a beautiful shade of peridot green.

Damon once asked if Gaia has always styled the bar like this. A sprite named Clover explained that this was *always* Mother Nature's favorite aesthetic, and she was the one who truly introduced it into the 1960s after thousands of years waiting.

Damon slides onto one of the few open barstools. Nights at the bar are always crowded. He scans behind the bar to see who is working, knowing at least one bartender will be Honey, his best friend.

Sure enough, she is currently pouring a draft beer, her signature infectious smile plastered on her face and her long ashy blonde hair up in pigtails. River is next to her, pouring a round of tequila shots for an excited group of angels.

After she hands the beer over, she scans the rail for the next customer, and her eyes brighten when she notices Damon waving her down. "Damon! How are you, love?" she calls as she walks to him.

He gives her a half-smile. "Same shit, different day."

She reaches across the bar and squeezes his hand, her gold bangles jingling when she moves.

"Draft or bottles tonight?"

"Surprise me."

She winks and then grabs a beer bucket. As she spoons ice into it, Damon admires her. Honey has grown into a good friend of his. Ever since he became a demon and struggled with the transition, she talked him down a lot and adjusted him to everything. She would calm his drunken panic attacks and help him toughen up, though she preferred his sweeter, softer side, which he only showed off to her. He could be his true self around her, not the demon version of him that everyone else saw.

Their friendship is the one thing that keeps him sane, and he is so grateful for that.

He never even considered sleeping with her—she truly is just a fantastic friend. Not that she isn't gorgeous with her big, kind peridot eyes; her amazing personality; or her tiny, toned body that she decorated with the best vintage fashion and body jewelry. Tonight, she is wearing a pair of dark high-waisted jeans and a sunflower yellow cropped halter top—and a lot of other men admire her, too.

She sets the now-full beer bucket down in front of him, the six bottles so packed into the ice that they don't even move. "Here you go!"

"Thank you."

"Oh, shoot. Is it already September?" Honey gasps, noticing the folder tucked under Damon's right armpit. "This summer has just flown by."

"You're telling me," Damon says, popping a bottle cap off his first beer and taking a long drink, the taste of barley lightening his mood instantly.

"How's the Missy thing going?"

He shrugs. "Fine. I finally told her the other day about what she has to do, and she was not thrilled."

"That's a surprise." Honey snorts.

"Yeah, well, the hardest part is over. Now it's just the convincing that I have to finish. I ended up pissing off The Boss at the meeting earlier. Like my new tattoo?"

Damon shoves up his jacket sleeve, and Honey cringes.

"Beautiful. I don't even want to know."

River calls for Honey to help him tray a few drinks. She smiles at Damon before bouncing that way. "Talk later!"

Damon grabs the bucket and his open beer and makes his way for the back table where his friends wait. He uses the term "friends" loosely—coworkers are more like it. The few people he considers his friends are Honey, William, and Chloe … although Chloe is iffy a lot of the time.

"There you are!" William says, grinning and tipping his glass of whiskey towards Damon. The other demons say quick hellos before returning to their conversations.

Damon sits on William's left and sets down the bucket and his folder. The others' folders are already all sprawled and searched through, and Damon can hear Ashley talking about her new operation.

"I've never possessed anyone before. I'm so excited!" she exclaims, slipping a little blue pill into her mouth and chasing it with her vodka. Ashley got into the wrong crowd during her human life and ended up being addicted to pills. She is the only one in the group who sold her soul to The Devil—for the ability to be high forever. That kind of devotion got her promoted to demoness quickly.

"Enjoy it now, because soon enough it gets boring," Felix says with a snort. Damon doesn't know his backstory well enough—Felix started dating Ashley recently. He is a big, burly man with many scars running all up and down his arms—obviously a fighter, a gang member, or worse, in his first life.

She shrugs.

Ben and Chloe occupy the other side of the table, and they are shamelessly flirting in front of everyone else. Ben is a stocky guy with a short buzz cut—a police officer on Earth who ended up killing many people with excessive force before a criminal shot him in the line of duty. He actually enjoys being evil and has admitted multiple times how much he loves being a demon.

William is a curly-headed ginger with a big, toothy grin. He fought in the Irish revolution, and that's where he was murdered. If a stranger met him on the side of the road, they'd just think William was a cool dude with weird eyes—he is the least demon-like out of all of them. To this day, he hasn't disclosed what he did to end up in Hell, but Jeremy says if William admitted it, no one would ever believe him. It was a running joke between the group to guess his crimes, and no one has ever gotten it right. That, or he was just an exceptional liar.

"Cannibalism?" Damon asks William out of the blue.

He laughs, used to the random accusations. "Nope. Although I am hurt that you'd think I was *that* gross."

Damon chuckles and finally opens up his folder, but he already knows mostly what it will say. Missy Lovington's name is highlighted and bullet-pointed through the document, and he skims it quickly.

Damon rolls his eyes and shuts the folder. The mission is ridiculous to him. The Devil has so many women who want to be with him, in the human world and spiritual world, but he has to make things difficult for everyone around him. Once every few years, The Devil falls in love with some random woman he meets in the bar, in the grocery store, wherever, and chooses a random unlucky demon to carry out his dirty work. The Devil came to him and instructed him to get this woman to be his wife, and that was that. If Damon fails and Missy doesn't want to marry him, then his afterlife will be over.

This year, The Devil chose Halloween as the date for this significant sacrifice. So cliché.

Convincing her to marry The Devil isn't the hard part. Convincing her to commit suicide is the real challenge. And she hadn't taken it well when he brought it up.

Then he has to worry about angels trying to stop them—their annoying, mighty selves always trying to squish evil and bring about good. They can really put a damper on this if they find out—but Damon is trying his hardest to keep it on the down-low.

He grimaces and leans back in his chair to rub his temples.

"What's on your mind, ol' chap?" William asks, watching a baseball game on the big TV in front of their table. The television looks out of place next to all the colorful peace signs and bright art decorating the walls. William is the sole reason it is there—he had to argue with Honey about putting it in the bar for years before Mother Nature finally caved.

"The stupid Missy assignment. Why does he need so many wives?"

William chuckles. "Who knows? He needs to share."

"Is it time to retire yet?" Damon grumbles.

"No way, that would be so much worse."

William is right. Demons eventually get the chance to retire their duties and become normal dead humans again. The Devil has a decent place in Hell reserved for all the retirees, and it's not that bad of a place—a little knockoff slice of Heaven—but then you cannot leave Hell ever again. Demons try to stay in their position for as long as they can, but the longevity period is only around two to five hundred years, depending on how good they are at their job, before The Devil forces them to step down. When Damon was promoted, another demon had stepped down, and when the next demon comes into the picture, the cycle will continue. The only exception is Jeremy, who will step down from head demon when he chooses to. He's been in that position for ten thousand years, though, and he doesn't look to be stepping down any time soon.

The night continues on, Damon drinking his beers and watching the baseball game with William. Honey brings him his second bucket by the start of the fourth inning, and he finishes those off even quicker. By the sixth inning, he is happily drunk.

Chloe interrupts his TV time by sitting on his lap. "Baby?" she coos, wrapping her arms around his neck and squishing her chest onto his. "Why don't you take me home?"

Damon rolls his eyes. "After you've been flirting with Ben all night? No thanks."

William snorts.

Chloe shoots William a glare that would make Medusa

proud before turning her attention back on Damon and pouting. "I was just doing that to see if you'd come over. You didn't, so I had to."

"Well, I'm still not taking you home. You're drunk."

She wrinkles her nose. "So are you."

Damon looks over her. She looks good, and they both know it. And he knows that he will go home with her tonight.

He makes a feeble attempt at saying no again, but he is lonely. Just as lonely as she is. "I thought we'd agreed that it's not good mixing business with pleasure?"

She leans in close to him, grazing his ear sensually with her mouth and whispering, "Why does it matter, when we aren't good?"

Chapter 4

Chloe's naked body is pressed against Damon's, her head tucked into his neck. Soft snores are escaping her lips as she sleeps. Damon is wide awake next to her. His drunkenness wore off during their hours-long sex session, and now he lies awake, sober and unable to sleep.

Damon already loathes himself for taking her home again. It'll just come back to haunt him in the long run. Plus, nighttime in his apartment is the only chance he really has to be alone, and he knows that Chloe will linger as much as she can.

Night, after coming home from the bar or some random woman's house, is his favorite time. He loves being alone when he can—away from the other demons, away from his looming duties, the always-plausible ending of his existence if The Devil just felt like getting rid of him. He likes doing hobbies he loved on Earth—painting, listening to music, even reading sometimes to keep his head level. The longer a person is in Hell, the worse they become. He will still have a little, tiny sliver of his real self in his soul, but it will be consumed with selfishness, hate, and wickedness. Damon has a long way to go for that to be the case—William is still a good guy, even after all his time down here—but he can feel his true self slipping away more and more.

As the clock ticks away, Damon's pain resurfaces. He thinks about his new life and how he ended up this way. His heart aches for the man he was in the last few days he was on Earth, and then his heart aches even more when he thinks about his family and how much he misses them—

BZZ BZZ.

Damon's phone jolts him out of his thoughts. He reaches over Chloe to grab his phone. She wakes slightly, rolling over to her side and away from him. Damon groans when he reads the address that popped up on the screen.

"What?" Chloe yawns.

"Ouija duty. I just got my first call," he says, hoisting himself out of bed.

"Well, have fun," she mumbles, snoring again a few seconds later.

Damon sighs and rummages through his dresser for a clean pair of boxers and a new tee. He slides on the clothes, jeans, and jacket. He steps into his sneakers, smooths down his sex hair, and teleports to the address.

He stands in front of a dark gray house. All the lights are off inside, giving the impression that there is no activity happening between the walls. But Damon can feel the Ouija board calling to him, begging for him to answer. Like a phone that is constantly ringing. He steps again and appears in a basement where the culprits lie. Three young girls sit in front of the Ouija board, a small hand from each on the planchette.

Damon rubs the sleepiness from his eyes and sits on a leather couch, right in front of them. The TV is off, but Ariana Grande's voice is blasting from one girl's phone.

"Maybe you didn't say it loud enough?" the scrawny girl whispers.

The girl with her hair in long braids sighs. "I don't think that matters, but I'll try again." She clears her throat. "Is anyone there?"

The third one stays silent, her eyes widened in fear.

The girls can't see him—he is invisible unless he chooses to appear to them.

Damon lights a cigarette. Reaching down to grab the planchette, he slowly slides it up to yes.

The girls scream.

The second Damon touches the planchette, worlds away, Angelica Beck's phone screen lights up with the same address. She is sitting on her couch, eating a late-night snack, and watching *The Notebook*, which she now pauses.

Her phone screen is red for this call, meaning that someone is in trouble.

She quickly smooths down her fuchsia dress and teleports to the house in Minneapolis. When Angelica opens her eyes, she quickly takes in her surroundings. She is standing in a nice basement with beige walls, a huge entertainment center, leather couches, and a pool table. On the other side of the pool table, in front of a couch, three middle-school-aged girls sit, staring at the planchette that is moving around the Ouija board.

The hair on the back of her neck stands up when she notices the being responsible for their terror.

A demon.

His bushy eyebrows are furrowed, and a cigarette hangs out of his mouth as he concentrates on communicating with the girls. Raven-black hair waves around his face and stops right above his shoulders. His face structure is strong, and a stubbly beard surrounds his cheeks and lips.

Angelica is taken aback by how handsome he is. She learned in her angel classes that demons weren't the ugly, creepy things portrayed in horror movies, but she didn't expect him to be *that* handsome.

She shakes her admiring thoughts away and steps around to where they sit, into his view.

He looks up at the sound, and his face turns down into a deadly glare. "What the hell are you doing here, angel?" His voice is low, husky, and matches his dark handsomeness perfectly.

"Stopping you," she says as if it were obvious. Angelica squats down to the girls and tries to touch one of them, but her hand stops inches away. A dark bubble surrounds the demon and the four girls. She tries to push through, but her hand will not go any further.

"Nice try." Damon smirks. "But this is none of your business. I got here first, plain and simple. You can't stop me."

"It's literally my *job* to stop you."

He shrugs, spelling out more words with the planchette.

"Whose soul should I steal first!?" the third girl with glasses reads from the board, tears forming in her eyes. "I told you this was a bad idea, Claire!"

Claire—the girl with the braids—starts crying, too. "I thought it was just some dumb game!"

Angelica's heart aches for the poor girls, and she wishes she could touch them and help. She frowns at the demon. "Look, you've had your fun, now let them go. They're kids."

"Kids who are playing with a powerful item," he says, extinguishing his cigarette on the bottom of his sneaker.

"They don't know that. Again, they're *children*."

"I don't care."

Angelica lets out a long sigh. She sits cross-legged between two of the girls, directly across from where the demon sits on the leather couch. "Fine. I guess I'll just have to steal them from you."

This makes him laugh. "Good one." He snaps his fingers, and the basements lights flicker.

All three girls cry even more hysterically, hugging each other.

Angelica meets his gaze with pleading eyes. His dark eyes are arrogant.

She shakes her head, knowing there is no use trying to argue with him any longer. Closing her eyes, she takes a few deep breaths. Her powers came from her soul, and she places her hands on her upper stomach, calling on them for help. Her toes tingle, and then the sensation crawls up her entire body. Angelica envisions light seeping from her, overpowering the darkness that filled the room. When she opens her eyes again, the lights stop flickering.

She reaches over to touch the bubble again, and it bursts the second her fingers graze it.

"What the hell?" Damon gapes, his smirk wiped away.

Angelica touches Claire on the shoulder and whispers into her ear.

"Guys! We have to tell it goodbye. Once we do, the scary ghost will leave us alone!"

Angelica grins at Damon, her eyebrows raised in triumph.

He shakes his head, lighting another cigarette. "Save your face, Barbie. I still have the house marked. Ending the call and stopping the lights won't change that."

"GOODBYE!" the girls scream in unison.

Angelica closes her eyes again and whispers, "Protect this house with all I have, don't let the demon steal their paths." When she exhales, she knows the tether to the demon has been cut, and angel dust now covers the house, protecting it.

Damon exhales a long breath of smoke as the girls stand, grab all their belongings, and run up the stairs—leaving the Ouija board behind. He felt it when she interrupted his connection, and he knows that she has beaten him.

"That was fun." Angelica giggles, standing and dusting off her maxi dress.

Damon doesn't respond. He is pissed. He's heard of

angels beating demons, but this is the first time it has happened to him.

Both of their phones buzz. They glance at their respective screens, confirming what they both already know. Angelica's shows a smiley face, flashing *House Saved!* Damon's isn't as exciting—it just shows a black *Mission Failed.*

"Well, I really should be going," Angelica says. When she looks up to the demon, she flinches when she realizes he is now standing only inches away, glaring at her hard.

She glares right back. He is only a few inches taller than she, and they are so close that they feel each other's breath.

Angelica runs her glaring eyes down his face, noticing features she couldn't see when he was far away. A few freckles decorate his pointed nose, and his eyes are the same black shade as his hair. Although his mouth grimaces, she can see his teeth, and they are perfectly straight and sparkling. If he wasn't giving her a look of hate, she probably would've blushed.

"I don't know who you think you are," he spits, his vision red with anger, "but next time I'm working, you better stay the fuck away from me."

Angelica can feel the anger radiating off him.

"Or what? You're going to hurt me?" she scoffs.

He leans even closer to her, their noses almost touching. "Worse." He growls.

The look he gave her makes her stomach queasy. He definitely seems to be the guy one doesn't want to piss off … which is a little late for her.

But then a new feeling appears that steals her attention. It grows slowly but is strong enough to overpower all the other ones. Warmth fills her, and it's as if she is being pulled closer to him, her soul wanting to touch him.

Damon feels it, too, and he doesn't know what to make of it. His anger subsides, and he surveys her. Long blonde hair, petite frame, pink dress. Thick eyelashes framing big, colorful eyes. And soft pink lips that his eyes linger on for a few long moments.

Angelica recognizes that look and finally steps back, shaking her head. "Were you about to kiss me?"

"No," he says repulsively, stepping back as well. "Your breath stinks."

She gasps. "No, it does not!"

Damon chuckles and looks her up and down slowly. "Trust me, angel. If I wanted to kiss you, you would know it. And you'd be thrilled."

"Ew, I would not." She gags, walking over to scoop up the Ouija board in her perfectly manicured hands. Before teleporting back to Heaven, she turns to wave at him with a bright smile on her face. "Have a blessed day!"

Once she disappears, Damon stares at the empty space and shakes his head. A quiet chuckle escapes his lips as he leans down to grab the half-smoked cigarette he threw on the ground in anger.

He lied—he totally was thinking about kissing her.

Chapter 5

Angelica strolls into the angel's office building, prepared to throw the Ouija Board into the hazard bin. She yawns as she sits at her desk, finishing up her end-of-day paperwork. Even though she is bone-tired, happiness floods her as she scribbles down the details of her eventful day: saving a choking woman's life, giving out a bunch of warm hugs, reading to cancer patients, and finishing with saving the girls from the nasty demon. She writes legibly but quickly and drops off her report, yawning again. The clock strikes four a.m.—overnights are not her favorite.

When she arrives at her home—a spacious, intricate mansion—she grabs a late-night snack from the kitchen before walking up the stairs to her bedroom. Her huge California King bed waits for her, looking as soft and warm as ever. Angelica crunches down on the rest of her granola bar before stripping out of her dress and into an oversized t-shirt. She slides in between her pink sheets and sinks into the mattress.

As she falls asleep, the weird, indescribable feeling she

felt with the demon keeps popping up in her mind. She never felt it before, and it intrigued her. At the same time, she knows that it doesn't matter—she will never see him again. It is probably just some demon magic that will fade when she wakes up.

Only six short hours later, the sound of birds singing and light seeping through her curtains awakens her. A cloudless blue sky is waiting when she opens her eyes. Angelica stretches and sits up, yawning loudly before wrapping her long blonde hair into a messy bun on the top of her head. She rolls over to the edge of her bed and slides her fuzzy slippers on before standing.

"Good morning, world!" she sings.

Even though she only got a few hours of sleep, she feels refreshed and ready to take on the day. She prances to the window and flings it open. The sound of the birds grows louder, and she revels in their songs. "Another perfect morning, right?" she calls to them, and a few zip by the window excitedly.

But, of course, every day is perfect when one lives in Heaven.

Angelica walks out of her bedroom and glides down the stairs, ready for breakfast. She waltzes into her kitchen and starts her coffee maker, her mouth watering as the warm brew fills her nostrils.

When people get to Heaven, they have everything they need waiting for them. Father has their dream homes planted in their own realms. Imagine an apartment complex, different apartments all stacked together, except they can't see any neighbors unless they directly teleport to their place. And each "apartment" is their dream life. Tiny houses tucked away in the mountains, old-timely mansions in the south, even penthouse suites overlooking the city. Everyone has different dreams and different tastes.

Her coffee finally finishes brewing, and she pours herself a heaping cup, mixing caramel creamer into the brown liquid. She lifts the cup to her lips and takes a sip, sighing happily as she feels the warm brew flow down her throat.

Her mug in hand, Angelica steps out of the kitchen to her big, ornate French doors. Opening them wide, the sun shines down on her in hello, and she inhales the scents of fresh air and flowers. She heads down her front steps and to the right, stepping onto a smooth dirt path that weaves between her flower gardens. Roses, hydrangeas, daffodils, camellias, tulips, peonies, magnolias, and her favorite, dahlias, stretch as far as the eye can see. She always loved flowers growing up—her mother and she would go to the farmers' market, and every time, she was allowed to pick out a few to take home. She loved those moments with her mother, and that love of flowers carried over to Heaven, where now she gets to see the beautiful blossoms every day. As she admires them, she picks up a stashed pair of pliers and cuts a few dahlias loose for her kitchen vase.

Besides the flower gardens, Angelica also has a produce garden filled with every kind of vegetable and fruit imaginable. They are always plump, perfect, and pickable—there will never be a bad tomato or watermelon. Angelica had a lot of time in Heaven before becoming an angel, so she learned how to cook delicious, elaborate meals. Her favorite is quinoa-stuffed squash with walnuts and pomegranate.

Angelica greets a few bees that buzz around her. When she finishes her last bit of coffee, she returns to her mansion, gracefully walking through the front doors. She sets her empty mug in the kitchen sink and snags a piece of chocolate from the stash bowl before heading to get ready for work.

She takes her time showering and pampering her body and opts for a more casual look today—a white jean skirt, a lacey tank, and a magenta cardigan. It is still technically summer, but depending on where she answers house calls, it can be chilly outside. She pulls her hair into a high ponytail, dons a gold watch on her left wrist, and secures her favorite gold locket around her neck. Right before walking out the door, she swipes on some lip gloss and mascara before winking at herself in the mirror.

Perfect.

"Good morning, Angelica!" Gabriel grins as she walks up to his desk. Gabriel is Father's right-hand man, the one who carries out important messages and hands out all the angels' work assignments.

"Good morning to you, too," she says, returning his smile. "What do you have for me today?"

He browses through the files on his desk until he comes across a manila folder with her name on it. The tall stack of similar folders wobbles as he slides it free and hands it to her. "You've been doing a fantastic job at spreading joy hugs, so probably some more of those!"

Angelica's heart swells at the compliment. "Great! Thanks, Gabriel."

He nods and motions for the next angel in line.

Angelica walks to the angel lounge and sits at one of the empty circular tables. Groups of angels gather at the other ones—some looking through their assignments, some having conversations, even a few eating an early lunch.

Angelica opens her own folder and scans the contents. On her to-do list today is hugging three hundred sick people to give them relief, talking to a few depressed teenagers who need support, and being on-call for any critical Ouija board clean-ups.

"What's up, sexy bitch?" Cora catcalls, plopping down in the chair across the table. The other angels all look at her when she swears.

"Cora," Angelica warns through giggles.

"Oops." She looks up and covers her mouth with her hands innocently. "My bad!"

The eyes all turn away. The girls giggle some more.

Cora is Angelica's best friend and one of the wilder angels. She is a short, curvy Latina woman who is loud, fun, and always down to have a good time. She does her job perfectly, earning many awards for her service over the years, but after work, she can always be found at Gaia's or another bar, dancing on the rail and outdrinking a sailor.

Cora sets down her folder. "Busy day today. I'm so ready for the weekend already."

"You do know it's Tuesday," Angelica points out.

Cora groans. "Thanks for the reminder. What are you planning for the weekend, *chica*?"

"Nothing planned yet. Although I don't wanna do anything too crazy."

"Let's go out!"

Now it's Angelica who groans. Angelica isn't as big into the party scene as Cora is, but she is always dragged out to be her wing woman. Angelica died at 19, her freshman year of college, and she partied enough that year to cover the rest of her life. Especially since the last time she ever got wasted in college, it didn't end up well for her, and that fear was always in the back of her mind when she drank. However, Cora always takes care of Angelica, even when she is completely intoxicated. Knowing that makes the whole thing easier, so Angelica goes out with her 90% of the time. While it ends up being super fun, the hangovers are something she regrets every time.

"We went out last weekend."

"And? We are young! Let's make crazy memories and have fun!"

"Relaxing and reading is also fun."

Cora rolls her eyes. "Girl, we have eternity to read. We don't have forever to go to Earth and party!"

This is true. Once Cora and Angelica retire from being angels, they will not be able to leave Heaven again. They can stay angels as long as they want, but once they turn in their figurative wings, they are done for the rest of forever.

"I guess you're right," Angelica says, coating her lips with fresh lip gloss.

"Of course I'm right." Cora twists a chocolate brown strand of hair around her finger. "But I figured you'd want to go out this weekend because ..." She dramatically pauses, building suspense. "it's Garrett's birthday."

Angelica blushes a deep red. Garrett graduated in her angel class with her a few years back, and she has had the biggest crush on him ever since they got paired up for group studies. He is tall and handsome—and could be Michael B. Jordan's twin. Besides his gorgeous celebrity looks, he is one of the sweetest and bravest people that Angelica has ever met. He is an Army veteran who died in action trying to save one of his fellow soldiers.

For the longest time, Angelica felt like he liked her, too, but then he started dating Lucy Truman. Angelica went through two tubs of ice cream that weekend she found out.

"Well ... I guess I could make an appearance." Angelica grins.

"Yesss," Cora cheers, dancing in her seat. "We are stopping by Gaia's first, of course, and then we will probably go to a human club and have some fun. I can go home with a cute human man, while you can have Garrett all to yourself."

"Yeah, right. He is with Lucy, remember?"

Cora shakes her head, her purple eyes sparkling behind her reading glasses.

"What?! They broke up?"

"A few weeks ago, now. I can't believe you haven't heard about it yet." She wiggles her eyebrows. "Yeah, he's single. So, we need to make sure that you look crazy hot. *Caliente loco!*"

Angelica agrees excitedly, although thinking about a freshly single Garrett makes her palms sweat. He already induces weakness in her knees, but now that he is available, she is terrified. Angelica switches topics.

"Speaking of crazy hot … I saw a demon last night."

Cora reacts the way Angelica knew she would. She widens her eyes theatrically and swoons before leaning over the table towards her. "You did!? And you didn't *tell me!?*"

"I'm telling you now."

"Spill the details!"

Angelica explains exactly what happened that morning, not leaving a single detail out. Cora somehow can always tell when she forgets to mention something—even if it is completely unimportant, like the color of a shirt.

Cora listens intently, nodding and facially reacting when applicable. Finally, Angelica finishes and takes a deep breath before opening the floor up for questions and comments.

Cora doesn't hesitate. "First of all, you are *killer* for swiping those girls out from under him. Second, the rest sounds all fine and dandy, but the most important thing is … what did he *look* like?"

"Do you really want to know?" Angelica teases.

Cora grimaces, unamused.

"Kidding!" Angelica laughs. She puts her finger up to her chin, making a big show of thinking and building suspense. "He had black irises, of course. Bushy eyebrows and long lashes framed them. His charcoal black hair matched his eyes, and it was long and wind-blown around his face. Freckles on his sharp nose. A stubbly beard. Though I couldn't see his body much, I could tell that he was toned and muscular through his tight black shirt." She straightens up and lets out a breath. "Very handsome."

Cora wiggles her eyebrows again. "I'll say. He sounds smokin' hot!"

"Smoking hot, and a total ass."

Cora laughs. "Yeah, most of them are, but that bad boy persona draws you in."

Maybe that explains the weird feeling and the tension, Angelica thinks.

"There's more to the story …" She squeaks.

Cora's eyebrows raise.

"Right before I left, when he was glaring in my face … I could've sworn it looked like he wanted to kiss me."

"What!?" Cora shouts, causing more angels to look at them. "Sorry!" she apologizes again and turns back to Angelica, grabbing her arm. "He did what?"

Angelica fills her in.

Cora sits back in awe, sucking on her teeth. "Hmm."

"What's that mean?"

"I think that you should've got his number and found out if he really wanted to kiss you." She grins devilishly.

Angelica's mouth plops open. "You can't be serious."

"Hey, I've had a few nights with demon men ... trust me, it's a good time."

Angelica's nose wrinkles up in disgust. "Well, that's you, not me. I could never date a demon, no matter how gorgeous he may be. Ew." Demons are horrible beings, nothing like anyone she should like. They are evil, vile, gross, and she will never let herself get involved with one. She doesn't care what Cora does, but she will never. Even if she's curious to know what kissing him would really be like…

Cora shrugs. "Yeah, well, there's a difference between dating someone and spending the night with them."

Angelica is no longer enjoying the conversation. She is a virgin, after all. "Okay, Cora. I should probably get to work."

Cora sighs and stands. "Don't get your panties in a wad. I'm just messing with you." She turns to go but winks at Angelica over her shoulder. "But if you ever see him again, get his number for *me*."

Chapter 6

Friday night, Damon drops off his completed weekly paperwork and heads straight for the bar. His usual group of friends are already there and piled into a corner. Damon nods at them, and William hops up to meet him at the bar rail.

"How was the rest of your week?" he asks, setting his empty glass down on the counter.

Damon shrugs. "Same old shit. Missy didn't talk to me much; I think she's still upset about the other day. Ouija duty wasn't too eventful—I only had three calls total."

Honey notices the two of them as she hands a beer to another customer.

"Yeah, whenever I get Ouija duty it's pretty boring. I know it's supposed to be a punishment, but it's nice to fuck off for a few days." William laughs before his smile turns impish. "Get any company?"

"Oh, yeah. An angel came by and stole my house the first time," Damon says, shaking his head and grinning.

"I figured you'd have at least one. Was he annoying as hell?"

"She," Damon corrects.

William's eyebrows shoot up his forehead. "Ohh, you got a *woman*. Lucky bastard."

Honey walks up to them with a smile. "Hey, guys. Who's the lucky bastard?"

"That's me, darling." William leans over the counter. "You look gorgeous as ever tonight."

Honey laughs, used to his brazen flirting. "You always flatter me, William. What are you two drinking?"

Before Damon can answer, William orders for both of them. "Two Jack and cokes."

Damon raises his hand to object—he usually stuck to beer—but William shoos his hand away. "Come on, you always drink beer. Get out of your comfort zone."

Before he can complain again, Honey extends her arms, two finished drinks in her hands. Her grin is even wider than before.

Damon sighs and gives in, reaching for the glass. "You guys are bad influences."

"I'll take that as a compliment," William says. "So, tell me what she looked like."

"Who?" Honey asks.

Damon rolls his eyes and sips his beverage. "I had an angel steal a house from me this week."

Honey's eyebrows now match the height of William's. "Interesting, although not uncommon."

"She was annoying, of course. You know how high and mighty they are. But she was a looker, at least—young and blonde with a sexy body."

Honey just shakes her head. "You men," she says.

William nods in approval, ignoring her disdain. "The blonde angels are the best." He turns to Honey. "And the blonde sprites."

Damon looks around at the bar, which is filling up fast. "Something going on tonight?"

"It's one of the angel's birthdays," Honey informs, wiping off the counter next to them.

"Why do they even celebrate birthdays?" Damon asks, rolling his eyes. "We are dead. We don't age anymore."

"Don't be such a sourpuss. Let people enjoy things," William chides, slurping down his alcohol.

Damon snorts but surveys the huge group of angels all laughing, dancing, and drinking in the middle of the room. ABBA is playing over the stereo, and a few girls in the center are screaming the words to "Dancing Queen." It is easy to recognize them—all the angels have striking, color-changing opal eyes, just like how all the demons' eyes are black and sprites' green. Besides their eyes, they are all drop-dead gorgeous. Chloe is neck and neck with some of the angels in beauty, although she argues that she is—and always will be—the superior.

Thinking about beautiful angels, Damon remembers the one he saw on Ouija duty. He would never admit this aloud—especially around Chloe—but she was the prettiest woman he ever saw. And blonde women weren't his usual type.

She unwillingly popped in his mind a few times since their meeting. A tiny part of him was disappointed that she didn't appear at his other house calls. He was sure he could overpower her quickly as long as he didn't mess with the caller like he did last time ... he wanted to wipe that smug grin off of her face. Then convince her to come home with him.

Plus, there was something about her that he couldn't forget about. Like the weird feeling she gave him.

Not weird as in bad, but just ... different. He couldn't put his finger on it, and he was dying to scratch that itch. Although he figured it was just an angel thing—they were known for bringing men to their knees with their power and beauty.

She got under his skin, but he'd love to get under her.

Honey disappeared during his thoughts, bustling behind the counter to fulfill all the drink orders. William claps him on the back, and they walk towards the corner table to join their small party.

Around the same time, Cora knocks on Angelica's front door. Three minutes go by, and no answer.

Oh, no. This brat is not standing me up tonight.

She already knows that the door is unlocked, so she pushes it open. "Angelica?"

Her heels clack on the floor as she searches through

the house. After coming up empty on the first floor, Cora makes her way upstairs.

She finally finds Angelica sprawled on her bed, staring at the ceiling with glassy eyes.

"Cora!" Angelica slurs in surprise. "What are you doing here?"

"Are you drunk?"

She blushes. "Maybe a little ... I had one bottle of wine." She lazily motions to the empty bottle sitting on her bedside table.

Cora puts her hands on her curvy hips. "Did you forget we were going out for Garrett's birthday tonight?"

Angelica responds by pulling her covers over her head. "I can't go! I'm too scared!"

"Oh, don't be such a baby." Cora sighs, walking over and whipping the covers off her. "Why are you scared?"

"I don't know what to say to Garrett. He makes me so nervous. I thought that if I loosened up and pre-gamed before we left, it would help, but now I just feel stupid and don't want to go at all."

Cora, who is a tough-love gal, rolls her eyes. "*Ay caramba*! We are going. I already told everyone we were, and we are not disappointing them. Get up. You will be fine talking to Garrett. Maybe he won't even talk to you, then you don't have to worry about it."

Angelica is stung by her words and doesn't move.

"Angelica Nicole, put on your big girl pants and let's go."

She cringes as Cora says her middle name but finally

gets off the bed. "Okay, fine, Mom." She wobbles over to her closet. "But I have no idea what to wear!"

Angelica turns to inspect Cora's outfit for inspiration and bursts out laughing. "We are going to Mother Nature's bar, and you are wearing *that*?!" She motions to Cora's sexy outfit, both of them knowing Gaia's is a hippie bar full of bright colors and lava lamps.

Cora looks down to check out her little black dress that ends a few inches below her butt. "Hey, Mother Nature can appreciate a sexy outfit. Besides, we are going to a few clubs after, and you know how those human girls like to dress." She enters Angelica's huge walk-in closet, surveying its contents.

She returns with a skintight, mauve mini dress that is very similarly cut to her own, and a pair of black kitten heels. "What about these?"

Angelica takes them without complaint. "Perfect!"

After the dress is on, hair secured, and makeup retouched, the girls admire themselves in the mirror.

"Your boobs look amazing," Cora says in approval.

"My little B cups don't do much." Angelica laughs, although she agrees that they do look great in the dress.

"It's not the size that counts, but how you accentuate them," Cora reassures, poking Angelica in the side.

"Says the woman with DDs."

Cora laughs. "We can't all be blessed like this. Okay, I think we look as hot as can be. Are you ready to go?"

Angelica looks confident in the mirror, but her stomach squeezes. She wishes she drank more wine. "Let's do it."

Cora grabs her hand, and together, they step to Gaia's. They push through a huge crowd of people to get remotely close to the bar. Angelica holds Cora's hand, so she doesn't get separated from her. Cora is only five feet tall, and even in stilettos, she is quite a bit shorter than Angelica, who is five-foot-eight and a half in her heels. It's easy to lose her in a big crowd.

When they finally hit the bar rail, a woman covered in rainbow-colored beads and an orange flared retro dress smiles at them.

"Honey!" Cora shouts above the noise. "How are you?"

"I'm good!" she hollers back. "What are you drinkin' tonight?"

Cora points at the displayed alcohol and says something too low for Angelica to hear, which she knows is a bad sign. Angelica watches Honey pour a few different liquids in a cup before shaking it up and pouring it in a glass filled with ice. When she's finished, Honey hands her the red liquid.

"What's this?" she asks wearily.

"Just drink it," Cora says. "You'll like it. It's called sex on the beach."

Angelica takes a drink. When the vodka hits the back of her throat, she cringes. Cora and Honey giggle at her sour face. Angelica's eyebrows raise when she realizes it really isn't bad; it just isn't the sweet wine she was drinking before.

Angelica prefers wine, sometimes a spritzer, and mimosas, but Cora loves to torture her with hard liquor.

Cora orders a dirty martini—"You *won't* like this,"

she promises Angelica—and then they dance over to their friends. When the girls get close, everyone cheers. They know, now that Cora is here, the night will get so much better.

Angelica gets wrapped up in a wedding planning conversation with her friends, Lily and Connor. They just got engaged a few months prior, and Lily wanted to get married in the spring, so planning is full-on. Cora gives them her love before bouncing over to flirt with Liam.

Angelica sips her drink sparingly, trying to warm up to the vodka, but after a while, she notices her tipsiness wearing off, so she chugs the rest. It is only eight, and, thanks to previous experience, she knows Cora will keep her out until the sun rises.

"Excuse me," she says, smiling at the happy couple before heading back to the bar rail for a refill. Honey is busy, so the other bartender comes up to help Angelica.

As she waits for her refill, she looks around the bar for the tall, dark, and handsome birthday boy she is terrified, but hoping, to talk to. She comes up empty and sighs, pulling out her phone and refreshing her work email.

Moments later, a throat clears behind her. "Angelica," a deep voice says.

She blushes before she even turns around.

Garrett's perfect white smile glows against his dark skin. "Hey, I've been looking for you."

She swallows hard, trying to keep her composure. "Garrett, hi."

He looks her up and down, his smile widening. "You look amazing."

Her eyes shyly dart to her pink toenails. "You are so sweet, thank you. You look equally dashing." She giggles.

"Thank you."

Dawn returns with Angelica's refill and takes Garrett's order before flitting away.

"I wanted to come say thanks for coming out tonight. I meant to do it earlier, but I've been wrapped up talking to people."

"Oh, not a problem," Angelica says, sipping her drink. The vodka doesn't hit her as hard anymore. "I'm glad I came."

He cocks his head to the side. "Oh? Why's that?"

Her fading blush returns. "Um, well, I had to see you, of course. For your birthday and all."

"Ah, I see."

Thankfully, Dawn drops off his drink, and Angelica jumps at changing the conversation. "What's that?" she points to the glass, full of cubes and brown alcohol.

"Buffalo Trace—a damn good whiskey." He holds it out to her. "Want to try?"

Angelica scrunches up her nose and shakes her head.

He chuckles, pulling out the barstool in front of them and motioning for her to sit. "Shall we?"

They both get comfortable on the bar stools. Angelica glances through the crowd and spots Cora dancing next to Liam, giving her a thumbs up and a wink.

"So, are you having a good night so far?" Angelica asks him.

He nods. "Yeah, it's been great. The whole day has been. I took the workday off and hung out with a few buddies before coming here." He tilts his glass, playing with his whiskey and smiling. "I never thought I'd be celebrating turning thirty in Heaven, but I couldn't imagine it being any better."

"Well, if it's any consolation, you look amazing for thirty." Angelica can feel her brain fogging up more from the vodka. It also makes her more forward, apparently.

Garrett raises his eyebrow. "Hey, now. Aren't I a little old for you?" he teases.

Angelica's heart flutters. "Technically, I'm twenty-three, if we are still counting birthdays. Seven years isn't *that* big of a difference …" She sucks vodka through the blue straw. "Unless you think so."

He laughs and shakes his head. "Seven years is nothing. My parents were thirteen years apart, and they are still just as in love as they were the day they met."

"Well, that settles that," she slurs and then giggles.

Garrett reaches out and grabs her hand.

Angelica's fluttering heart stops completely.

"Look, Angelica, I don't mean to be forward but … I was looking for you because I wanted to see if you'd like to get dinner sometime."

If Angelica could die again, she would've on that bar stool. "Oh yeah?" She squeaks.

His lips tilt into a warm smile. "Yeah."

"What about Lucy?" The question is out before she can stop it, and she quietly scolds herself. *Idiot, don't bring up his ex!*

He shrugs, unfazed by the question. "That wasn't serious. We ended a few weeks ago on a good note."

Angelica tears her eyes away from his, trying to think clearly. It isn't working. "Well, that's good."

"So, would you like to go out sometime? Whenever you are ready, of course."

She turns to give him a bright, sparkling smile. "Yes, I'd love to."

He lifts her hand to his mouth and kisses it softly. A flawless gentleman. "Perfect."

At that moment, Liam and Cora approach them. Liam holds a cigar out to Garrett. "Time to go outside, man. Hey, Angelica."

"Liam." Angelica nods.

Garrett lets go of Angelica's hand and stands. "I look forward to taking you to dinner, sooner rather than later." He winks, and then he and Liam disappear in the crowd.

Cora takes his seat, her half-moon eyes all-knowing. "What was *that* all about?"

"Oh, he just asked me out on a date," Angelica says nonchalantly before they both burst into excited screams. A few of the people sitting next to them shoot them questioned looks.

"Hell yes!" Cora says. She waves down Dawn. "Two tequila shots, please!"

"Uh, *no!*" Angelica protests—she isn't drunk enough for shots yet.

Cora doesn't listen and hands her a lime and saltshaker. "Suck it up, buttercup. It's time to celebrate."

Dawn drops off the shots and the girls grab them in their left hands.

Cora clears her throat. "To Angelica, who not only is my best fucking friend and the second hottest angel in this bar—" She winks, and Angelica snorts. "—she just got one of the handsomest angels to ask her out on a date. *Salud!*"

The girls lick their salted hands and shoot back the shot, hurrying to get the lime in between their teeth before cringing.

As Angelica sucks on the lime juice, she can feel her brain go from the slightly drunk threshold over to the *definitely* drunk threshold. She looks around the room as Cora orders another martini.

Her eyes sweep over the crowd, looking for no one in particular.

Then they connect with a pair of eyes that she recognizes.

A dark, cold, black pair.

Chapter 7

Angelica has to turn away quickly, her stomach lurching as she spits the lime out of her mouth onto the counter.

"Girl, are you okay?" Cora asks.

"Oh my god, Oh my god, Oh my god," Angelica hastily whispers.

"Are you gonna puke?"

She closes her eyes. The initial look of awe when he noticed her quickly hardened into disgust as he realized who she was, and that look sent anxiety to her alcohol-soaked stomach.

"No, I'm fine," Angelica says, taking a deep breath. "*He's here.*"

"He who?" Cora looks around the room.

Angelica nods in his direction, thankful that he is currently talking to another demon and not glaring in her direction.

Cora follows her nod, scanning the corner. Suddenly, her eyes widen. "Is that the demon from the other day?"

Angelica nods.

Cora whistles loudly, but it is drowned out by the music and the crowd. "You were not kidding; he is drop-dead *smokin' hot*."

"Stop staring at him!" Angelica hisses, slapping Cora's hand.

Cora chuckles, turning away. An ornery grin slides on her face. "No wonder you talked about him so dreamily."

Angelica glares at her.

"Oh, come on, Ang. Just ignore him …" She giggles, looking back in his direction. "Or go get his number. Or introduce us. Whichever you prefer." She purrs.

"This isn't funny," Angelica says, although she is giggling, too.

"What are the odds that you two would both be here tonight and see each other? It's kind of funny."

"It's Gaia's. Everyone sees everyone."

"But you've never seen each other here before."

"Maybe we have; we just never recognized each other."

Cora sighs. "Fine. Just ignore him," she repeats. "Let's go back to our friends and dance. But before we do, you need another drink." She turns and waves down a bartender.

Angelica stares at the almost-empty glass in her hand. *Yes, Angelica, ignore him* … she knows that he is nothing but bad news, especially since he probably hated her for stealing his house.

Another thought pops into her head.

Maybe it is because of the vodka, or that she is

unexplainably attracted to him, or both, but Angelica decides to do something entirely different.

"I'm going to go talk to him," she says confidently and stands.

"You're what!?" Cora grabs her arm.

Angelica focuses on the handsome man she is about to confront. "I don't want him to hate me. I didn't mean to upset him; I was just doing my job. I want to explain that to him, and hopefully, he will respect that."

"He won't! He is a demon, Angelica. The worst kind of being imaginable, remember?" Cora warns. "Only go over there if you're trying to bang him, not apologize. That will not go over well, I *promise* you."

Angelica shrugs, her mind already made up, but when she notices the group of demons around him, her confidence wavers. A redheaded man is laughing and appears nice enough, but a beefy guy with a buzz cut looks totally intimidating. Her stomach churns even more when she sees the breathtakingly beautiful demoness with ebony skin and long black hair.

She shakes her head and resumes her trek towards them. Her steps are slower and her head heavier than she thought they would be, but she doesn't stop or turn around. She stares at the man standing in the corner, determined for him to hear her out.

Damon doesn't notice her arrival; he is busy trying to push a very drunk Chloe off of him. It isn't until his friends all stop talking and their eyes narrow to something behind him that he turns and sees her right next to him.

What was I doing, again? Angelica thinks, forcing a smile onto her face. "Uh, hi!"

Chloe is the first to speak, wobbling over to get in her face. "What are you doing over here, bitch? You aren't welcome."

Father knows that Angelica wants to run back to Cora, teleport home, and never set foot around these terrifying people again, but she refuses to back down. She ignores Chloe and steps around her. "Excuse me."

William chuckles at Chloe's bewildered expression.

Angelica clears her throat a few inches away from Damon. "Can I talk to you?"

"Why?" he asks, although it sounds more like a statement. His dirty look is unsettling.

Her stomach turns. She takes a deep breath, which is a mistake. She is so close to him that she can smell him, and the scent of cigarettes, cinnamon, and whiskey warp her brain even more than what it already was.

"I just … wanted to apologize for what happened a few days ago."

He laughs. "Apologize for fucking up my job?"

Angelica cringes at the hate in his voice. "Yeah. I want you to know that it wasn't personal; it's just my job."

"And I care, because?" he asks, setting his glass down on the table and pulling his raven hair back into a low ponytail.

Angelica has to tear her eyes away from his toned arms. "You don't have to. I just wanted to clear the air. My mistake."

Damon pulls his cigarette carton out of his back pocket, squinting at her. A part of him wants to say thanks; it took some balls to come do what she did. But the other part of him loves watching her squirm. Seeing her so up close, especially in that skintight dress, is fun.

His friends are no longer staring, but he knows that they are eavesdropping on him and the sexy, drunk angel that is trying to keep the conversation going.

"Look, Barbie," Damon says, putting a cigarette between his lips, "what's done is done. I don't want a fake apology." He lights the stick and then blows smoke directly in her face. "You're right, it was your mistake. Now, go away."

Angelica stands there, dumbfounded. *Did he really just …*

Her polite smile rolls into a furious glare, and she puts her hands on her hips. Anger mixed with alcohol gives her another boost of confidence. Even though angels are supposed to "turn the other cheek," she is not someone who enjoys being treated poorly. Especially since she is trying to be nice.

"I'm not sure if you know this, but you don't always have to be such a dick."

Silence falls over the group. Once the shock of what she said wears off, William bursts out laughing next to Damon. Even some of the others grin.

Damon's eyebrows raise, and a small smile plays on his lips. He is impressed.

He runs his tongue over his bottom lip, planning his

next move. "Well, well, well." He looks at William. "This angel has a little sass on her."

William wiggles his eyebrows.

Damon looks back to a very angry Angelica.. He steps closer to her, as close as he was to her in the basement. "I like my girls a little spicey."

Her mouth plops open. "You just insulted me, and now you're hitting on me? As if you'd *ever* have a chance with me."

Damon smirks. He extinguishes his cigarette in the ashtray on the table behind him and then turns back to her. With his own level of extra courage from the hard liquor, he reaches out and wraps his arm around her waist, pulling her closer to him.

The second they touch, a warm, electric spark connects them.

Angelica gasps at the feeling of fire.

Damon's body buzzes with sparks, and his heart beats faster.

Time slows down, and everyone else in the bar fades away as their eyes stay locked.

Since they aren't that off from height, their faces and lips are only mere inches from each other's. Damon makes a point to look over her plump lips before meeting her gaze again. "If you do ever want a taste of the dark side, little angel, let me know." His voice is like melted butter, and he reaches to catch a piece of her hair and tuck it behind her ear. "I promise you; it will be a night to remember."

In this moment, Angelica *does* want a taste of the dark

side. She examines his lips and imagines what they would feel like pressed against hers for the second time that week. Does he kiss soft and sweet? Or hot and heavy? She searches his eyes for any sort of clue, and the feeling of recognizing him returns as if she could see into his soul. It's as if they are old friends who have met again after being apart for many years. But it feels as if ... they're more than friends.

She imagines doing things with him she has never done before, and her cheeks turn pink as her thoughts turn R-rated.

Damon is feeling the same thing. As he looks at her, he feels as if she is something he has been missing. Not just the wanting to get in her pants, see that blonde hair sprawled around her naked body, but more. Like she is the answer to all his prayers.

He looks down to her lips again and bites down on his own.

The tiny, sober part of Angelica's brain registers what is about to happen, and she quickly regains her composure and steps out of his grasp. The second she does, the buzzing feeling stops. Shaking her head, she clears her throat. "I wouldn't get your hopes up." She sticks her tongue out like a five-year-old. "And, for the record, I rescind my apology."

She straightens her dress and sticks her nose in the air before walking back to Cora, whose jaw is on the floor.

As soon as Angelica sits back down, Cora pounces on her. "Bitch. That was hot! I watched the whole thing. At first, it looked like he wanted to murder you—I was seriously about to come beat his ass when he blew that smoke in your face—but then, whatever that thing was with you two touching ... he looked like he wanted to fuck your brains out but make love to you at the same time."

Angelica doesn't know what to say to that. "Ew, Cora. No way."

Cora shrugs. "I don't know, girl ... the way he looked at you ... I wish someone would look at me that way."

Angelica glances back at him, but he was turned back to the redhead.

"Did you feel something?" Cora asks. "Your back was to me, but you tensed up when he touched you. And not necessarily in a bad way, if that makes sense."

"I ... don't know," she admits. "I'm pretty drunk."

"Well, good, keep drinking," Cora says, handing Angelica her refill before slapping her ass and dancing back over to their friends.

Angelica looks down at her drink, trying to register how drunk she really is. What she felt was just a chemical reaction of some kind, or maybe her drunken mind made the whole thing up. Even as she thinks that, she knows it's a lie. She felt an instant connection with him when they first looked into each other's eyes a few days ago, and after touching, it was raised one thousand percent.

Across the bar, Damon is thinking about the exact same thing.

Chapter 8

Damon wakes the next morning with Chloe's legs entangled with his. He silently groans and rubs his eyes with his hand. A pounding headache echoes between his ears.

He thinks back to last night but not much comes to mind. The bar. William belligerently drunk-singing an ABBA song. Then Chloe's naked body under him.

He looks at her sleeping soundly and sighs. *Dude, stop sleeping with her!*

Damon eases off the bed slowly, so he doesn't wake her. Luckily, they are in her apartment, so he can sneak out and go back to his place alone. Gathering his clothes quietly, he tiptoes out of her bedroom and shuts the door behind him. Dressing in last night's clothes, he walks out her front door and heads towards his apartment. He knows he can teleport, but sometimes it's nice to take his time.

The demons don't exactly live in luxury. They all live in a huge, run-down apartment complex, and each has its own small one-bedroom apartment. It's shitty. Damon figured that they would've at least had something nicer to live in, considering they were The Devil's favorite workers, but that isn't saying much. The Devil doesn't give a shit about anyone but himself. The doors don't even have locks on them. While it's nice that they don't have to worry about keys or anything, it's just another reminder that they have no privacy and belong to someone else.

He walks up the steps to the third floor and down the hall to his apartment on the right. Once inside, he immediately heads to the bathroom and turns on the shower. As he scrubs his physique of spilled alcohol, Chloe, and dirt, he relaxes. He tries to remember more of last night, but Jack Daniels got the best of him—he blacked out.

It isn't until someone flushes a toilet in the building, causing the water to go scalding hot, that a memory resurfaces.

His body felt something similar last night when he touched the angel.

The angel.

A grin spreads across his face as he coats his hair with shampoo. She was adorable, coming up to him drunkenly last night to apologize as if they had a fight on the school playground. Her wide eyes—although glassy from alcohol—looked innocent and kind. And then when she got an attitude with him, he saw her sexier side. Not that she wasn't already sexy in her tight pink dress. It impressed him that she didn't take his shit. Usually those kinds of people just walked away, but she stood her ground. He never talked to an angel so close before, but he definitely has never heard of one being as sassy and spicy as she was.

When they touched and that odd, warm fire spread through his body, he knew that she was special. Special how, exactly? He didn't know. But he should start trying to find out by getting into her pants. There is no reason behind how much he craves her body. It must be a polar opposite thing, light and dark coming together, making a chemical reaction?

Who knows? But he will sure as hell find out.

As he turns off the showerhead and starts drying himself off, he devises a plan on how he can get her alone. He heard stories about another angel who liked to play on the dark side a few times, and he was certain it was the brunette that was with her all night. He even watched them talk about him once and could've sworn the brunette whistled at him. Maybe she could help.

Damon wraps his towel around his waist before brushing his hair. The wet, dark strands tousle together and hang almost to his collarbone. He brushes his teeth, swipes on deodorant, and shuts off the light before walking out of the bathroom.

And almost jumps out of his skin when he sees Jeremy sitting on his living room couch.

"Dude!" Damon exclaims. "What are you doing here?"

Jeremy looks up from the book he is reading to glance at Damon as if this were a normal occurrence. "He wants to see you."

"Now? It's Saturday."

"I'm just the messenger," Jeremy says, his face grim.

Damon huffs. He knows there is no use trying to argue.

What The Devil wants, he gets. Damon takes his sweet time getting ready, dressing himself in his usual faded jeans, a dark-colored tee, and black boots. His hair is still dripping when he meets Jeremy by the front door, and they begin the walk to the office building down the road.

"Why is he bothering me on his day off?"

Jeremy shrugs. "Not my business."

"Come on, you must have some idea?" Damon presses.

Jeremy stays tight-lipped, keeping his eyes in front of them as they walk.

Damon steers his gaze in front of him, waiting for his eyes to adjust to the night. It is always dark in Hell, the only light emitting from the surrounding fires. The Devil and his demons sit on a tall plateau, surrounded by the chasms and the suffering humans. Lucky for Damon, he has finally learned how to tune out their screams.

They arrive at the building and walk through it in silence. Damon glances at Jeremy's face again to see if he can give anything away, but it stays hard as stone.

Drake nods at them when they come into his eyesight and opens the door for the men to walk through. Even though Damon is confident that he has nothing to worry about, he is still a little nervous as they walk into the office. Even if The Devil is still pissed about what happened at the meeting last week, and maybe a little annoyed at him for losing his first house to an angel, he still wouldn't exterminate one of his best demons …

Would he?

"Welcome, Damon," The Devil says, lounging on a

couch to the right of his desk, not far from where Damon and Jeremy walked in.

They both bow, and The Devil signals for Damon to sit. "Thank you, Jeremy. I dismiss you."

Jeremy bows again before heading swiftly out the door; it shuts loudly behind him. Damon sits on the chair opposite to The Devil, crossing his leg over the other and resting his arms on the back of it.

"How is your day going?" The Devil asks as if they were old friends.

"Great, thanks. Too early to do much," Damon says, knowing not to buy into his friendly antics—he is there because he wants something.

"Any plans?"

"Probably going to Gaia's later. The usual."

The Devil nods. He holds a whiskey glass in his left hand and brings it to his lips. The ice clink together when he lowers it again. "I always loved Gaia's. My sister sure does know how to throw a party."

Damon nods.

The Devil stands and walks to his desk, grabs a folder, and sets it in front of Damon.

He recognizes it instantly—it's his end of week paperwork.

"I see you lost your first house this week to an angel, is that correct?"

Damon tilts his head up and down once.

"Would you like to explain what happened?" The Devil says, plopping back down on the couch.

Damon doesn't want to, but he knows he has no choice. He quickly runs through the whole situation, starting with getting the call and ending right after she stole the house. He doesn't mention the last few moments of their staring at each other.

When Damon concludes his story, The Devil grins. "She sounds like a handful."

Damon nods again. He knows it is better to be silent and respectful than vocal and accidentally cop an attitude. The burn from The Devil's hand still throbbed, and he doesn't want another.

The Devil sets down his drink, pushes his palms together, and presses his lips against his pointer fingers. "So, I have a new mission for you."

Here we go, Damon thinks. "Yes, sir?"

"I want her," The Devil demands, his black eyes glimmering.

Damon uncrosses his legs and straightens up. "I'm sorry?"

"I want her to be one of us," he clarifies. "A demoness. I think she'd be a significant advantage to us."

"Why?" Damon asks. "Angels steal houses from demons all the time, yet you don't want all of them to join us. What's so special about her?"

The Devil's eyes flash with anger. "Do not question my reasons, Jones. I said I want her, and that is all the reasoning you need."

Damon swallows. The painful burn on his arm flares up. "Yes, sir. So, you want me to …?"

"Do I have to spell it out for you?" The Devil snaps. "Your new job is to convince her to become one of us. I don't care how you do it—befriend her, seduce her, whatever."

Damon looks down at his hands. "So, you want me to convince Missy to become your wife and this angel to become a demoness."

"Correct," he says coolly.

This is bullshit. He never gives this much work to one of his subordinates. Especially two dire *missions such as these. Why is The Devil so out to get me?* Damon thinks, grimacing. Even though he knows the answer to what he is about to say, he asks, "What happens if I fail?"

The Devil's lips turn up in a sinister grin. "Oh, I think you already know that answer."

Damon gulps.

If he were to fail—which was a huge possibility—he would either be thrown into the flames and burn with the other humans for the rest of eternity, or he would be murdered and turned into dust. People always say that they only die once and then spend the rest of eternity in Heaven or Hell, but they're wrong. You can die again. But once you do, that's it. You will not go to a new place; you will cease to exist. Forever.

"Now, run along. Keep me updated on both, though I understand this angel job may take a while."

Damon stands, his hands in fists. "As you wish, my lord."

He bows and turns to go, but The Devil stops him. "Damon! One last thing."

Damon looks back over his shoulder.

"If you try any funny business, anything at all, I will give you the worst possible death imaginable. Are we clear?"

Funny business? Like what? Damon thinks.

Physically, he nods. "Crystal."

Chapter 9

Angelica wakes late-morning and rushes to the bathroom, sure that she is about to throw up all the alcohol that she consumed last night. After she dry heaves for minutes and nothing expels, she lies down on the cool tile floor, closing her eyes and praying that the room will stop spinning.

"You okay?" Cora calls from her bedroom.

"No, I feel like absolute ass," Angelica croaks just loud enough.

She takes slow breaths, trying to calm her stomach. Footsteps echo down the hall until Cora's bare feet appear in the doorway. Opening one eye, Cora grins down at her.

"You know the best way to cure a hangover?"

Is this a trick question? "Sleep, coffee, and a shower?"

Cora shakes her head.

Angelica closes her open eye and rubs her temples. "Please enlighten me."

"Drinking more!"

A feeble laugh escapes Angelica's lips. "You can't be serious."

"Oh, come on, Ang! It's Saturday! Let's go out again!" Cora cheers, obviously not feeling sick.

Angelica curses the fact that Cora never has hangovers. She, however, seems to be a magnet for them, as she lies in her pajamas on the bathroom floor. "Hard pass."

Cora crosses her arms. "We could start with some … brunch and mimosas." She sings the last part of her sentence, knowing they are Angelica's favorite.

That was the perfect thing to say. Angelica's stomach growls at the thought of warm, buttery French toast drenched in syrup, crispy bacon on the side … and juice filled with champagne. She makes a point to sigh heavily before agreeing. "Okay, fine. Brunch it is."

"Yes!" Cora exclaims and wraps her robe around herself tightly. "Okay, I'm going to head home to shower and get a fresh pair of clothes. I will be back in twenty minutes." She teleports away for a few seconds and then reappears with a glass of water and three ibuprofens. "Here, take these."

Angelica gratefully takes the medicine and chugs the water before slowly standing. The spinnies are starting to subside. She reaches to turn on the showerhead, and when she turns back around, Cora is gone.

She shuts the door, trapping in the hot steam coming from the scalding water that is waiting for her. Glancing in the mirror, she notices all traces of makeup from the night before are gone, and she laughs, impressed that her drunken self took the time to take it off. She steps into the tub and shivers in pleasure as the water hits her cool body.

The water bounces off her back, her arms, and her neck for a few minutes before she washes herself religiously.

Angelica thinks back to last night as she rubs lavender soap along her legs. After Gaia's they ended up at a random cowboy-themed bar in Texas. She doesn't remember much but the taste of tequila and flashes of memories—Cora dancing on a bar rail, another shot, the whole bar singing happy birthday.

She blushes as a memory resurfaces. Her getting dared to give Garrett a lap dance.

Luckily, she doesn't remember every detail, probably saving her a lot of embarrassment. She does remember the music and Garrett sitting in a chair, his shirt unbuttoned, revealing dark, chiseled abs. And she is quite sure it wasn't even a good lap dance, just an awkward, drunken sway of her body against his.

Angelica shuts off the water and reaches for her towel. Drying herself off, she tries to remember more of the dare, but her brain is too foggy. She makes a note to ask Cora about it at brunch.

She dresses herself in the comfiest clothes she has—a pair of yoga pants and an oversized crew neck—and twists her wet hair into a French braid. As she tucks a stray hair behind her ear, the memory of the same thing happening last night jumps out at her.

Only it wasn't she who tucked the hair, but the demon.

She sits on her bed, remembering their entire encounter. At first, she remembers him being a major douchebag who she never wanted to see again. But then when they touched ... she felt this intense yearning she had never felt before. She didn't ask for it, nor did she want it—her body took over, as if it recognized him. A feeling erupted in her stomach as if she were being pulled to him, wanting to touch him, kiss him, become one with him. Not even just sexually ... soulfully.

Before they left Gaia's, she snuck quite a few glances at him. The drunker she became, the more frequently she peered over her shoulder. She watched him laugh with his friends, smoke many cigarettes, and soften when talking to Honey. She even noticed a handprint that was burned into his left forearm. Watching him from across the bar, she thought he looked normal. Which was dangerous. She couldn't allow herself to think that.

He's a demon. A vile, gross, evil creature. Don't forget that. She warns herself as her heart softens at the thought of his smile and intense, smoldering eyes.

She loves romance movies, and now something correlates to them ... all of her favorite ones, the cheesiest of course, talk about finding "The One." How what you feel makes little sense, but it's something you've never felt before and can never feel with another person.

A wave of disappointment flows over her as she realizes that Garrett gave her no buzzing feeling. Nothing out of the ordinary besides butterflies. Nothing as intense as the demon did.

Angelica meets her eyes in her vanity mirror. She raises an eyebrow tentatively. "Is he ..." she whispers, "... my soulmate?"

As soon as she says the words, she falls back onto her bed in a fit of laughter. *Come on, that's ridiculous!*

She does her best to ignore the nagging feeling that is now etched in the back of her brain—the feeling that is trying to convince her that it may not be as ridiculous as she wants it to be.

Luckily, Cora returns and interrupts her pondering. She looks just as casual and comfy as Angelica does, and they head to breakfast—a small place right outside of Nashville, Tennessee, that serves bottomless mimosas and a delicious breakfast. The girls love to try new restaurants every time they eat out, but this place they return to frequently because of the amazing food and staff.

As soon as they are seated, Lannie, their favorite server, drops off two bottles of orange juice and a freshly popped bottle of champagne. The girls thank her, order their usual breakfast, and pour themselves large glasses.

After taking a huge sip, Angelica sighs, setting down her flute. "I needed that."

"Agreed," Cora says. "So, what do you want to do today?"

"Nap and relax." Angelica answers, laughing when Cora's nose scrunches up in disgust.

"Are you really just an eighty-year-old who took marvelous care of her body?"

"You caught me."

"Seriously, you need to have more fun while you're young!"

Angelica snorts. "I will be young forever, remember? So I have plenty of time."

Cora rolls her eyes, knowing Angelica is right. "Fine.

Napping and relaxation can happen, but we are going back out tonight! *Sin excepciones!*"

As much as she wants to argue, Angelica knows it'll be no use. "Okay, fine. But nothing as crazy as last night. I had way too many tequila shots." At the mention of tequila, her stomach turns queasy. Thankfully, a whopping plate of French toast arrives just moments later, and she digs in, moaning after shoving a huge bite into her mouth.

"Speaking of moaning ..." Cora says, biting into a piece of bacon. "Garrett really likes you."

Angelica swallows and blushes. "Did I really get dared to give him a lap dance last night, or was that a drunk hallucination?"

Cora wiggles her eyebrows suggestively. "I wouldn't call it a lap dance ... but it was an attempt. And yes, it happened."

Angelica groans.

"But don't be upset! He loved it. He was pretty drunk, too."

"And he really likes me? Who told you that?"

Cora spears a piece of omelet and downs the rest of her mimosa. "He did."

Angelica pauses, looking at her with wide eyes. "He did?"

Cora grins and nods.

"What did he say, exactly?"

"When I was about to teleport us back to your place, he stopped me and whispered, 'Take care of her and make sure she gets home safe. I really like her.'"

Angelica looks back down at her plate of food. "That doesn't mean anything. He could mean as friends."

"Oh, bullshit." Cora finishes her second glass and refills it. "He *likes* you! But I assume you don't care anymore."

Angelica notices her change of tone and squints her eyes. "Why do you say that?"

"Because of that sexy demon."

Angelica shakes her head and laughs but cannot hide the color creeping onto her cheeks. "No way."

"Aha!" Cora notices the blush. "I knew you liked him! You kept staring at him at Gaia's."

Caught. "There is nothing to like!" Angelica defends herself.

"I told you. The way he looked at you last night ..." Cora whistles.

"Well, he can look at me however he wants. It doesn't change the fact that he is a demon, and nothing is going to happen in a million years," Angelica says, shoving more of her breakfast into her mouth. She decides not to tell Cora about the weird feeling she had when they touched. She wants to figure out exactly what it was—a side effect of their atoms touching possibly, or maybe even the alcohol. Cora is very overdramatic, and she doesn't need her hounding her about it every time they hang out. Once Angelica can disprove her earlier theory about him possibly being her ... soulmate ... then she will tell her.

The only problem is, how will she figure that out?

Chapter 10

That entire afternoon, Damon tries to plan out a strategy on getting the angel to become a demon … and fails. Nothing comes to mind. Why would an angel, living a happy, perfect life, ever want to come to Hell?

He finishes the water bottle he is drinking and crushes it down between his hands.

An uneasy feeling has been sitting in his stomach all day that he can't shake. Like The Devil is setting him up for failure, just so he can kill him …

Damon grabs a jacket to go talk to his favorite person about the whole situation.

Since it is Saturday, the bar is packed. He squeezes between the warm bodies, sighing quietly to himself.

Honey immediately notices his annoyed face and meets his eyes with a curious look. "What's wrong?"

He sits on the barstool directly in front of her, resting his forearms on the counter. "I'm just getting bored with drinking all the damn time. Not that I'm not excited to see you, but it's so boring."

She nods. "Why don't we go on a trip soon? I can talk to Gaia and get you and me a few days off of work," she suggests, a warm smile spreading across her face. "We could go see the beach, maybe hike in the mountains?"

Damon gives her the smile that is reserved only for her. A big, toothy grin that touches his eyes. "I'd like that very much."

Sunshine, the other bartender of the night, places a beer in front of him. Damon nods at her and she winks, both of them remembering the night they shared many moons ago. He watches her walk away, her purple jumpsuit hugging her in all the right places.

Damon looks back to Honey. "I need to talk to you about a new mission I was just assigned."

"I'm listening." She cocks her head to the side, her oversized daisy earrings dangling in the wind.

Damon reminds her about the angel that stole his house and then relays the whole conversation he had with The Devil, finishing with being assigned the impossible task of getting her to join Hell. He explains that he was trying to come up with a plan the entire afternoon but had nothing good.

She listens intently, not interrupting or exposing any emotion. When he finishes, her eyebrows furrow sympathetically. "Wow, that's tough."

He sips on his beer. "Yeah."

Honey dries off a clean glass and sets it on the shelf behind her. "So, The Devil wants you to get this girl to become a demon …" she repeats.

"That's the plan," Damon grumbles.

"Why? What's so special about her?"

He shrugs and rolls his eyes. "When does he ever give me exact reasons?"

"Touché."

Damon watches her clean, thankful that he has someone to talk to about this who will not judge him, even if she doesn't agree with what he is doing. "Do you have any ideas on how I can go about this?"

She shakes her head. "I have no ideas. Did you come up with anything at all?"

He leans forward and rubs his eyes. "I thought about getting her to sleep with me, then fall in love with me, then I would tell her that the only way for us to be together is if she became a demon like me."

"Sounds ideal." Honey snorts and then sighs. "Honestly, I don't like this plan."

Damon's eyebrows raise. "You actually have an opinion?"

"I have opinions on many things, but I know it isn't any of my business." She smooths down her yellow dress. "However, this one just feels wrong. You know how unhappy you are being a demon, yet you want to damn one of the kindest, sweetest, most caring types of beings around? That girl doesn't have a mean bone in her body."

"I don't know, she was pretty sassy with me last night," Damon objects, chuckling.

Honey doesn't laugh.

The humor in his voice dries up. "I don't really have a choice here."

She frowns, her green eyes twinkling behind her fashion glasses. "There is always a choice."

Damon runs his hand through his hair. "So, what? You suggest that I should just tell The Devil I can't do it and die again?"

"Not necessarily," she says.

"Never in a million years would I sacrifice myself for someone I don't even know. Especially not a perfect, prissy, stupid angel. She's had enough goodness in her life, she can learn to live in Hell." He growls.

Honey backs away from him, her hands raised. "Hey, don't freak out on me." She turns to help another customer who raised their hand. "But what you just said proves that you are exactly where you deserve to be."

Damon is shocked that she just called him out so easily. He watches her fill an empty glass, a bitter pang in his stomach. Deep down, he knows she is right. He chugs the rest of his beer. Though it doesn't happen often, he can be a dick to his best friend once in a while. He stares into his empty glass, guilt spreading through him. This mission is wrong, and he knows that ... he just doesn't give a shit at this point. In the end, he's where he is and a demon for a reason.

If young me could see me now ... he'd be so disappointed.

After a few minutes, Honey returns with a fresh beer.

Damon wraps his hand around hers as she sets it on the counter. "I'm sorry, Honey."

She nods, a small smile on her lips. "I know. Me, too." Stepping back from his grasp, she crosses her arms. "Now, how can I help?"

"I have no idea." Damon sighs. "I guess the first question is ... how do I get her to talk to me?"

Honey puts her pointer finger on her cheek, making a big show of pretending to think of the perfect answer. "Ooh, I know! Maybe go up and apologize for being a dick to her?"

Damon chuckles. "Yeah, no. I think I'll just buy her a drink."

"How original."

"I don't hear any better ideas. I need to gain her trust; I can't do that if she thinks I'm a scummy demon."

"But you are a scummy demon." Honey giggles, handing a mixed drink to another demon a few feet away from Damon.

"Yeah, but she doesn't have to know that." Damon picks at a chip in the side of his beer glass.

Honey clears her throat and nods towards the entrance. "Well, think fast, because she just got here."

Damon turns in his seat. Sure enough, the gorgeous, albeit annoying, angel just walked in the front door, a gleaming smile on her face. The same brunette she was with last night is next to her.

"She is so gorgeous," Honey says. When Damon turns back to face her, she notices his face is a little flushed. "You look nervous," she teases.

"Oh, shut it," he says, definitely a little nervous.

"What does Chloe think about this mission?"

Damon studies his beer glass again. "Uh, she doesn't."

"You didn't bother to tell her?!"

"It hasn't come up! Besides, she isn't my girlfriend, so it doesn't matter." He is *not* ready to have that conversation with Chloe. They already argue about being exclusive regularly, and if he had to explain to her that he might seduce an angel to get her to join the dark side, that would not be good.

Honey narrows her eyes at him but keeps her mouth shut.

"So, what can you tell me about her?" Damon asks. Sprites know everything about everyone since they work for Gaia—they are literally the eyes and ears of the Earth.

"If I tell you, don't you think that's cheating?"

"Come on, just a little?" He bats his eyelashes.

She laughs and shakes her head. "Okay, just a little." She leans in closer, lowering her voice. "Her name is Angelica. Cora's her best friend, the brunette. She's been an angel for about a year now, and she is honestly so sweet whenever we talk. She doesn't really like to drink the hard stuff, but Cora loves to drag her out to the bar and make her try different cocktails."

Damon glances back at the girls, who are busy chatting with River. The brunette woman, Cora, has a short bob and a curvy, busty body. She is definitely attractive, too, and he recognizes her. Preston, another demon that he isn't close with, has definitely made out with her a few times.

"Okay. I'll give it some time before I say anything. Make sure she has a drink or two beforehand."

"Good idea," Honey says before disappearing behind an avalanche of drink orders.

Damon lies low, watching the girls out of the corner of his eye. Angelica is gorgeous, but he already knows that. She is gorgeous in a way that he isn't used to admiring—the demonesses are all gorgeous in dark, mysterious ways. She is smiling, carefree—beautiful like the sunshine. Her long, golden hair cascades down her back and rests right in the center, curled on the edges. Her body is just as killer as he remembers. She is toned and obviously was an athlete in her first life, but has a curvy ass. The light blue dress she is wearing looks like it was designed just for her. He assumes Cora made a joke, because moments later she laughs, and, wow, that smile …

Damon internally gags and turns away from them. *Dude. What!? You are on a mission. Get her to join us and get in her pants. That's it.*

The girls finally say goodbye to River and walk up to the bar rail, signaling for a drink. They are only a few seats away from Damon, but it is so crowded that they don't even notice him. Cora looks around, surveying their flirtation options.

"Ooh, look at him …" she motions to a tall man in the corner with dark blond hair and green eyes.

"A sprite?"

"Hey, I don't mind. I love all men, no matter what kind they are. Sprites, humans, spirits, angels … demons." She says the last word with a wink.

Angelica shakes her head. "We don't always have to be on the lookout for guys, you know."

Cora's eyes playfully widen. "Oh, are you saying you want to swing the other way tonight? I'm not opposed."

"Funny. No."

Cora wiggles to the music as Sunshine takes their order. Angelica orders a glass of white wine while Cora orders a Manhattan.

"Cheers!" The girls clink their glasses together and then find a table in the corner. They recognize a few of their friends and wave them over. People gush about how fun last night was, and Angelica blushes when they tease her about her *cute lap dance* until Cora takes the conversation over. She excitedly talks about her upcoming Halloween Party. It is the ultimate extravaganza of the year, always wild, crazy, and a night to remember … if they can after all the booze they drink. Last year was the first time Angelica attended—since it was on Earth—and she danced and drank so much that her head and feet hurt for a month straight after.

"Where is it going to be this year?" Isla asks.

"Hmm, I don't know! I was thinking about Vegas or Australia. What do you guys think?"

The group of angels all toss in their ideas for locations. Angelica finishes her glass of wine and then heads back up to the bar for a refill, squeezing through the crowd to get close. As she leans between two people sitting on the stools to signal for a bartender, she bumps against the person to her right.

Zap.

She bounces back.

Damon smirks at her. "Hey."

"Are you stalking me!?"

He rolls his eyes. "Uh, no. I come here almost every night, and I've only seen you twice, so you're the one stalking me."

Angelica's lips curl back in disgust. "Never in a million years."

"You sure about that?" he asks, raising an eyebrow and shamelessly trailing his eyes up and down her body slowly.

She tries not to think about how hot that movement was. He was confident, she will give him that. "Definitely." She turns away from him and watches Honey, Sunshine, and River bustle behind the bar, praying that she will be next.

"Look, I know we got off on the wrong foot, but I'm not just some asshole. I'm actually pretty cool."

"That sounds like something an asshole would say."

Damon straightens up in his chair and leans closer to Angelica, making sure he doesn't touch her. "Come on, give me a chance. Let me buy your next drink."

Now, this makes her scoff and turn to him. "Seriously?"

His smoldering dark eyes meet hers. "Seriously."

Even though they both know that 'buy' is a loose term—they don't have to pay for anything at this bar—Angelica tries not to blush under his intense gaze. But she can feel heat in her cheeks. *Maybe one drink won't hurt ...*

She looks him up and down. Black V-neck T-shirt. A black leather jacket with a pack of cigarettes poking out of the pocket. Faded jeans and black boots. Handsome face, charming smile. Hair that seems jet black but has a few streaks of dark chocolate brown in the dim light of the bar. Her eyes finally meet his again, and they are unmistakably black. And she remembers what their color represents.

No. Bad news.

She turns back to the bar because when her eyes are connected with his, she can't think clearly. "I'm good, thanks."

He shrugs and picks up the phone that is sitting on the rail. "Okay, then. Your loss."

Angelica stands there awkwardly, surprised at how unphased he is by her rejection. She is still waiting for Honey to come up to her, but now she is on the other side of the bar rail, talking to one of her friends. The other two bartenders are too busy to even notice her standing there. She glances at Damon, but he is not interested in talking to her anymore, instead playing a game on his phone.

She sighs and then leaves the rail without a drink in her hand.

"Is that who I think it is?" Cora immediately asks when Angelica resumes her seat.

"Yeah," she says, staring at the back of his head wearily.

"What did he want?"

Angelica shakes her head, still confused by the quick affair. "He said that we got off on the wrong foot and … he wants to buy me a drink?"

"What!? What did you say?"

"No, of course!"

Cora throws her head back in annoyance. "Girl, why not? Get that free drink!"

Angelica flicks a curled strand of hair behind her shoulder. "*Because*, Cora, he is a *demon*."

Cora holds out her hand. "And? That excuse is getting pretty old. It's not like you're going to get married or anything," she laughs. "Get a taste of the dark side. Live a little. I know you like him, and I know that you *actually* really want him to buy you a drink. You can't pull the wool over these eyes." She wiggles her fingers.

Angelica shakes her head but stays silent, thinking over Cora's words. She knows she is right ... he totally intrigues her. She doesn't like him—that is ridiculous—but he is the first demon she has had this much communication with, and she craves more. Anxious questions run through her mind.

Why does he want to be nice all of a sudden? Is this a trick? Is he just trying to get some? Can demons actually be nice just to be nice? Or is he planning something bad? Or is this because of the feeling we felt last night? The last question poses a bigger one ...

What does he think that feeling was?

"Hello, earth to Angelica!" Cora says, bringing her back to reality.

She takes a deep breath, glancing at him again. "Okay, fine ... one drink won't hurt, right?"

"*Si, muchacha!*" Cora cheers. Angelica loves when she randomly speaks Spanish. Cora told her once that she couldn't speak it fluently but was taught certain phrases and words by her grandmother. Plus, she doesn't like confusing

Angelica, who knew little-to-no Spanish. "Okay, look at me." She makes Angelica stand and turns her around in front of her.

"Cora, stop." She blushes but complies.

Her best friend adjusts her dress and fluffs up her hair. "One last thing ... do that boob trick."

"*Cora*," Angelica whines.

"Do it!"

Angelica sighs but does what she is told, cupping her boobs and pulling them up in her dress, making them pop a little extra. A classic trick.

"So sexy." Cora smacks her butt as she turns. "Go get him, tiger."

Angelica takes a deep breath and makes her way back to the bar rail, where the suave demon is waiting for her. *Be confident. You are sexy*, she reminds herself. She marches right up to him, and when he turns to look at her, she gives him a fearless smile and says, "I'll have a glass of sparkling Moscato, thank you."

Chapter 11

~~

Damon raises his eyebrows at her, then smirks and signals for Honey. He wasn't sure if his tactic would've worked but … she came back.

Honey immediately approaches them and smiles, her daisies swaying again.

"A glass of your best Moscato, please, Honey," Damon orders.

Angelica stands there, her confidence slowly evaporating as Honey quickly fills and drops off the wineglass in front of her. *Now what?*

"Would you like to sit?" Damon asks, pulling out the surprisingly empty barstool to his left.

Angelica does without saying a word. She sips her drink.

He gives her a lopsided grin. "So, what made you come back?"

She bites her lip. She couldn't really say *the undeniable attraction and connection I feel with you that needs to be answered.* "My friend, Cora. She's kind of a bad influence on me."

"I'll say." He chuckles, running his hand through his hair.

"So, why did you buy me a drink?"

Damon adjusts his sitting position, resting his feet on the lower bar of the stool, thinking of a good excuse since he can't tell her the real reason. "I wanted to talk to you." *Not a total lie.*

"Why?" she asks, her multicolored eyes narrowing.

He shrugs, realizing that he has to be a good guy to get her even remotely interested in him. She isn't into the typical bad boy persona that all the other girls he courted were. "Well, honestly, you have been running through my mind all day."

This gets her attention. "Oh?"

His smile turns coy. "Yeah. I couldn't stop thinking about how cute you were last night, coming up to me and apologizing for ruining my mission. It was … sweet."

Angelica looks away from his intense gaze while Damon swivels his head to the side and silently gags.

"I was just trying to be nice; it was no big deal," she reassures him, her face red. She swallows some more wine.

"Well, I liked it. And then when you got all sassy with me, it made it even better." He raises a dark, bushy eyebrow. "I like a girl that can handle herself."

She laughs. "I am sorry about that. I try to stay as nice as possible and turn the other cheek and all that, but sometimes I can be a sassy little shit."

"Don't worry about it ..." he trails off, not sure if he should call her by her name since he technically shouldn't know.

She picks up on his hesitation. "Angelica," she says, beaming. Her smile slips right off her face as he starts laughing.

"Angelica the angel? That's cute."

She sticks her tongue out at him but then chuckles. "Hey, my parents just knew I'd be saving lives one day. What's your name?"

Damon's face reddens. He shouldn't have laughed. It's not like his name is any better. "My name is Damon."

She raises her eyebrow and brings her wineglass to her lips, sipping it slowly. Lowering it and resting it on her cheek, she tilts her head and gives him an endearing smile before saying, "Damon the demon? That's cute."

Honey, who has been eavesdropping, snorts.

Damon raises his eyebrows, impressed by her again. "You know, you don't seem like a normal angel."

"What do you think a normal angel is?"

"I don't know."

She finishes off her drink. "We aren't just perfectly pious, ramrod straight beings. Even though there are those kinds. We do have personalities. Just like how not all demons are evil, soulless assholes."

He props his hand under his chin and grins. "Are you saying that you don't think I'm an asshole?"

She looks away from his handsome, bearded smile. "Well, you certainly showed you can be something *besides* that." She giggles, shaking her head and standing. "It was nice to officially meet you, but I should be going."

"Wait." Damon instinctively reaches out to grab her arm. When they touch, that familiar, startling buzz of electricity zaps them. "You're leaving already?"

Angelica looks down and then frees herself from his grasp, clearing her throat. "Yeah, I finished my drink, and I should get back to my friends."

"Do you want another?" He turns to look for Honey, who disappeared again.

"No, that's okay. Thank you, though."

He meets her gaze, his eyebrows furrowed. "Well, when can I see you again?"

"What? You want to see me again?"

The hand that Damon used to halt her now reaches out to brush a blonde hair out of her face. "Of course, little angel."

Angelica's breath hitches in her throat at his sweet gesture. She forces a polite smile on her face. "I'm sorry, but … I just don't date your kind."

"My kind?"

She raises an eyebrow.

"Ahh, right, because I'm a demon." Damon nods, playing into the game. "What would make you go out with me?"

Her forehead crinkles and she crosses her arms across her sky-blue bodice. "Is it really that big of a deal? You want to go out with me that bad?"

"Yeah, I do," he says, completely serious. "So, tell me what I have to do."

Angelica is speechless. *Who is this guy?*

She knows she shouldn't trust him, or even consider the idea of seeing him again. This time is already a bad idea, but another time ... that can mean more. Especially since every moment they spend together, the more and more she becomes intrigued by him. More under his dark, mysterious, handsome spell.

An idea pops into her head, and a smirk slowly spreads across her face. "Okay, I have an idea."

He opens his hands, waiting.

She leans over close to him, just inches from his face. "If you want to take me out so bad ... become an angel."

Damon stares into her sparkling sunrise eyes and doesn't back down. "Done."

Angelica's heartbeat races. She raises her eyebrows but doesn't back away. "Done? Just like that?"

A smile dances on his lips. "Just like that. I want to get to know you. And if becoming an angel is my ticket to doing that, then slap my ass and give me a halo."

She finally leans back, her cheeks warm. "How do I know I can trust you? That was too easy."

"Believe it or not, being a demon isn't all it's cracked up to be," he says. There is no way in hell that he will actually end up becoming an angel, but she doesn't know that. Although this wasn't in his original plan, he can see it playing out perfectly—she trains him, he gets her to fall for him, he fails the tests, and the only chance she can be with him is if she becomes a demon, too … and she would rather do that then let him go.

This is going to be a piece of cake.

His smiling face (although smiling for other reasons) gives her hope. She straightens and smooths her dress. "Okay! I'm excited for you. Just know that becoming an angel isn't easy. You have to completely change what you've been programmed to do, study and pass a series of tests, and then be appointed by Father himself. The transition will make you feel physically sick, since it's against everything you've been doing as a demon. Are you sure you are up for this?"

"Oh, trust me, I can handle this," he promises confidently. He finishes his drink and bites down on his lip. "So, are you going to be my teacher?"

Angelica falters. She didn't think of that. "Uh … if you'd like me to."

"Well, of course."

She looks him up and down with narrowed eyes. Taking a deep breath, she reaches out her hand for him to shake. "No funny business. This is strictly work. Promise me you won't waste my time. I'm putting faith in you."

Her serious tone gives Damon an uneasy feeling since he knows he is lying through his teeth. He reaches out to shake her hand anyway, winking. "I promise. But after I pass, you have to go on a date with me."

"Fine. Deal," she says, quickly letting go of his hand and trying not to focus on the feelings his ornery smile and electrified touch gave her. "We will start next week; the tests are only four months away."

She pulls her phone out of her dress pocket and hands it to Damon. They exchange numbers and then hand each other's phone back. Angelica looks at him one more time and picks up the wine glass Honey refilled without asking. "I will see you later … Damon." Even saying his name gives her chills.

He tips his beer toward her. "Till next time, little angel."

Chapter 12

Damon wipes his hands on his jeans, smearing paint all over. His phone just buzzed, and he has been on edge all week, waiting for Angelica to text him. He hasn't seen her at the bar since they decided to train together.

He spent the beginning of the week talking to Missy and working on her openness to the possible job. She wasn't pissed off at him anymore, but every time he tried to bring up Halloween, she shut the conversation down. Although annoying, Damon wasn't worried—he still had plenty of time to convince her to join them.

Once Damon realizes the text isn't from Angelica, instead from his friend group chat, he exhales and picks his paintbrush back up.

He has always been a painter, ever since he was a child and got his first art kit for Christmas. It became his hobby and then his passion—he loved taking nothing and creating something beautiful from it. He had even earned a fine arts degree in painting and drawing a few months before he died.

After he arrived in Hell, he didn't paint anymore. It was too painful for him, thinking of all the things he had planned to do in his lifetime with his degree—all the art shows he would miss, his family's adoration each time he showed them a finished piece, art auctions—so he just stopped altogether. It wasn't until very recently that he forced himself to pick up a brush again, and it was nice. The feeling of the brush smearing paint across a blank canvas was something that he dearly missed.

Streaks of blue and purple decorate the canvas. The beginning stages of becoming ... something. He has no idea what he is working on, which is the beauty of painting for him. It usually isn't until much later in the painting when he figures out what he is doing. Something abstract, maybe?

He continues brushing and coloring, letting his mind wander without limitations or judgment. After a while, he steps back and looks at his work.

A close up of a woman's bodice. Prominent collarbones and a cap-sleeved dress colored with blues, pinks, and purples. A wine glass in an upright hand on the edge of the painting.

Damon groans and sets down his brush. It is unmistakably the angel.

How is she this stuck inside my head? I've never thought about painting Missy.

He notices his phone clock reads 12:28 p.m. Lunchtime is the perfect excuse for getting out of painting and his questions surrounding it. He cleans up all his supplies and shoves them back into the hall closet. Since he has little space, he paints in a small corner of his living room. He prefers going out in the world to paint—like a relaxing beach or a quiet park—but this morning he is feeling lazy.

Even though he is annoyed by the painting, he carefully tucks it away.

The frying pan sizzles as he turns on the stove. Damon isn't a particularly good cook by any means, but he knows how to make an amazing BLT, which he eats almost every day for lunch. He shoves two pieces of bread in the toaster as he starts frying the bacon.

As he bites into the crispy sandwich, there's a knock on his front door. "Come in," he mumbles through his full mouth.

Chloe struts in the room with a furious look on her face. "Were you not going to call me?"

Damon rolls his eyes. He is *not* in the mood for her right now. "I'm sorry, Chlo. I've been busy. You know you could've called me, too."

She ignores the last sentence, jutting her hip out and resting her hand on it. "Uh, huh, I've heard you've been *busy*."

"Oh yeah? Heard what?"

She narrows her eyes and points at him with her other hand. A blue topaz ring twinkles on her dark brown finger. "Allll about your new little mission to get *miss angel* to become a demoness."

Damon swallows his last bite and walks to the sink. "Then you know it's not my choice. It's just a job. Don't make it personal."

"How can I not?" she whines. "You are going to be hanging out with an angel all the time. A woman angel!"

Chloe doesn't get jealous often, so when she does, it's horribly unpleasant.

"Because it doesn't matter. It's none of your business," he says, turning on the sink and rinsing his plate.

Before she can snap back, his phone buzzes again. She struts over to where it rests on the counter.

"It's probably just the group chat. Did you see what Ashley said this morn—"

She gasps. "Who the fuck is Angelica?"

Damon hangs his head. *Impeccable timing.* "The angel."

"And why is she texting you?"

"I got her number. Obviously, we will have to talk in order for me to convince her to be a demon, Chloe."

"Okay, but she says—'Hi! I hope you aren't busy tonight! Meet me at blah blah address at five? Excited to see you!'" Chloe spits through gritted teeth.

She's excited to see me? Damon thinks, biting down on his lip so he doesn't grin. "Right. We need to hang out so I can *convince her to become a demon.*"

Chloe sets the phone back down and crosses her arms. "Sounds like a load of shit. Why didn't you tell me when it was assigned?"

"Chloe," Damon raises his voice, looking over his shoulder to glare at her. "Because it was assigned to me and not you. Why would I have told you?"

"Why wouldn't you have? What if she takes things too far? What if she tries to sleep with you or something?"

"Then I'll sleep with her."

Her nostrils flare. "Excuse me?"

His plan wasn't to piss Chloe off, but now it seems to be the only way she will get off his back. He takes his time turning around, putting his hands together in a praying motion. "Chloe. Again. It's none of your *fucking business*. We aren't an item! I don't know why you always 'forget' that."

"Maybe because you take me home all the time? Or does our sex mean nothing to you?"

He doesn't answer. She already knows.

Her stone-cold eyes soften a little. "Damon, I love you."

He scoffs, "Oh, don't even. No, you don't. You're just trying to manipulate me. I've told you a thousand times that I don't want to be with you for anything more than sex. We will never be together." He calms down when he sees the hurt in her eyes. "Look, I'm sorry I keep having drunken sex with you. I know it's not fair. But don't come in here claiming that you love me when you fuck our boss more than you do me."

Her mouth gapes, anger replacing all traces of the hurt Damon just saw. "Wow. Okay." She straightens and sticks her nose in the air, giving him a disgusted sneer. "Next time you are drunk, do not even think about talking or looking at me."

"Okay." He shrugs.

She storms out of his apartment, slamming the door behind her.

Chapter 13

At five on the dot, Damon appears at the address that Angelica texted him earlier. He looks around at the public park until he spies Angelica sitting on a park bench. She is wearing a pair of dark jeans, a graphic tee with the words *Bee Kind* and a bee on it, and pale pink sneakers.

She pops the last grape of the snack pack she is eating and stands. "Nice to see you again."

He raises an eyebrow at her. "No dress today?"

She sticks her tongue out at him and walks to a nearby trashcan. "Nope. We are getting dirty today."

He raises his other eyebrow. "Oh yeah? Like making out dirty?"

She laughs and tosses her empty grape bag away. "You wish." Angelica surveys him. She wishes she would've given him a dress code, but she only saw him in dark clothes thus far, so she didn't even think about it. She starts nervously braiding her hair when she realizes that he dressed up to see her. "You look very nice today ... but that may be *too* nice."

Damon looks down at his maroon button-down shirt.

"Not a problem. I have a t-shirt underneath. I'll just take off the button-down."

When he starts unbuttoning his shirt, Angelica tears her eyes away before her thoughts can get off topic. The way he looks in that shirt with his sleeves rolled up to his elbows … it is something. She didn't notice his half-sleeve tattoo before, and it made him that much sexier. She would be lying if she said she didn't think about his toned body during the week while she nervously worked up the courage to text him … and she doesn't need to think about him like that anymore. At least until he becomes an angel. Once that task is completed … her thoughts are free to roam.

"Okay, I'm ready," Damon says, his shirt bundled up in his hand.

Angelica gently takes it from him, folds it up, and zips it up in the bookbag she brought with her.

The initial adrenaline from seeing her again is evaporating, and he is starting to feel awkward. "Thanks."

She examines the half-sleeve tattoo, shocked that she hadn't noticed before. It was the famous Starry Night painting in black in white—beautiful and intricate. "I like your tattoo. It looks awesome."

"Thanks." He says again.

"Anytime." She clears her throat and the bright, happy smile she normally keeps on her face reappears. "Are you *so* ready for your first angel day!?"

Damon forces himself to smile. "Let's do this."

Angelica sees right through him. *He must be nervous,*

she thinks. "I know this feels weird to you, but you will get the hang of it. She holds her hand out to him. "Trust me."

Damon hesitates. Her hand lies outstretched in front of him. *There must be another way ...* his eyes leave her hand and meet her gaze, and she is still smiling. He sighs and finally grabs her hand.

She pulls them through dimensions until they are standing in front of an old building. Paint peels off the sides, a large fence lines the property, and a huge sign out front reads PAWSITIVE PALS.

"An animal shelter?" Damon asks skeptically. *This is what she meant by getting dirty.*

"Yes!" she squeals.

His lips curl down in disgust. He has never been a big fan of animals; he had an old cat growing up, but she was always mean to him.

"Get that nasty look off your face." Angelica laughs. "This is what you signed up for! Being an angel isn't all fun and games. It's hard work, remember?"

He nods once, still grimacing.

"So, what do sheltered animals make you think of?"

"Smelly cages? Sad, old animals? Poop?"

Angelica laughs again. "I mean, kinda. That's part of it. But that's not what we are focusing on. One of the most important values of being an angel is ..." She dances in place before creating a rainbow with her hands and singing the next words. "Compassion and patience!"

This was not a good idea. "I didn't know you were a singer."

She straightens and flicks back her braid. "I won my seventh-grade talent show because of it. Back to the matter at hand."

He chuckles and rubs his hand over his mouth.

"So, technically, being compassionate is one of the fundamental rules in being an angel, but patience is also important. We will encompass them both today."

Damon looks back to the run-down building. All he can hear is barking coming from inside. Lots. Of. Barking.

"So, what is compassion?"

"Oh, now you're asking me more questions?"

Her smile turns into a grimace. "If you are studying to take the angel *tests*, wouldn't you think that I would quiz you from time to time?"

"I just like getting under your skin, sassy."

Angelica rests her hand on her hip, waiting.

Damon clears his throat. "Okay, compassion? Uh …" He racks his brain. It's been a long time since he's thought of anything besides being a dick, taking people to Hell, drinking, carrying out his work, and sex. Compassion … "Isn't it like caring about other people?"

She waves her hand in the air as if trying to guide his words. "Can you be more specific?"

He can feel his face turning red. He thinks about the animals, how they are mostly old and sad and nobody wants them … oh, wait—"Is it caring about other people or animals that no one wants?"

"Warmer. What should you feel when you look at these animals?"

My god, this is so fucking embarrassing. **Damon** knows he is blushing now. "Bad?"

Angelica gives him a pitiful smile. "Close. Being compassionate means caring and feeling bad for people who are suffering, but *also* wanting to help them. Wishing that they had a better life or hoping you can do something to improve it." She turns and throws her hands up in front of the building, her voice rising a few octaves. "And volunteering to help poor, innocent animals who have no one is a perfect example!"

Before he can leave—which he really wanted to do—she loops her arms through his and directs him toward the building. The buzzing feeling returns, and this time it almost calms him as they walk inside. The walls are lined with pictures of dogs, cats, and even some birds. Under each picture is a plaque that says the name of the animal and the date they were adopted.

Angelica greets the woman behind the check-in counter while Damon looks at a picture of a beagle puppy.

SAM
11 MONTHS OLD
ADOPTED 8/2/2014

"Hi!" Angelica says cheerfully. "Angelica and Damon, here to volunteer!"

"Great! Welcome." The middle-aged woman with graying hair peers at them before grabbing a few pieces of paper and pens, which she hands to Angelica. "Read the first paper and sign the second."

They skim and sign, Angelica way more eagerly than Damon.

"Thank you." The woman files them away in a manilla folder on her desk before beckoning them towards a side door. A sign above the door read STAFF ONLY. "You two can follow me."

The woman, who introduces herself as Karla, walks them through the shelter. Angelica is basically skipping as they follow her, while Damon is sulking.

"First thing to do is walk the dogs," Karla instructs loudly as they enter a room filled with cages and barking dogs. "One dog per person at a time. They usually walk for about fifteen to twenty minutes. Follow the path right outside that door." She points at the green door to the left. "After you finish the walks, come back in here and bathe the dogs with blue collars. Then, when you are all finished with that, come find me." She hands them two leashes and smiles before disappearing out the door they came in through.

Angelica hurries over to scope out the cages. "Who wants to go on a walk first?" she coos.

She locks eyes with a beautiful German Shepherd mix. "Hello, Balto. Do you want to go on a walk?" The dog answers with a joyous yelp and wags his tail vigorously.

Damon's disgusted look returns to his face as he scrutinizes all the dogs. *Eyes on the prize, eyes on the prize ...* he chants to himself. He walks to the cage next to Angelica's. An old mutt is snarling at him, baring its teeth with its fur raised.

"Do you think it knows what I am?" Damon asks nervously.

Angelica shrugs. "Maybe he's just mean?" She clicks the leash on Balto smoothly before coming over to check on Damon. As soon as the mean mutt sees her, he stops snarling and wags his tail. She giggles. "No, he definitely knows that you are a mean ole demon."

"Ha," Damon says flatly. "What do I do now?"

"Try being nice to him!"

Damon gulps. *This dog is going to eat me alive.* He reaches for the lock on the gate. "It's okay …" He glances at the information sheet hanging next to his cage for the name. "Killer." *Ha-ha. Funny.*

The dog continues to growl. "Don't worry, I won't hurt you." Damon tries to sound as sweet and kind as Angelica did, but it comes out monotone and awkward.

Angelica giggles quietly to herself. *He looks so adorable right now.* "Hey, it's okay. You got this!" she encourages.

Damon tries to keep his composure, although this dog is starting to really piss him off. Actually, the whole situation is pissing him off. The fact that this is even his mission is one thing, but having to pretend to want to be an angel and be good is another. He's accepted his fate, knows he is anything but good, and has no desire to be that. Plus, he is beginning to feel physically sick—this is against his nature.

He pauses when he recognizes that thought. *She said that would happen …*

He lets out a long whoosh of air, then crouches down

close to the dog's face, his teeth gritted. "Look, dog. I know I may be a demon, but I'm trying to be nicer, and I would really appreciate it if you'd let me take you on a walk."

Killer stares at him with beady eyes. Damon encourages the standoff, knowing he will not be the loser. After a solid three minutes, Killer looks away and makes a huffing sound, letting his fur fall back to its normal place. Damon grins as he swings open the gate and clasps the leash onto his collar. "Good boy!"

Angelica, who has been watching the whole encounter, feels her heart warm when she sees Damon soften. The emotionless grimace that usually rests on his face is no longer there. A small smile—his teeth barely showing—is in its place as he pets Killer. She holds open the door and they all walk out, Killer sprinting at full speed and pulling Damon behind him.

Chapter 14

Damon and Angelica walk their dogs down the gravel path that Karla showed them. Both of the dogs take every opportunity to stop, smell the grass, and pee a little. Neither of them speak except to get the dogs to move or laugh at their antics. Damon wants to talk to Angelica and get to know her, but he is enjoying the quiet. No screaming humans or loud bar music here. The barking dogs quieted down, and they all wait inside patiently for their turn to walk.

Damon will never admit it aloud, but walking the dog, getting some sunshine, and not being stuck doing bad things to people is actually nice. A part of him feels warm and fuzzy inside.

They finish walking Balto and Killer and then leash new dogs. Damon picks Daisy, a pretty girl who, according to her information sheet, is a mix between a lab and a pit bull. This time it doesn't take him nearly as long to coax her. He is feeling better than he has been in a long time.

Back outside, Angelica speaks up. "How are you doing?"

"I'm fine," he replies, brushing his hair back with his hand. The September sun is beating down on them.

"You seem a lot lighter today," she says, trying not to stare at him and his rustled hair.

Damon frowns. "Lighter?"

"You know what I mean. Like a weight has been lifted off your shoulders?"

"Sure."

"Never mind." She sighs.

Silence falls on them once more, until Damon's phone buzzes. He ignores it. Thirty seconds later, it buzzes again. And again.

"Are you going to get that?" Angelica asks. "I don't mind."

He slips his phone out of his back pocket and groans. Chloe is blowing up his phone with angry texts, obviously still upset about earlier. He turns it on silent and shoves it back out of sight.

Angelica gives him a quizzical look. "Everything okay?"

"Yeah, it's nothing." Daisy pauses to sniff a broken stick, and Damon leans down to pet her.

"What, is it your girlfriend or something?" she jokes, her stomach tightening at the thought of him being unavailable. As soon as that feeling registers, her brain scolds her. *That shouldn't matter to you!*

Damon hesitates before shaking his head. "No. I don't have a girlfriend."

Angelica sits on a bench right off the path. "You don't sound so sure."

"Trust me. It's just ... complicated."

She tilts her head to the side. "How so?"

One thing that always throws Damon for a loop is that Angelica always seems to genuinely care about what he has to say. Which is ridiculous. He never enjoys talking about himself because he knows no one gives a shit. But with her ... it is nice to be with someone who actually wants to know. Plus, he knows that opening up to her is the key to getting her to want to be with him and eventually become a demon. He needs to show his softer side, even if it makes him feel small.

She is still waiting, eyebrows raised. Her dog, Princess, is lounging in a sunny patch of grass next to her.

Damon sighs. "Well ... she wants to be exclusive. Like date, get married, the whole shebang. But I don't want to. To be honest, the whole thing is ridiculous to me. Is The Devil going to officiate the ceremony? Does she want to have demon babies that wreak havoc like us? Our afterlives and our jobs aren't really made for monogamy and raising children," he says, his eyes turning up to the sky in exasperation.

Angelica's face turns sympathetic. "I get that."

"But I'm a dick and like to fuck her when I'm drunk, and vice versa. She confronted me earlier about not calling her after our latest ... session," he ends awkwardly, almost spilling the details of the fight and blowing his cover. He pulls a cigarette out of his pack and lights it quickly to stop talking.

"You know, smoking is bad for you," Angelica says, her nose scrunching up.

He rolls his eyes. "I'm already dead. What's it gonna do, kill me?"

She doesn't answer—he got her there. She watches him exhale smoke, his other hand lax at his side as he holds the leash. His long hair is beaded with sweat on his forehead. Daisy is sniffing something a few yards away.

As he puffs on his cigarette, he has another realization—this is the first one he's smoked the entire time they've been there. He hasn't been anxious and felt the need to smoke. Once he realizes why, he internally complains. It is because he is around her—an angel. She is making him feel better. That nagging, empty feeling in his soul has subsided for now, hence no need for smoking.

He forces himself to finish the stick of tar, regardless.

Angelica waits, petting the little chihuahua she has leashed. She moved from the grass onto her lap, tired from all the excitement. Little muddy pawprints now garnish her jeans. "Here's an idea … why don't you just tell her you can't see her anymore? Set healthy boundaries. But you have to stick to them." She raises her eyebrows sternly at him, her eyes a mix of shades of green.

He laughs and tosses his cigarette on the ground. "Okay, Mom. Although I don't think she'd take it well, and I definitely don't want my balls being ripped off."

A sly grin creeps onto her face. "Well, good thing you won't need them anyway. No kids, remember?"

Her joke takes Damon by surprise, and he laughs, a toothy grin escaping onto his face. She laughs with him, and he looks over her a few moments. Honey was right—she is sweet, caring, and the more Damon gets to know her, spunky. And he likes it.

They smile at each other until the bad person in Damon's brain reminds him of his true reasons for being there. He turns away, tugging the dog with him.

Angelica watches him walk away. Even though she keeps trying to ignore it, she is becoming more and more attracted to him. Which feels completely ridiculous to her, since she knows barely anything about him. However, she wants to know everything about him … who is this guy, really? "Want to play the question game?"

"What are we, twelve?" He snorts, shoving a stick of cinnamon gum into his mouth.

She sticks her tongue out at him again. "No. I just feel like if we are going to be hanging out, I need to know you better. Ya know, to make sure you will not murder me or kidnap me and take me to Hell or something."

Damon laughs a little too forced. "Okay, fine. What do you want to know?"

"Hmm … what's your favorite animal?"

"That's what you want to know?"

"Well, it's a good start." She bumps into him as they walk to get a new set of dogs. Every time their skin touches, they are shocked. They have stopped reacting to it physically, but Angelica gets butterflies every time.

Damon isn't sure of what he feels just yet.

He thinks about her question. He hasn't been asked that in years. "Probably the tiger."

"That's a good one." Angelica nods in approval. "Your turn."

"What's your favorite animal?"

They return their dogs to their crates. "Oh, no, no, no!" Angelica wags her finger at him. "You can't ask me the same question right away. That's against the rules!"

"That's stupid," he says.

Angelica's shoulders slightly sag in defeat. They return to the gravel path, two new excited dogs strapped to their leashes.

Damon glances at her through his peripheral vision and curses himself when he sees her defeated face. "Okay, um … what's your favorite color?"

She grins. "Pink … obviously."

"Yeah, I could've guessed that one." He chuckles.

"How old are you?" Angelica asks.

Damon remembers that the angels celebrate birthdays, so he quickly adds two years onto the age he was when he died. "Twenty-four."

"I'm twenty-three!"

They continue asking simple questions. Damon finds out that she used to practice ballet growing up, her favorite flower is the dahlia, she really loves to sing—she's been told she sounds like a Colbie Caillat—and she's never broken a bone.

Angelica learns that his favorite color is green—which surprises her, since she has only seen him wear black, gray, and now maroon—he is a fan of older nineties bands, he's sprained his ankle skateboarding before, and he doesn't like tea.

But when Angelica asks him about his family, he shuts her down.

"Not something I want to talk about," he says firmly as they finish walking the last dogs.

"Why not?"

"Because I said so." He gives her a deathly glare, and she shrivels away from him. Damon has not talked to anyone besides Honey about his family, and he isn't ready to open up to Angelica like that, mission or not.

She doesn't argue. She understands that they are still basically strangers, hence the reason for the game in the first place.

They prepare the large outside bathtubs for the dogs with blue collars. Even though he is feeling better and talking to her, he still feels a little awkward. The demon part of him despises what he is doing, but the tiny, good part of him—the real him—is actually enjoying himself. Being with Angelica helps—her natural sunshine and love for life are contagious.

But then when he remembers that he is a wolf in sheep's clothing, he just feels stupid.

While they are washing the first dog, Angelica splashes water on him. He laughs and splashes her back. As they flirt, he takes a moment to admire her. Her clothes are damp as she sprays the hose on the dog, and she is covered in splotches of dirt and animal hair. Even though he has seen her all done up at the bar, Damon can't help but think how effortlessly gorgeous she looks in this moment.

"So, what exactly do you do as a demon?" she asks.

He presses his lips together. "Do you really want to know?"

"Well … can you just give me a rundown and spare me all the gory details?" She shivers thinking about all the evil possibilities.

"Well, The Devil is the boss, as I'm sure you know. We do all kinds of things. Ouija duty is the easiest job we have. We possess people, run cults, kill people …" He pauses for a moment when he sees her face twist in terror. "… and a bunch of other things."

She swallows, definitely wishing she didn't asked. "Did you have to take a test to become a demon?"

Damon clenches his jaw. "No. When I got to Hell, The Devil asked me."

"Was it easy for you to say yes? Do you … enjoy … what you do?"

"It was easy after he threw me in the fire for a few minutes." He sees her shift uncomfortably. "But it's not like I really enjoy what I do," he admits. "I just do it because the alternative is far worse." He motions to the area around them. "It's nice being able to walk around Earth and live normally, even if it's only a few times a week."

She looks back to the dog, focusing on soaping him.

Demons are bad people on Earth who are chosen to continue their life in a bad place. Their mission was to be just that—bad, evil people. To ruin lives, to create pain and suffering. She wouldn't understand; it's so alien to her. She is on the complete opposite part of the spectrum; angels literally save lives, make people happy, and *are* happy. People who do good on Earth get to live their afterlife in the most perfect place on Earth.

"Lucky bastards," Damon mutters.

Damon notices her staring at his burn. It is starting to blister as it heals, and it is ugly, peeling, and red.

"Did your boss do that to you?"

"Yeah."

"Why?"

"Because he was angry I wasn't doing my job quick enough," Damon says quietly.

She looks away from his arm and ruffles the dog's ears. "I'm sorry."

He shrugs. "Don't be. It's a part of the whole demon thing."

She purses her lips. "I can see why becoming an angel was so easy for you to consider."

He nods, faking a smile for her. "Yeah. Exactly."

A new thought pins into his brain.

What if I ... actually try to become an angel?

He thinks about the possibility. Getting out of Hell. Saving people's lives instead of ruining them. Being genuinely happy, like he is slowly feeling now ... being around her, which would be a major plus ...

Before he can think about it too much, the looming thought of The Devil finding out crushes his soul and erases the possibility. He would not be happy, and if he had the slightest inkling of what Damon was doing, he would kill him in a heartbeat. Damon quickly hardens back up.

It seems easy for him to leave his old life behind and start this new one. But it isn't. Even if The Devil wouldn't end up killing him, Damon is in Hell for a reason, after all. A reason that he is ashamed of, and he knows deep down that he doesn't deserve to go to Heaven and live out his life in peace. He is right where he deserves to be.

"So, what do angels do?"

Her face brightens. "Oh, so much good! I give out a lot of hugs, talk people out of depression, suicide, hurting themselves or others. Save lives, mainly."

"Gotcha. And what are the tests like?"

"If I give it all away, what fun would that be?" She winks. "There will be a written test, and then you will be given a series of practical tests. If you pass, Father himself will appoint you."

"Father?"

"Father, God, Creator, The Universe, whatever you want to call him. He is in charge. He is the one who oversees all the angels and humans in Heaven. The Devil's brother, Gaia's brother. Did you know they were triplets?"

"I didn't, actually. No wonder my boss is always so pissed; he definitely got the short end of the stick there. Who created them? Do they have parents?"

"No one knows. They've just always been there, or so the stories are told."

"Interesting …" Damon frowns.

Angelica watches him. "What are you thinking about? You look awfully serious."

"Just making sure this pooch gets enough soap," he lies.

"I see." She doesn't believe him but doesn't snoop anymore. She picks up the hose to rinse the dog. "So, do you think you understand the purpose of today? Compassion and patience? You definitely showed it earlier with Killer."

Damon nods as the dog starts shaking, water splashing on both of them. They laugh.

"How are you feeling about all this?"

He doesn't meet her gaze. "Honestly, I feel weird. A part of me feels great, but the other part feels like I'm doing something wrong. Which is stupid. I'm just washing dogs."

"First of all, you aren't just washing dogs. You are being helpful, compassionate, and patient!" She smiles warmly at him. "What you are doing is against everything they have programmed you to do. It's going to feel weird at first. Second, I am so proud of you. Above anything else, you are actually trying. I can tell you understand the impact you are putting on these animals. You are doing wonderful work!"

A lump forms in his throat at the way she is looking at him. "Thanks," he mumbles shyly. He hasn't heard *I'm proud of you* since before he died. It is ... nice.

Once they finish the bathing, they dry off their hands and make sure all the pups are accounted for. Angelica sneaks them all an extra treat before they check out. Karla sees them out, earnestly thanking them for all their hard work. Damon smiles awkwardly before heading out the door while Angelica hangs back to hug Karla and promise to return.

The sky is an array of colors from the setting sun.

"Day one complete!" Angelica cheers, raising her hand for a high five. Damon's hand meets hers with half of her enthusiasm. She laughs and continues, "I think you did very well. I definitely think you have what it takes to pass the test and become an angel. At least the easy parts." She winks.

Damon nods, silent again as he looks up to the sky.

She takes his silence as worry. "Hey." She grabs his hand, igniting the fire between them. Meeting his charcoal eyes, she smiles encouragingly. "It's normal to doubt yourself. I promise it'll all be okay."

He looks down at her small hand intertwined with his. It looks so out of place—hers perfectly manicured and petite, while his is calloused and rough. She has a sun ring on her middle finger that he runs his index finger over.

Angelica watches him stare at their hands. Something about the way his eyebrows furrow together in concentration, the way his damp shirt clings to his toned chest, and the buzz from their touching makes her knees weak. The slight burning turns warmer, no longer mere sparks, but now electric flames … and she is overcome with the overwhelming feeling of wanting to kiss him.

Even though they didn't touch when they first met in that basement, she understands why he may have wanted to kiss her that night.

Damon looks up and meets her gaze. Her opal eyes have turned into a glistening chartreuse color, and it is unlike anything he's ever seen before. He raises his eyebrows at her and the intensity in her gaze.

She blushes. "Can I ask you something?"

He nods.

"Do you feel that?"

He doesn't have to ask her to clarify; he knows what she's talking about. The voltaic feeling that Damon has been thinking about ever since their first time touching. He nods again.

Angelica's mouth twists into a small smile, and she forces her eyes away from his fierce gaze. She lets go of his hand and steps back. When their skin separates, the buzzing doesn't just stop completely but lingers before fizzling out.

Damon clears his throat. "Well … thank you for teaching me today. I actually had fun."

She clasps her hands together in glee. "Great! I'm so glad."

"When will I see you again?"

"I don't know. I can text you when I get some free time to train you again. Does that sound okay?" She reaches in her backpack to give him his shirt back.

"That sounds good." He takes the shirt and winks at her. "Bye, little angel."

She waves before disappearing.

Damon stands there for a moment before teleporting home as well. He strolls through his apartment, sits on his bed, and tries to ignore the gnawing feeling in his stomach.

Damon tries multiple ways to block out his

throughs—turning his stereo all the way up, watching mindless TV, and even debating jacking off. Unfortunately, nothing seems to help.

He sighs and lies back after a while, finally letting his thoughts wander.

Angelica really is a good person. Which pisses him off. She isn't an angel who acts like she is better than everyone else; she genuinely is kind, sweet, funny, and someone he enjoyed being around. She even made him laugh multiple times with her spunkiness. Even though he has only talked to her a few times, hanging out completely alone for the first time today, he feels more compelled by her each time.

If he was being completely honest with himself, she was exactly the type of woman he always dreamed of finding someday.

Now damning her to Hell just seems unfair. She doesn't deserve it in the slightest.

He groans and rubs his temples. *Is this what it's like to want to be good?*

A tremendous sadness fills him after that thought. He really is a bad guy if walking and washing a couple of mutts can turn his world upside down like this.

Snap out of it. The bad part of him returns to the surface. *You have to do this. It's just a job. Would you rather die?*

He opens his eyes and stares at his ceiling. "No," he answers aloud. "I'm not dying for her. I will get her to become a demon, and that's final."

Later that night, Damon ends up at a human bar and quickly finds an eager woman to take him home. He wants to get his mind off his guilt and torn soul, and a sexy brunette distracting him is just what he needs.

Until after, when the woman is sleeping in his arms and he is stuck awake.

The only thing on his mind ... Angelica Beck.

Chapter 15

"So, what was your first day of training like?" Cora asks, shoving a piece of brie into her mouth. The weekend has finally arrived, and the girls are sitting at Cora's kitchen table, making the invite list to her annual Halloween party. It is her biggest bash of the year—she loves encouraging everyone to dress up and have a wild night together.

"It wasn't bad. It was kind of awkward, and he isn't much of a talker on his own, but he really seemed to understand the lesson."

"Well, good. The sooner he becomes an angel, the sooner you can admit you like him."

Angelica's head snaps up from the list she is reading. "I do *not* like him."

"Bullshit," Cora provokes.

"We went over this already. I can't like him like that. I barely even know him!"

"What about the weird feeling you get when you touch? Don't you think that means something?"

Angelica groans, regretting telling her about it before she could figure out exactly what it was. Cora coaxed her to spill about the weird feeling after a few drinks the other night. She reacted exactly how Angelica had imagined—throwing out the words "soulmate" and "the universe wants you to have sex" and even more ridiculous things.

"I don't know. It means nothing to me," she coolly lies.

Cora gives her a sarcastic *uh huh* look.

"Don't give me that. Fine. I might just … think he's attractive …" Angelica trails off, thinking about how he looked yesterday. His button-down hugging his body perfectly and his sleeves rolled up, his black and white tattoo. His damp T-shirt sticking to his chest, his long hair pulled back in a low ponytail as they washed the dogs. "Really attractive."

Cora leans over the table towards her, whispering in a sexy voice, "Maybe his congratulation present for passing the tests can be your virginity."

Gasping, Angelica slaps her on the arm, making Cora burst into laughter. She wipes a tear from her cheek when her cackles subside. "When are you seeing him again?"

"I'm not sure. I told him we would text about the next training day. We still have plenty of time to train, so I'm not in a hurry."

"Okay, when do you *want* to see him again?"

Angelia sighs, knowing Cora will not let the conversation go. "I don't know. But … I almost kissed him yesterday."

Cora makes a big show of fake choking on her drink.

Angelica rolls her eyes and drums her fingers on the table, waiting for her to stop being dramatic.

After a good minute, Cora composes herself. "What!?"

"Okay, you are the most ridiculous person I've ever met, Cora." Angelica laughs. "Second, almost kissed him is a bit misleading. I wanted to kiss him at least. It was weird. When we were touching and just staring at each other ..." She blushes and looks down. It was usually Cora spilling the spicy details and not her. "The warm, tingly feeling was so intense. Then he looked at me and licked his lips, and I wanted to kiss him right then and there." She watched his tongue gently sneak out of his mouth to wet his bottom lip, and she was sure he didn't do it on purpose. But she saw and *wow*.

Cora fans herself. "*Dios mio*! Why didn't you go for it?"

"I didn't know how he'd react. Plus, we promised strictly business."

"Boooo."

"No! I can't be kissing him."

"Keep telling yourself that."

"I will ... but let's just say that he tries to kiss me ... what do I do?"

Cora shoves another cracker smothered in cheese into her mouth, a look of confusion on her face. "Why are you asking me as if you've never kissed a boy before?"

Angelica sighs. "Because I've never kissed a *demon* boy before. I know it's not a good idea, but I want to. Should I let it happen? Or reject him if he tries? Should I wait until he becomes an angel, or since he's in the process, would it be okay?"

"Thank you for finally admitting that you like him, at least." Cora winks. "But talking around it won't make it any better. If the opportunity presents itself, let it happen!"

Angelica huffs, her baby hairs blowing up on her forehead. "Okay, you're right."

"Of course I am." She laughs, but then her voice lowers. "Are you scared to like him because of … you know?"

"Maybe? I don't know."

"Baby girl." Cora reaches over to squeeze her shoulders. "It's hard. I understand. But don't jeopardize something that can be amazing because of something that happened years ago. Don't punish Damon for that man's mistakes."

Damon isn't … him, Angelica reiterates internally. "You're right," she says again.

Cora claps her hands together. "I never get tired of hearing that."

They giggle and return to their lists. Angelica tries to breathe through her stomach, which twisted into a big nervous knot at the mention of her ex. Even though it's been years, and she finally forgave him (a lot in thanks to her angel heart), it still traumatizes her.

Damon isn't the same asshole. He is actually trying to be better, not really a horrible man trapped in a "good guy" persona.

Right?

Even though he is a demon … and he is in Hell for a reason she doesn't know yet …

She shakes her head, erasing both of the men from her thoughts. She has been thinking about Damon way too much since she saw him two days ago and needed to stop. Pronto.

Chapter 16

~⁀~

"How's it going, dude?" Jeremy asks, walking up behind Damon, who is sitting on a bench in front of Missy's house. The demons conveniently placed it there for easier house watching.

"I'm bored," Damon says. "I've been here a few hours, waiting for her to show up. She won't answer my texts."

Jeremy parks himself next to Damon on the bench. "I understand, house watch is the worst. I'm glad you're here, though ... we've got company." Jeremy nods to behind them.

Damon turns around and makes eye contact with a man walking down the street. He isn't looking at them, but Damon can see his multicolored eyes.

"Get out of here; this isn't your territory," Damon growls at the angel.

The man turns toward them and tips his hat before disappearing.

"Damn angels." Jeremy sighs. "I knew it was only

a matter of time before they noticed our mark on their house."

"Do you think they will sabotage the mission?" Damon asks, a cigarette between his pointer and middle finger.

"Possibly. We will have to see. We still have enough time to get them off our backs."

They sit in silence, listening to the autumn breeze rustling through the trees.

"How is your other mission going?" Jeremy asks.

Damon sucks on his cigarette. He hasn't really spoken to Angelica since he saw her last week. He has debated texting her a few times to check in, but he still feels weird about the whole situation, so he is just putting it on the backburner for now. Even though he can't get her smiling face out of his mind.

"It's fine."

"It's been what, two weeks?"

"Yeah."

"Any progress?"

Damon shrugs. "A little. I don't want to freak her out, and The Boss isn't in a huge hurry. We've talked at the bar twice, hung out alone once. She thinks I want to become an angel, which is the only reason why she's talking to me."

Jeremy cackles. "You? An angel?"

Damon joins in his laughter. "Yeah, she isn't very bright."

"So, what's your game plan?"

Damon flings his cigarette into the street. "I take the

tests and fail. By that time, she will be so in love with me that becoming a demoness would be better than letting me go forever."

Jeremy shakes his head. "Good plan. You know women. If they think it's their idea, they will be more opt to do it."

Damon nods. He feels a small pang of guilt talking shit about Angelica after how kind she has been to him.

"Speaking of women ... have you talked to Chloe lately?"

Damon rolls his eyes. "No. I haven't. Why?"

"You may want to. She is super pissed at you."

"I know. We got in a fight when she found out about the angel mission."

"Yeah, she was bitchin' about the fight and you avoiding her since."

Damon sighs. "I just don't know why she can't leave me alone. I've told her countless times I don't want to be with her, yet she still doesn't listen to me."

"This is why I don't shit where I eat." Jeremy shrugs.

Damon narrows his eyes at Jeremy but doesn't comment. He knows he is a blunt person and isn't trying to rouse him.

At that moment, Missy's red Corolla pulls into her driveway.

"Duty calls," Damon says, standing.

Jeremy follows suit and claps him on the shoulder. "See you later. If you need anything, let me know. If not, I'll see you soon for the October meeting."

"Thanks, man."

Damon walks up to the house alone, popping his gum. He has been hanging out in the Middle—between the human and spiritual realms. He can choose whether or not he wants to be seen by certain humans. Damon makes sure Missy can see him as he ducks into the garage. "Hey, Missy."

She jumps, almost dropping the bag of groceries she just picked up. "Damon! Shit. You scared me. I didn't know you'd be coming over tonight."

He smiles at her. "Sorry about that. Let me help with the groceries." He opens the car back door and stacks grocery bags on his arms.

"Thanks," she says, and they head inside the house. They unload all the groceries in silence and put them inside cabinets and in the fridge. Once everything is in its place, Missy grabs a pint of ice cream and offers Damon a spoon. He declines, and she shrugs before walking into the living room and turning on the television.

"How was your week?" Damon asks.

"It was fine. I failed my chemistry test, but then my friend and I went to see that new movie Poster Girls and it was decent."

"Isn't that the movie about the two girls who find out they've been kidnapped and missing their entire lives?"

"Yep, that's the one." She shoves a heaping bite of Moose Tracks into her mouth. "What about you?"

Damon knows he can't be honest about how annoyed he is with his job currently—it can harm his chances of her accepting his proposition—so he keeps it vague. "Boring, really. Worked and then went to the bar."

"Is that all you do?"

"Eh, not all of it. A big part of it, though."

Missy snorts. "And here you are on a Wednesday night, hanging out with the woman you're trying to sacrifice."

Damon exhales sharply and turns his attention to the sitcom that is playing on the TV. After she spoons a few more bites of ice cream into her mouth, he clears his throat. "Speaking of … have you thought more of what we talked about?"

She shrugs, her relaxed face turning fearful. "I don't know."

"You don't know if you've thought about it, or you don't know if you wanna do it?"

"I don't know if I wanna do it."

"I understand," he says. "It's a big step."

She scoffs. Her big brown eyes are full of annoyance. "A big step? Having a baby is a big step. Moving across the country is a big step. Killing myself so I can become The Devil's wife? That's more like a *ginormous* step."

Damon leans back into the couch. "You're right."

She takes another bite of ice cream, clearly not in the mood to discuss it further.

Damon looks over her. Her copper hair is pulled up in a messy bun and her toned body is clothed in running shorts and a hoodie. He notices a small floral tattoo on her ankle. His chest aches with pity as he stares at her. It is a shitty situation. He wishes he can tell her to forget it and move on, but his life is on the line. Plus, she will literally become a queen and have some magical powers like The Devil does. She'll turn out okay.

"What are you staring at me for?" she asks, setting down the now-empty tub of ice cream.

His eyes meet hers. "I was just thinking about everything. I'm sorry that it's such a hard decision." He reaches over to hold her hand. "But I promise you. Dying isn't that bad. It only hurts for a little."

She looks down at his hand on hers but doesn't pull away. "I'm not so scared of the dying as much as abandoning my family. What would they think when they found my body? They'd be heartbroken."

"Your family may not understand right away. They might never understand, to be honest." Damon says. "But you would be in our new family, and I promise that we would take such good care of you. The Devil is so excited to see you again. He can't stop talking about when you two met."

She blushes. "He hasn't?"

"No. He loves you." Damon forces himself to smile. He is lying through his teeth.

Missy doesn't answer for the longest time. Finally, she answers, "Can I have a little more time to think? Halloween still is a ways away."

"Of course. I just need to know your answer a week in advance so I can get everything situated. Deal?"

"Deal."

Missy walks back into the kitchen and throws away

her empty container. Damon listens to her bang about the room until she returns to the couch with a bag of potato chips and turns on a movie. He hangs out with her for a while longer since he has nothing better to do. He tries to let his mind get lost in the rom-com she picked out and forget his missions or his looming failure, but when a gorgeous blonde goes on a date with the main character, Angelica returns to his thoughts.

His eyes dart to his phone. He hasn't seen her in almost a week. Maybe he should talk to her. The food on the TV looks delicious, and he hasn't eaten yet … and he is supposed to be getting to know Angelica more …

Before he can stop himself, his phone is in his hands, and he shoots her a text. **Hey. What are you doing?**

His phone pings a few minutes later with her reply. **Right now? Just getting home from work. Is everything okay?**

Damon's heart quickens as he types out the next text and sends it just as quickly. **Do you have dinner plans? I'm starving.**

I do not have dinner plans.

He shakes his head at her formality. Is she really going to make him ask? **Well … do you want to get dinner with me? As friends.**

This time, her reply isn't instant. He stares at the TV for a good ten minutes, anxiety buzzing through his veins. With each passing minute, he feels even more stupid.

Until his phone pings again. **Sure :). Give me ten minutes to freshen up. Where are we going?**

A grin spreads across Damon's face as he reads the text and sends her back a restaurant and address.

"I don't think I've ever seen you smile that big," Missy comments, raising her eyebrow.

He stands. "I don't smile often."

"Got a hot date?"

Damon winks at her, his mood surprisingly elevated … especially since he knows that he shouldn't be this excited to see her. "Something like that."

Chapter 17

Angelica hurries upstairs to change out of her sweats and into a cute outfit. Not that she is trying to impress him, since it isn't a date, but she still wants to look nice. She throws on a jean skirt with an emerald green blouse and flats. Angelica combs her hair quickly and throws it up into a half-updo before swiping on some more blush and lip gloss.

When she appears at the diner, she lets out a nervous breath when she realizes he isn't there yet. *Good*.

The hostess walks Angelica through the old-fashioned diner and sets her in a little booth. She looks around the room, admiring all the vintage parts about it. The floor is checkered, and the booth she sits in has blue sparkles in the leather. Records, magazines, and mirrors adorned the walls, and she starts reading the magazine cover closest to her. Dolly Parton is posing on it.

She hears the jingle of the front door and looks as the hostess points Damon toward their table. Angelica smiles and raises her arm.

Damon smirks back and walks toward her.

"Hey," he says as he slides into the booth. "Sorry I'm a little late."

"No problem. I just got here."

The waiter approaches the table and gives Angelica a double-take before clearing his throat and asking for their drink orders. Angelica orders a water while Damon orders a Dr. Pepper. The waiter leaves and returns with their drinks quickly.

"Are you ready to order?" The waiter asks them.

Angelica looks like a deer caught in the headlights. She hasn't even looked at the menu. "No. Do you, Damon?"

"I get the same thing every time. Double cheeseburger and fries."

"Ooh," Angelica says, her stomach grumbling. "Make that two!" She smiles at the waiter. "Can I also get a chocolate milkshake?"

"You sure can." The waiter smiles.

"Make that two," Damon says to the waiter but winks at Angelica. The waiter scribbles in his notepad and disappears.

Angelica leans back in the booth. His wink makes her stomach dance. "So, why'd you ask me to dinner?"

He shrugs out of his jacket. "Friends get dinner together all the time. I was hungry and didn't want to eat alone tonight."

She puts a hand over her heart and swoons. "I didn't know you considered us friends."

Damon raises his eyebrows. "Do you not consider me a friend?"

Her face heats. "No, that's not what I meant!"

He raises a hand to cut her off, but his voice is playful. "No, I understand how you really feel about me now."

Angelica shakes her head and laughs. He was playful and flirty with her a few times before, but this time she can tell he isn't feeling as awkward as he was at the animal shelter.

"So, I'm pretty sure it's your turn for a question," Damon says, taking a drink.

"Is it?" Angelica sits forward and thinks for a moment. "Hmm … how has your week been?"

"Boring. Working on another mission I have and then just hung out at the bar. I don't do much besides that."

"Do I want to know what your other mission is?" she asks.

Damon purses his lips and shakes his head. "What's your favorite animal?" he asks.

"Definitely the hummingbird. They are so fast and mighty for their size! And adorable, of course."

"Of course." Damon smiles.

Their food arrives and is set in front of them. Angelica douses her fries in ketchup while Damon takes a huge bite of burger.

Angelica tries not to stare at him, but something feels different about them hanging out this time. Maybe it's because last time they admitted they felt something weird when they touched. Maybe he has started feeling the same things that she does when she thinks about him ... like butterflies.

She glances up at him through her thick lashes. *Do guys even feel butterflies?*

"What is one thing that you can eat every day?" she asks him halfway through their meal.

"Fruit snacks. What is your favorite thing to eat?"

She gives him a look.

"Hey! Those are different questions. Close, but different." He smirks with a mouth full of food.

"Chocolate for sure. I have bowls of it all throughout my house." She makes a point to slurp down her chocolate milkshake.

Damon's face scrunches together, dumbfounded. "You have a house?"

"Yes! It's my dream home. It's a six-bedroom mansion, although I've turned a few of the bedrooms into a library and a craft room. It even has a home theater, and I have a huge flower garden. A small pool is outside ..." she trails off when she sees him set down his burger and stare at his plate. "Everything okay?"

"Yeah. Fine." He grumbles, in a totally different mood than the happy, playful one he was just in.

Angelica looks down. "I'm not trying to brag. I'm sorry. I assume things are different for you in ... where you live."

He looks up at her with a hateful glare. "Do you want to know what I live in?" He asks rhetorically. "I live in a tiny one-bedroom apartment with no locking doors. My kitchen appliances barely work. I have a bed, dresser, tv, couch, a few dishes, and a kitchen table all to my name, and that's it."

"I'm sorry, Damon."

He ignores her apology. "Does he watch you?"

She picks at a lukewarm fry. "Watch me?"

"Yeah. In Hell, we have no privacy at all. The Devil can watch us all the time as if he has hidden cameras set up everywhere. It isn't constant, but you never know when he might be watching you. The only place he can't watch us is on Earth."

"Oh. Yeah, Father does the same. He is always with each of us, but he doesn't necessarily always keep an eye on us. He respects our privacy." She glances at him but quickly looks back down when she sees he is still glaring at her. "He can't see us on Earth either."

Damon takes a deep breath, trying to calm down his anger. He hates the way that she looks right now. He can clearly see he made her uncomfortable, maybe even a little scared, with his glaring and snarling. It's not her fault that she has a ... *mansion* ... and he doesn't. Softening his voice, he tries to lighten the mood once more. "Oh, so he can't see us do inappropriate things?"

It works. She looks up at him, and when she sees his smile, a small one appears on her lips. "Easy, tiger."

The waiter returns with separate bills. Angelica fishes in her purse for her wallet, and Damon grabs his own. He debates on paying for both of them, but he knows she doesn't want it to be a date ... so he doesn't.

"Where do you get your money from?" Angelica asks him. "We just have it on hand whenever."

"Same. This sounds ridiculous, but we have a bank where we just get money to use on earth. There's a demon teller and everything."

Angelica laughs. As they walk outside, she rubs her full stomach lovingly. "That was delicious."

"I agree," Damon says, shoving his hands into his pockets. "Thank you for joining me."

"Well, thank you for inviting me."

They look at the ground awkwardly. Do they just say, "See you later?" Or fist bump? Hug?

Damon clears his throat. "Um, have you decided on a training day?"

She thinks for a moment. "How about next Monday?" She smiles. "I have a feeling you will like our next day *a lot* better than the dogs."

He can't help but grin back at her. Her smile is contagious. "That sounds perfect."

They smile at each other for a few moments, both of their hearts quickening. Both of them a little too excited to see each other again on Monday. Before Angelica can do something embarrassing—like try to hug him or even think about kissing his gorgeous face—she waves goodbye and disappears.

Damon sits on the curb to smoke a cigarette, sighing. He thought about leaning over to kiss her cheek before she left, but she vanished too fast. Probably a good thing ... he knows that he is getting into dangerous territory. As much as he tries to ignore it, he can't deny it any longer.

He is starting to fall for Angelica.

Even though tonight wasn't a date ... a part of him feels like it could've been. She was a little flirty with him. She looked cute—did she dress up for him? And the way she hesitated before she left ... was she reluctant to go?

The signs are there. Damon has been trying to stop thinking about her all week. He can pretend that it was all for the sake of the mission, but he knows that's bullshit. When he thinks about her, only half of the time does it concern bringing her to Hell. The other half of the time it's the melodic sound of her laugh, the way she lights up a room, and the way she looks at him like ... he is more than a demon.

He smokes the cigarette in his hand, thinking about how good she looked in that jean skirt. Until the demon part of him snaps him back to reality. *This is a mission, not a love story.*

Back in Heaven, Angelica thinks about the dinner. About their conversation, Damon's smile, and what Cora has been teasing her about.

Realizing that ... maybe ... she does kinda like Damon after all.

Chapter 18

"New York City?" Damon asks, looking around the crowded streets. The weekend finally passed—slower than a snail for both of them—and they are together again.

"Yes! The Big Apple!" Angelica sings. She dances and narrates about the people surrounding them. "Look! People hustling to get to work! That person is almost naked! That looks like someone I've seen in a movie before. Aww, look at those puppies! So many different lives go on here, and it is amazing."

Damon chuckles at her. "So, what does NYC have to do with our lesson today?"

"Come on, let's go find a cute little coffee shop to sit in, and you'll find out."

Damon follows Angelica as she weaves through the crowd. As much as he hated himself for it, Damon was looking forward to seeing her again today. He spent most of the weekend chilling at the bar, hoping she would come in through the door. Cora came a few times, but she was busy with another male angel. Damon thought about asking her where Angelica was, but he didn't want to be weird. Now, as he follows behind her, he feels at ease again, like how he usually does when he is with her. The wind blows, and he inhales the sweet scent of her perfume, smiling.

Dude.

As soon as he gives in to the slightest feeling he has for her, the evil part of him shoots him down. He feels like Dr. Jekyll and Hyde, except reverse. The good part of him is trying to emerge, but the evil part keeps pushing it down. It is exhausting.

They finally arrive at a small café tucked into a side road. Angelica walks in happily, making herself seen by the humans. Damon follows her lead.

"Good morning!" she says cheerily to the barista. "How are you today?"

Who talks to the baristas? Damon thinks.

"Good, what can I get you?" the barista asks unenthusiastically.

Angelica orders a latte and funfetti cupcake and then looks to Damon, who orders a black coffee with a blueberry muffin.

She snorts at his order as the barista prepares their drinks. "You are so boring."

"It's not boring, it's classic." Damon says seriously but cracks a smile.

Angelica giggles and shakes her head. "Okay, weirdo."

When the barista returns, Angelica tries to pay, but Damon cuts her off and reaches into his own wallet.

"I got breakfast," he says nonchalantly.

"Aw, how sweet." She smiles. The barista takes his money and Angelica whispers so low no human can hear. "Is there anything else you want to do?"

"Like what?" Damon asks, whispering as lowly as she.

"I can't tell you. Does it feel like anything needs to happen? Remember, our first lesson was compassion."

He draws a blank. "Yeah, but what does that have to do with me getting breakfast?"

Her helpful smile wavers into a grimace as she becomes more annoyed. "Do I really need to spell it out for you?"

His face burns. "Maybe?"

"Tip him."

"Tip him?" Damon says, his forehead wrinkling. "All he did was take my order and make some coffee. That's dumb."

Angelica forces a smile—*remember, you are training him!*—"Be nice. You never know who could use the extra kindness."

The barista places their coffees and treats on the counter before turning back to the register, counting the money.

Tip him? That's stupid. All he did was take my order and make me a coffee. Plus, he doesn't need extra money—not my fault that he is a coffee shop worker and not doing something better with his time. If he wants more money, he can get a better job. It's my money, and I don't want to spend it on some loser.

Damon freezes at his own thoughts. *Wait ... is this the evil in me? Am I being mean just to be mean?*

He watches the cashier count the cash. He can't be

much older than eighteen or nineteen. *Maybe he is going to school to do something better? Maybe he just moved here, and this is the first job he could find? Maybe this is his third job because he is struggling to pay rent? Maybe ... maybe it'd be nice if he got a good tip.*

Damon can feel Angelica's eyes burning into his profile as the barista holds out his change. Damon clears his throat and pushes his hand back. "Uh, no, man ... you keep it."

The barista—Brandon, according to his nametag—looks at him with wide eyes. "All of it? All seventy-six dollars?"

Damon picks up the coffees and nods uncomfortably. "Yeah. It's yours."

Angelica comes to his rescue. "You deserve it, Brandon! We see you working so hard."

After the initial shock of the huge tip wears off, tears fill his eyes. "You guys just made my whole week. I just moved here to be an actor and gigs have been low, so I've been struggling to pay rent, which is why I picked up this extra shift in the first place. And with this tip ... it's covered, and then some!"

Angelica praises him and asks him all about his acting gigs, while Damon bolts to a table in the corner. He sips on his hot coffee, feeling stupid that it took him that long to figure out what to do. He used to tip when he was a human; how could something so normal make him feel so dumb?

Angelica finds him a few minutes later, holding their breakfast and smiling from ear to ear. "That was an amazing thing you did, Damon."

"You told me to."

She reaches across the table to touch his hand. "Yes, but you didn't have to. It's ingrained in you to be selfish and not care about others. Was that easy for you to do, or did it take some convincing?"

He slides his hand out from under hers and under the table, his ears reddening. "It was hard. A lot harder than it should've been."

"That's all?" she asks, resting her face in her hands, waiting for him to spill more.

He looks up and gives into her angel eyes. "At first, I thought it was stupid. Why should I give him extra money when he chose this job, knowing that it didn't pay well? But then I thought that maybe he lost his job and is struggling, or maybe he was going to school, or something. It's not my job to judge him. I remember that's the thing with compassion, right? I feel bad and want to help him?"

"YES!" Angelica cheers, standing and dancing excitedly.

Damon jumps and looks around the café to see if anyone else is just as startled as he. No one moves a muscle.

She sits back down and returns to the human realm again. "Damon, you just said one of the most important things us angels believe. *It's not my job to judge him.* That is exactly what we preach! It isn't our job to judge—that's Father's job. Our job is to be as helpful and loving as we can be." Her heartstrings tug at each other as she looks at him. "I am so proud of you. You are learning so much so quickly. I guess getting peed on by dogs was exactly what you needed."

Damon smiles and looks down, picking at his blueberry

muffin. He doesn't normally smile, but when he's with her, it seems to be the only thing he does. It makes his cheeks ache.

Angelica's breath is taken away by him. He is not only being nicer to her but also being nicer to others—even if it took a little push. She is helping him. It is working. She examines his smiling face and continues with the lesson. "So, besides compassion, are there other specific feelings that came up?"

He leans back in his chair and watches Brandon talking to a customer. Gone is the sullen face. In its place is a toothy, happy grin. "I don't know if this is a feeling … but let's say that I'm a human and I need that money. Obviously, as demons and angels, we just have it on hand for Earth purposes and don't need it to live, but if I were a human, I would. My human self knows that I need that money, but I know he may need it more than I do, so I give it to him anyway. Even if I know that I may struggle later. Does that make sense?"

When she doesn't answer, he looks at her and is taken aback when he sees tears in her eyes. "What?"

Angelica blinks through her tears. "Damon, I could kiss you!"

She then turns redder than a tomato, bites down on her lip, and stares down at the cupcake between her hands. *Real smooth, Angelica!*

Damon's heart stops beating. He knows she probably doesn't mean anything of it—it is an expression—but a part of him hopes she means it …

Without thinking too hard, he reaches across the table and lifts her chin with his hand. "Do you want to?"

They lock eyes as the current flows through them. Angelica doesn't know how to answer. If she says yes, will he lean over and do it right there, in the middle of the café? Or will he laugh and let it go? God, she wants to say yes and feel his lips on hers. She melts into his charcoal eyes and slowly loosens her bite on her lip. When they part, she takes a short breath, about to admit that she does ... or lie and say she doesn't ... she isn't sure...

Someone drops a coffee near the entrance, and everyone's head whips to the loud sound. Angelica scoots back and out of his grasp, nervously giggling as she peels the wrapper off her cupcake.

Damon searches her face for a sign. Anything to show him that she does want to kiss him and he isn't just swept up in her perfection and the connection between them. She did ask about the weird feeling, which is a good sign ... and her face is red, another good sign ...

He lets it go, promising himself that he will ask her again soon, and drinks the rest of his coffee.

After taking a bite of her cupcake, a few sprinkles falling onto the table, Angelica speaks. "Today we will focus on humility and selflessness."

"Is that what I just described?"

"Just about! Humility is thinking of others and putting yourself last. Selflessness is acting on that. So, with Brandon, you thought about how he has it worse than you, and you gave him a generous tip—knowing that you could've used that money elsewhere."

"If I were a human and needed that money."

"Yes. If you were a human and needed that money."

"I get it," Damon says, finishing his muffin. "Wasn't the last lesson humbling, too?"

"More or less," she says, standing. She crumples her cupcake wrapper and shoves it into her empty coffee cup. "Are you ready to be an angel today?"

He smiles and nods, genuinely looking forward to spending more time with her, regardless of what they might do. He follows her out of the café and back onto the busy sidewalk.

Angelica looks around and gathers her surroundings. "Okay, we need to be on …" she murmurs, reading the street signs. "Follow me! We have a few blocks to walk before arriving at our destination."

Damon follows her once again. As they walk, he has to remind himself over and over his true intentions of being there. He isn't really trying to become an angel. He is there to convince her to become a demon. That's it. As if he needs another reminder, his burn aches, reminding him of The Devil's power and ability to kill him off if he even tries to get out. He can never leave. Damon's soul is owned.

"Who's turn is it for a question?" she asks as they turn a corner.

"I don't remember," he says flatly.

She gives him a sideways glance, confused at his change of tone. "Okay, I'll go then. What's your favorite season?"

He looks up to the gray sky. "Summer."

Angelica lets out a little giggle.

He narrows his eyes at her. "What's so funny?"

"I don't peg you for a summer guy. I figured you would've said winter ..."

"Because I'm cold?"

She shakes her head. "No! Because you always wear dark colors ... okay, and maybe because you're a little cold." She smiles at him playfully.

He looks down at his black t-shirt and shrugs. "I'm guessing yours is summer, too?"

"Nope! Fall. I love the changing leaves and warm sweaters."

Damon's eyes trail down her body. She is wearing a long pink sweater with tall, over-the-knee boots and a long gold necklace. It suits her nicely. "You don't say."

They approach a crosswalk and stop while the light is red. "That doesn't count as your question," she reminds him.

"Do you have any hobbies?"

"I actually like to write. Poetry, mostly. And then I like to read."

"Writing is fun. I'm not much of a reader." He swallows before admitting his own hobby that no one really knows about. "I paint."

"You paint?" Angelica asks, surprise laced in her voice.

"Well, not so much anymore. I just started getting back into it, but I was a big painter growing up. I have a bachelor's in art, and one of my paintings is hanging up in an art gallery in Los Angeles." He notices her bewildered expression. "What? Am I bragging?"

"No way!" She squeals and grabs his arm. "That's so cool! What do you like to paint? What's your art style? I want to know everything."

Angelica doesn't need to ask him twice. Damon talks all about his love for painting, growing up with it, everything. They walk through the streets as she listens to him intently, smiling and laughing at his stories. Damon opens up to her entirely and without worry. The only thing he doesn't admit is that his most recent paintings are about her. He started painting another one over the weekend of a woman walking a dog with sun-kissed blonde hair.

They stop at another corner, and Damon finally stops talking. He looks down sheepishly.

"That explains the Starry Night tattoo," Angelica says. "Do you like van Gogh?"

"Oh, yeah," Damon says, looking down at his intricate tattoo. "I knew I wanted that painting on me when I first saw it. I love the colorful version, but something about it being in black and white is awesome to me."

"I agree." Angelica reaches over to rub his shoulder. "Thank you," she says warmly.

"For what?" he asks, avoiding her eyes.

"For opening up to me. For being vulnerable and showing me a part of who you truly are." She reaches her hand up to trail her thumb across his cheek and then walks across the street with the crowd.

Damon doesn't move. He watches her cross the street, dumbfounded by her sweet caress. He opened up to her and showed her a part of him that only Honey knew about, and the sky didn't fall. She didn't reject him or call him stupid. She ... thanked him. He smiles and follows her.

Damon was staring at his feet the entire time he crossed the street, so he didn't see her stop walking. He barrels into her, and they both almost fall.

"Whoa, what the hell?"

Angelica turns to look at him, her phone in her hand, and her eyes widened in terror. "Shit, I gotta go, Damon."

He picks up on her alarm immediately. "What's wrong?"

"I'm on call and ..." She points to her phone anxiously. "Do you want to stay or go?"

"What?"

"Do you want to come with me or go home? I don't care either way, but I don't have time to wait for you to decide." Her opal eyes are a fierce mix of violet and magenta.

His stomach twists at her intensity. Curiosity fills him about what she does as an angel, and he wants to know what she is so worried about. What is she really like on the job? Even though a part of him is terrified, he looks at her confidently and says, "I'll go."

She grabs his hand and together they teleport out of New York City.

Chapter 19

Angelica and Damon open their eyes and take in their surroundings. They are standing in the corner of a young girl's bedroom. Posters of boy bands and movies are scattered across the walls. A CD player sits in the corner with a loud band playing—Damon recognizes it as Evanescence's "My Immortal."

And in the middle of the room, on a large bed, sits a teenage girl sobbing on her bed with a pistol in her hand.

Damon freezes.

Angelica rushes over to the young girl and sits on the edge of the bed. "Rose?"

She looks up with mascara-stained cheeks and sucks in a breath. "Who are you? Where did you come from?"

"I'm Angelica. I'm here to help you." She reaches over to hold her hand, but Rose shoves it away.

"I don't need any help!" she yells.

"I'm an angel, and I'm here to make you feel better. I give great hugs."

"You're lying," Rose says, tears sliding down her face. "You're a figment of my imagination. Fake, just like my mental illness."

"I promise you, I am very real. Can you tell me what's wrong? I'm a great listener."

"No. Go away."

"Please, Rose. I'm worried about you. Just ... give me the gun," Angelica pleads, reaching for the pistol.

"No!" Rose says, lifting the gun in the air.

Damon wants to move, to help, but he can't. He's frozen. This is too real for him. Too close to home.

Angelica takes a deep breath. "Rose, I know you think no one cares. I promise you that you are loved. You are needed on this earth."

"You don't know! No one at my school likes me. I get bullied all the time. I talked to the guidance counselor, and she thinks that I have depression. So, I told my parents, and they said I'm just trying to get attention." A sob escapes her lips. "Now everyone just calls me crazy at school, and my parents don't even care about how I feel anymore. No one will miss me if I kill myself. I'm just done."

"Oh, honey, no. I'm sorry you're getting bullied, and that your parents don't understand. I can talk to them and help them understand. I promise you they do care ..." Angelica says scooting closer to her.

Rose lifts the gun to her temple. "Don't come near me! Or I'll ... I'll pull the trigger!"

Angelica doesn't move or breathe. She can see just how shaky Rose is and doesn't want to scare her even more. She already said all the things that usually help and stop the crying, but nothing is working. Fear grips her as she thinks about failing this girl and letting her die.

Damon unfreezes in the corner. Seeing Angelica struggle ignites a feeling of courage in him, and he walks over to them. "Rose, trust me, you don't want to do this."

Rose, just now noticing Damon, glares at him through her tears. "How do you know what I want?"

Damon sits right next to Angelica and takes a deep breath. He looks at Rose sadly. "Because … I was in your position a few years ago. But I actually ended up pulling the trigger."

The girls both look at Damon with wide eyes. The only sound in the room is the sad music blaring from the speakers.

"You killed yourself?" Rose asks quietly, slowly lowering the pistol into her lap.

Damon nods. "I did."

Her eyes narrow skeptically. "How do I know you're not lying?"

He turns to the side and lifts his long hair. Above his ear, a scarred-over bullet wound is revealed.

Angelica covers her mouth with her hand. *Oh, Damon.*

"You really did kill yourself." Rose's voice cracks at the devastation of his news. "What happened? Why did you do it?"

"I was in a terrible place," Damon says. "I did something bad that hurt many people, and I didn't know how to make it right. I felt like no one would forgive me, and I felt like no one cared about me either. So … I did what I thought was the only option. But let me tell you … I saw my funeral. I saw all the people who I thought didn't care about me there. They all were crying and told my dead body how much they loved me and how sorry they were. My parents still cry over me to this day."

"But how do you know that's the same case for me?"

"I just know." Damon smiles at her. "Trust me. You are loved, and enough, and you can get through this tough time. I'm so sorry that your parents said that to you, but they just don't understand. Why don't you and your guidance counselor talk to them together? We can help you, too. Ignore the bullies at school—they are just unhappy with themselves and take it out on you unfairly. I'm sure you still have a few friends who truly care about you. Keep them close. The mean people won't matter when you graduate. When will that be?"

"I graduate in two years."

"And what do you want to do after? College?"

A small smile forms on her lips. "I want to be a veterinarian, so I can help animals."

"And you will be." Damon turns to Angelica, who was still in shock at his confession. "Don't you think she'll be an excellent veterinarian?"

She forces her eyes away from him and turns to Rose. "The best!"

Rose looks down at the gun in her hands and slowly hands it over to Damon, who puts it back on safety and shoves it into his waistband and out of sight. She looks to Angelica with a sheepish smile. "Can I have that hug now?"

Angelica smiles and scooches over to wrap her arms around Rose, who cries into her chest. Damon's chest tightens as if he would cry, too, but he shoves down the feeling and rubs Rose's back.

Angelica catches Damon's eyes and mouths a silent "*That was incredible.*"

After she finishes crying, Rose lets go and wipes her face. "Thank you. You two are the best angels ever."

Damon can't help but feel his heart warm.

With Angelica's help, Rose cleans up her face and goes downstairs to tell her parents how she feels and that she needs help. She relays what Angelica says through her so that she can tell them exactly how she feels with a clear mind. Rose's parents start crying when they realize how bad she has been feeling and apologize for saying the wrong things. They promise to take her to a counselor in the morning, and all three of them hug. Angelica touches them each before they leave, calming them down for the night.

"That was … amazing," Damon says as they stand outside the house.

Angelica doesn't respond but stares at him intently with her big sparkling eyes.

"Why are you staring at me like that?"

"Because Damon … what you did back there … it was so wonderful."

He looks down, embarrassed. "Don't sweat it."

An awestruck smile creeps onto her face as she stares at him. "You aced this lesson without me even explaining anything. You were selfless in there. And now, after that last statement, humble."

"How was saving her life being selfless?"

"If she died, you could've taken her to Hell before I took her to Heaven. You sacrificed your job to keep her living."

He looks up to the house, realizing she is right. But at that moment, he wasn't thinking like that.

"How did you know what to say?" Angelica asks quietly.

Damon shrugs. "I just said everything to her that I wish someone said to me."

"So … that's all true then?"

"Yeah, I died by suicide."

Tears fill her eyes. "I'm so sorry, Damon."

He shrugs again. "It's not a big deal anymore."

Without thinking too much about it, Angelica steps to him and wraps her arms around his torso in a hug. She lays her cheek on his shoulder and squeezes him tight.

After the initial shock—both literally and figuratively—he places his hands around her and hugs her back. They stand there for minutes, holding onto each other.

Damon is overcome with emotion, and a stray tear slips down his cheek. Angelica's eyes are closed, so she doesn't notice. He doesn't wipe it away to avoid drawing attention to it. Reliving his death was painful, but his mind is stuck on something different.

When Rose called him an angel.

After she said that and the whole situation was

resolved, the questions that had been stuck in his mind were answered. He truly wanted to become an angel. He was meant to be an angel—not a demon. And he couldn't damn this beautiful, kind, otherworldly angel that is currently buried into his neck.

The one he has romantic feelings for.

Angelica is in her own world, thinking about Damon. She just saw him save a young girl's life and heard his own tragic story. He isn't the evil demon that she once thought he was. Even at the animal shelter and dinner, she was still wary of his true reasons for spending time with her. But now she knows … he really is good. And she really, really likes him.

"Angelica?" Damon asks wearily, not letting go of her.

"Yes?"

"You never answered my question earlier …"

Her eyebrows scrunch together as she racks her brain for the question she missed. Surely, she answered them all, she wouldn't have just ignored—

Her face reddens as she remembers. "Oh." She leans back to look him in the eyes, just mere inches from his face. "About … if I wanted to kiss you?"

Damon nods, his intense black eyes smoldering hers. "So … what is it?"

Angelica is completely under his spell. She wants nothing more than to grab the back of his head and pull his face to hers, taste those lips she's been staring at for weeks now. And she has a feeling that he knows that's what she wants, by the way he softly licks his lips as he waits for her answer. Anyone that looked at them could see their desire for one another was palpable—Cora said it the first time they met, even before she started falling for him. And as they are touching, the warm sparks are shooting through her body, reminding her of the strange connection she only feels with him …

But she can't bring herself to completely fall. The only boy she ever loved on Earth scarred her for life. And how can she fully trust him? She knows him, but not enough. She doesn't know his true intentions. She doesn't want to kiss him just to kiss him. If she does finally let her lips meet his, she wants it to mean something to the both of them. Her heart can't take a mindless hookup. She is falling way too hard, too fast, and she has no idea if he really feels the same.

"I … I'm not sure," Angelica finally says, forcing herself to step out of his arms.

Damon deflates. "Come on, you're not the least bit curious to see what would happen?"

She shakes her head at him with a smile. "Strictly business … remember?"

He sighs, then chuckles. "Okay, yeah. Strictly business."

"Get home safe. I will talk to you later."

"Bye, little angel." He winks. "See you again. Soon, I hope."

Those butterflies return to Angelica's stomach. "I hope so, too." She turns to dissipate but then remembers something. "Oh! I almost forgot. I have homework for you."

His grinning face turns down in a frown. "Homework?"

"Don't give me that look." She laughs. "It'll be fun."

Damon sticks his hands into his jean pockets. "I've never had fun homework. What is it?"

She gives him a bright smile. "I want you to paint me something."

They stare at each other as Damon processes what she instructed. After a few moments, the big, genuine, toothy grin that only Honey has seen creeps onto his face. "Okay, I can do that. Give me a few weeks to figure it out. Any suggestions on what you'd like me to paint?"

Angelica forgets how to breathe at his magnificent smile but forces herself to wink before disappearing. "Surprise me."

Chapter 20

Angelica walks through the hospital, hidden from view in The Middle. The smell of sterile metal and air fresheners fill her nostrils. She double-checks the name and the room number on her phone. Doctors and nurses bustle about her, carrying patient files and discussing diagnoses. Angelica taps as many of them as she can because when an angel touches a human, they are filled with peace. As she touches a few of the stressed-looking workers, their worried faces slip into calm smiles.

Room 302 finally comes into her vision, and she peers inside. An old, frail woman is lying in the bed, her breathing shallow. Two women are standing in the corner of the room, conversing with tear-stained faces.

Angelica walks into the room and directly to the woman. "Margaret?"

The woman slowly creaks open her eyelids. When she notices Angelica, her mouth opens into a thin grin. "Are you here to guide me?"

Angelica sits on the chair next to her bed and nods,

smiling at her warmly. When humans are close to death and are in the beginning stages of crossing over, they know more than others. Angelica is still in The Middle, but Margaret can see her. The old wives' tale of angels coming to the bedside when someone is close to death is true. "I am here to guide you, Margaret," she says soothingly, taking her hands in her own. "No rush at all, just whenever you are ready."

Margaret lays her head back into her pillow and closes her eyes. "Did I do well in life?"

The two women standing in the corner peer at her with worried eyes. "She's starting to lose it, Janice," one whispers.

"Oh, the best. All ninety-three years of it." Angelica soothes her, knowing she can't hear the other women whispering about her. "Would you like to tell us about it?" she asks, looking at the two women and whispering for them to come closer and listen.

They walk over to the bed, unaware that their decisions are influenced.

Margaret tells her story. She talks about her childhood and how she was raised on a small farm in North Dakota with her seven brothers and sisters and bird dog, Charlie. When she graduated eighth grade, she didn't go to high school; she stayed home with her mother and helped her take care of the house. Until she was seventeen and met the love of her life, Thomas.

"Thomas was the son of the mayor." She chuckles. "His father didn't want us to be together because I came from a poor family, but we didn't care. We eloped after three weeks."

"Only three weeks?" Angelica asks.

"That was all it took. When you know your person, you know."

Angelica swoons at their romantic love.

"Thomas and I were together for sixty-three years until he died from a stroke. He gave me two beautiful girls." Margaret tearfully looks to Janice and Jaime, nothing but love in her eyes. "And those beautiful girls gave me even more beautiful grandchildren. As happy as I am here, I still miss him each day."

She closes her eyes, and her breathing slows even more.

"You will see him soon," Angelica promises, gently squeezing her hand.

"Mom, it's okay to go," Janice says, kissing Margaret's forehead. "We will be okay down here."

"Go, be with Dad. Tell him we say hi," Jaime musters out, her voice cracking.

Margaret nods but doesn't speak again. She is tired. She is ready for death.

Angelica, Jaime, and Janice sit in silence and watch her. A nurse comes in at the loud beeping, but the girls shake their heads and tell her it's time. The nurse puts her arms around Margaret's daughters as the machines go silent.

"Miss?" Angelica hears from behind her. She turns around and smiles, tears filling her eyes.

A beautiful woman is standing there wearing a green 1940s swing dress. Her dark hair is curled up around her young, tireless face. She looks down at her new body and twirls in a circle, giggling.

"Margaret, you are so beautiful!" Angelica gasps.

"Thank you," she says, tears filling her eyes. "I was in pain for so long. I'm so happy to finally be free." She hesitates before looking behind Angelica at her daughters, who are sobbing over her old body.

"They will be okay, I promise," Angelica says, walking over to hug Margaret tightly. "Now, come with me. There is someone who's been waiting for you!"

Angelica loops her arm through Margaret's and escorts her to Heaven. They enter through the big pearly gates and standing right behind them, holding a gigantic bouquet, is Thomas. He is looking just as dapper as Margaret in a neatly pressed suit and green bowtie. He might've died at eighty, but he doesn't look a day over thirty. When he sees her, he bursts into tears, drops the flowers, and sprints towards her. Margaret lets go of Angelica and runs toward him, too.

As if they are in a movie, he picks her up and spins her in a circle, laughing in complete bliss. Angelica looks away as they kiss. She hears them say, "I love you" and "I miss you," and Margaret teases him about wearing her favorite color to match. Angelica wipes away a rogue tear that slips down her face at witnessing their sweet love. Their true, pure, undying love.

"Thank you so much, miss!" Margaret calls to Angelica.

"My pleasure." Angelica bows to them. "Now, you two go enjoy the rest of eternity together." She smiles and watches them go; their arms wrapped around each other's waists. Margaret tells Thomas all about the things he's missed since he died, and Angelica watches until they are out of sight.

She glances at her phone. Her workday is now over, and she has the night off. When Margaret was talking about Thomas and how she knew he was the one, Damon appeared in Angelica's mind.

She hurries home and prepares to go to the bar, in hopes of catching Damon. Throwing on a casual outfit and fixing her hair and makeup, her heart swells.

Sure, she hasn't known Damon long. Yes, he is a demon. Yes, she has no idea if this will work out, or if he feels the same way, but ... she can't deny it anymore.

When you know, you know.

And she knows.

Chapter 21

"Honey, I don't think I can do this anymore," Damon admits, puffing on a cigarette.

"Do what?" she asks, peering at him over her funky purple glasses.

"The mission. Getting to know Angelica, I realize that she really is ..." He thinks of the right word to describe her, but not one could do her justice.

"Amazing?" Honey offers, giggling.

"At least," he says, extinguishing his cigarette into the ashtray.

"Sounds like you may have developed a little crush on her."

He rolls his eyes. "What am I, fourteen?"

She pops a peanut into her mouth. "I'll take that as a yes."

Damon looks around, making sure no one he knows can hear what he is about to admit. "Okay, fine. I like her. But ... I don't know." He sighs. "I feel stupid. Especially since I'm secretly trying to get her to join the dark side ... even though now it doesn't feel right."

"Have you told her how you feel?"

"No," he scoffs, as if that's the worst idea possible.

"Why do you say it like that?" Honey asks.

He drinks the last swig of beer in his glass and hands it to Honey. "We promised each other to keep things only about the training. Even last night, when I tried to kiss her, she shut me down, reminding me about our vow. If I told her I liked her, it may jeopardize the whole thing."

Honey hands him a fresh beer. "But if you like her, don't you think it's already compromised?"

"Touché."

She leans on the rail and props her head up with her hands. "So, what are you going to do about the mission then?" Concern laces her words; she knows just as well as he does the consequences for failing or backing out.

Damon's hand traces the top of the glass. He has been debating that since he realized he was falling in love with her. "Selfishly, I want to continue so that she will be with me. But then I think about how she would be so miserable as a demon ... so I don't know. I can try to get out of it ... but there's the probability that I will die. And I don't know if I'm ready for that, even if it means that it saves her."

She reaches across the bar and grabs his hand lovingly. "Damon. As much as I would hate to lose you, I want you to know ... whatever you decide, I am here. If you go through with the mission, I won't be upset with you. I understand your job isn't easy, and I know it will be hard for you to finish it. If you decide to sacrifice yourself for her, I will miss you like crazy, but I will forever be proud of you for doing the right thing."

He squeezes her hand and smiles gratefully. "I love you so much, Honey."

She beams back. "I love you, too."

Another customer waves her down at the opposite end of the counter, and she goes to take the order. Damon watches her flit behind the bar and then checks his phone notifications. Chloe has finally given up on trying to contact him after he ignored her 172 calls and messages, and he is relieved to see that she hasn't texted him all day.

His fingers itch to press on Angelica's contact and text her, but he knows that she wants to keep things work-related, which is why she rejected his advances yesterday. He needs to leave her alone. Right?

He doesn't notice Honey return until she clears her throat. "Uh, Damon …"

"What?" he asks, looking up to see her grinning.

"Boo!"

Damon jumps and whips around, catching Angelica cackling behind him.

"Scared ya, didn't I?"

His startled face relaxes into a grin. "What are you doing here? You know it's a weekday, right?"

Angelica sits on the open stool next to him and shrugs nonchalantly as if this were something she did often. "Oh, I know. I had a good day at work and wanted to celebrate."

Honey gives Damon a side-eyed look, sending him a message.

He tilts his head down in a slight nod, understanding.

That means she came to see you.

"Well, then, let's celebrate." Damon's grin widens. "Glass of Moscato?"

"Please and thank you."

Honey doesn't hesitate to fetch her wine. Once it's set in front of Angelica, she hurries to the other side of the bar to give them privacy.

"So, what happened at work today?" Damon asks, resting his elbow on the bar and holding his head up with his hand.

Angelica swoons before picking up her glass. "Oh, it was the most romantic thing ever. I helped an old woman cross over, and her husband was waiting for her. They had been married for sixty-three years until he passed, and he waited for her over a decade in Heaven, hoping she would return to him soon. Their reunion was so sweet it brought tears to my eyes."

"That is sweet."

She tilts her head to the side. "Do you believe in true love?"

Damon's dark eyes soften as they gaze into hers. He doesn't hesitate. "Yes."

Angelica melts and takes another drink of wine. "Good."

They tear their eyes away from each other, both feeling color warm their cheeks. They chat about nothing in particular—continuing the question game, of course—with butterfly-filled stomachs. Angelica finishes her first glass of wine and excuses herself to the bathroom while Honey refills it.

She walks past a group of demons to get to the restroom, and all their eyes follow her. After completing her business, Angelica passes them again and hears a sneer behind her. She glances back to a tall, gorgeous demoness who is giving her a dirty look. She recognizes her from the first night she talked to Damon in the bar. "I'm sorry, what was that?"

Chloe doesn't miss a beat. "I said, 'Barbie called and wants her life back, fake bitch.'"

Angelica laughs. "Okay, then. Someone had a bad day. I hope tomorrow is better." She blows a kiss and walks back to Damon. Not even a rude demoness can ruin her good mood.

Damon looks at her warily as she sits. "What did she say to you?"

"That demoness? Oh. Nothing important, just some snide comment." She waves him off, picking up her glass again.

He glances back at Chloe, a glare uglier than death on his face. Chloe flips him the finger with a smile.

Angelica watches them and then puts two and two together. "Wait! Is that your not-girlfriend?"

He nods.

Her heart drops. Now that rained on her parade. *How can I compete with her? She is literally the most gorgeous woman I have ever seen.*

Damon sees the concern on her face. "What are you thinking?" he asks, his eyebrows raised.

She doesn't look at him. "Just that ... she is very beautiful."

Before he can stop himself, he starts laughing uncontrollably.

Angelica glares at him, blushing again. "What are you laughing for?"

He wipes away a tear, his laughter turning into small chuckles. "Angelica. Have you seen yourself? She may be beautiful, but she could never compete with you. And she knows it, which is why she hates you."

Her blushing face turns twenty shades darker, and the butterflies in her stomach race around even faster. *Oh.*

"You are literally perfect in every way. She is a very flawed person. Don't sweat her at all," Damon continues, reaching over to brush his hand over her cheek. "Don't you ever get bored with being too perfect?"

Angelica pushes his hand away and laughs. "Trust me. I am not perfect. You remember my sassy side, remember?"

"And? That isn't a flaw. I like girls who can handle themselves, remember?"

"So, you like me?" She winks.

He flounders. "I didn't say that."

Angelica sips her wine and laughs again.

"For real, though. It's as if you're *too* perfect. Don't you ever need to feel a little wild?" His voice lowers, sounding like smooth velvet.

"I don't know. I can get wild."

"I have a good way you can ..." he says, biting down on his lip.

Angelica doesn't let herself focus on the sexy way he is biting his lip; instead, she rolls her eyes. "Let me guess ... kissing you?"

"How did you know?"

She slaps him playfully, and he finishes his drink. As he orders them another round, she thinks about what he said. *You're too perfect. Don't you ever need to feel a little wild?* She twists a blonde lock of hair around her finger, thinking of ways to show him that she can be wild and fun, not all perfection and priss. She looks at him and then his elaborate tattoo ...

She stands quickly. "Let's get tattoos!"

Damon is stunned at her sudden excitement. "Tattoos?"

"Yeah! You said I should be a little wilder." She grabs her purse and places her hand on her hip, smirking. "So, let me show you just how wild I can be."

Although impressed, Damon shuts it down. "I don't think that's a good idea."

Angelica raises her eyebrows and pouts. "What, are you scared?"

"I have a huge ass tattoo on my arm. No, I'm not scared." He laughs and stands, too. He takes a long drink of the fresh beer he is about to waste and sets the glass on the counter. Damon gives her a sarcastic smile. "I just think it's a little early in the relationship to get matching tattoos."

Honey, always the eavesdropper, walks by and raises her eyebrows at the confrontation.

Angelica rolls her eyes. "We aren't getting matching tattoos, dummy. I've always wanted one, and you obviously need to see that I am so much more than a perfect angel." She sticks her nose in the air. "So, I will. At a tattoo shop. Right now."

The buzz from her two glasses of wine is helping with her boldness. She definitely would not be jumping at this opportunity sober.

Damon looks over to Honey, who is grinning, then back to Angelica. "Fine. Pick a place and let's go."

"Honey!" Angelica turns to her quickly. "Know of a good tattoo shop?"

"I got this one at Lotus." She points to the intricate butterfly tattoo on her upper arm. "It's just a few miles down the road."

Angelica turns back to Damon. "Great! It's settled. After you." She motions to the door, and Damon turns as instructed.

Chapter 22

Once outside, Damon and Angelica teleport to Lotus Tattoo and Piercings. After they appear outside the building, Angelica confidently struts inside while Damon follows her warily. Drawings and pictures of tattoos line the walls, and a glass display in the corner features hundreds of piercing options.

The tattoo artist, who is staring at his phone, looks up. When he sees Angelica, his eyes bulge out of his head. He notices Damon next, who is tempted to pull Angelica closer to him as if to say, *She's with me*. He quickly composes himself and stands, walking towards them and clearing his throat. "Can I help you guys?"

"Hi! We are here to get tattoos," Angelica says cheerfully.

Damon snorts—*obviously*—and she shoots him a glare.

"Sounds good. Do you know what you want?"

Angelica falters a bit. "Uh …" She searches the walls for inspiration, but nothing catches her eye.

Damon comes to her rescue. "I still need to figure out what I'm doing. Can we look over your books for a while?"

The artist drags his eyes to Damon's huge arm tattoo and motions to the waiting area. "Not a problem. My name's Tony—let me know when you're ready."

Damon walks over to a couch and picks up one of the many books on the table. Angelica sits across from him, smiling gratefully. "Thanks."

"Anytime." He winks.

She picks up a book and starts flipping through it. Lots of skulls, knives, and flowers adorned the pages. "Any ideas?" she asks Damon after a while.

"How about this?" he asks, showing her a picture of a cat wearing a top hat and glasses.

She bursts out laughing. "Cute. That'll definitely get all the ladies." She continues browsing through the pages and then sighs. *Maybe this wasn't such a good idea.*

Damon notices her fallen face. "You better not be backing out on me," he says.

"I'm not!" she lies. "I just don't know what to get."

"Something meaningful, maybe? A favorite quote? Something pink?"

Angelica thinks back to her college days. Everyone was getting tattoos. Her roommate was a devout Catholic who had never even sworn before college, and three months into the school year, she got her half-sleeve done. A few other friends all had matching four-leaf clovers for good luck. She has a few quotes in mind, but he would most likely tease her forever if she got a nerdy book quote on her permanently. She has to do something fun, something to surprise him …

A thought crosses her mind, and an ornery smile creeps onto her face. "You know what ... I know what I want."

"Oh yeah?" Damon asks, tilting his head to the side. Her sultry tone intrigues him.

Angelica stands without another word and marches straight up to Tony. "Okay, sir, I know what I want."

Tony looks up from his phone. Both he and Damon wait for her to spill the details.

"I want a small heart ... on my ass."

The room goes so silent that they could hear a pin drop. At first, Damon rolled his eyes—a heart, how original—but when she said the placement, his mouth dropped open in shock.

Tony shrugs. "Well, alright. Outline? Filled in? What color?"

"Just a black outline, please."

"Do you want a partition?"

"Sure." She turns to smirk at Damon, who is still frozen. "But he can come stand with me."

Tony goes to grab the partition and leaves her waivers to sign.

Damon closes his mouth. *Okay. Who the fuck is this woman!?*

He gets off the couch and approaches her. "Uh ... did I hear that right? You're getting a tattoo on your ..." His eyes slide down her body and rest on her perfectly shaped behind.

"Yep, you heard that right. Why do you look so shocked?" Angelica asks, then giggles.

"Uh, I don't know, because you're an angel?!"

She rolls her eyes. "And? You wanted to see my wild side."

"Little angel, getting a tattoo was enough to prove that point. Hell, even suggesting it proved me wrong. But your ass?" Damon sucks on his teeth suggestively. "That is something I didn't expect."

"I guess I'm just full of surprises," she says, leaning down to sign the waiver and flicking her long blonde hair back behind her shoulders.

"I guess so." Damon chuckles. "Why the ass placement?"

She shrugs, standing up straight again and adjusting her purple off-the-shoulder sweater. "Well, I wanted it to be something fun for one. I don't know something really meaningful to do, so I thought this would be a good idea. I saw a model with it once and thought it was adorable. Plus, I think my future husband will enjoy it." That ornery grin is back when she says the next sentence. "And I'm sure you'll enjoy watching him tattoo it on me."

Tony calls her back, and she winks before walking to him.

Damon has to inconspicuously adjust himself after thinking about her naked ass ... bare on a table ... getting tattooed ... while he watches.

This girl is going to kill me.

Even though Angelica is totally freaking out on the inside, she keeps her cool and confidence. She doesn't know why she has this need to prove to Damon that she can be more fun and flirtier and not just a stuck-up angel, but she has to. By his reaction to the whole situation, she knows she is accomplishing it perfectly.

She stares at Damon while asking the next question. "So ... should I just slide my jeans down a little or take them off completely?"

Tony isn't fazed. "Whichever you prefer."

Damon, however, is completely stunned. He has an epiphany. The feelings for Angelica, the ones he kept pushing away and denying, squeeze his heart. He realizes that he does truly like her. He likes her for the sweet, innocent, caring woman that she is ... but now that he sees her darker, wilder side ... he is a goner.

Angelica hesitates with her hands on her pants button. *Am I really going to do this!? It's not too late to back out, change the placement, or something ...*

But she doesn't listen to her worried thoughts. Instead, she confidently unbuttons her jeans, slides them down to her thighs, and lays stomach-side down on the table. *Thank God I am wearing cute panties today!*

Both of the men are mesmerized by her ass so much that she has to clear her throat to snap their attention back to the matter at hand. The artist blinks a few times before sheepishly grabbing the razor and cleansing wipes and swiping them on her butt, making sure not to bother her pink underwear.

"Damon ..." Her voice lowers. "Will you come hold my hand?"

Damon walks to the chair that is next to the table and pulls it up to where her head is. She reaches her hand out as he sits and holds it, that familiar warmth running through both of them.

"Are you nervous?" he teases.

"A little," she admits.

Damon gives her a lopsided grin. "It'll be over before you know it."

She leans her cheek on the table and smiles up at him. She curses herself for having feelings for him, but as she looks into his dark eyes and admires his breathtaking smile, she can't blame herself.

"Are you ready?" Tony asks.

She gulps, all traces of certainty erased as the tattoo gun buzzes inches away from her bare ass. "Yes."

"Hold still," Tony instructs, and moments later, the needles are digging into her skin.

"Ow."

"How does it feel?" Damon asks as her face twists into an uncomfortable grimace.

"It's not that bad … but not exactly pleasant," she says through gritted teeth.

He glances down at the black curvy line that Tony is creating. "I'm impressed."

"Told you I could be a little wild."

He grins and shakes his head. "And you proved that."

They stare at each other. The only sound in the shop is the tattoo gun and cars that drive by.

Every time she looks at him, Angelica notices something

new. This time, she observes a slight scar under his right eyebrow. "What's that from?"

"Skiing accident."

She raises an eyebrow. *He must've been an athlete. He already looks toned, and I bet underneath his shirt he is ripped* .... She blushes and studies their intertwined hands. His tan skin makes hers look even paler. Proud of herself for going through with the tattoo, Angelica finally has the extra confidence needed to ask the question that she has been dying to.

"So, what do you think that buzzing is?"

Damon quirks a brow. "Are you bringing this up again?"

She nods.

"I don't know," he says honestly, rubbing his thumb across her sun ring. "Maybe it's because we are polar opposites? An angel and a demon?"

Angelica nods again, although she doesn't think that is just it. She is falling rapidly for Damon at a pace she never thought was possible. Nothing like she has ever experienced before. After watching romance movies her whole life and being in love with love, she can't help but think about what the weird feelings might mean ... he is her soulmate. Maybe Cora wasn't too far off with her dramatics. It was the first thing Angelica thought of after they had touched. Even though it sounded completely ridiculous in the beginning of their relationship, now it isn't as silly. Especially if he does become an angel and they can really be together forever ...

As she stares at him now, into his black eyes—once cold and full of hate, now smoldering her with affection—she really believes that it is true. He has to be her soulmate.

She doesn't voice any of these thoughts, however. "Yeah, maybe."

Damon nods, thinking about his own possibilities. What started off as an improbable mission to get her to become a demon just became so much more impossible when he realized that he liked her. A lot. And he couldn't kill her.

But if he gives up and The Devil murders him, he can't even be with her. So, what is the point?

Angelica notices his furrowed brows. "What are you thinking about so intently?"

Damon looks up to smirk at her. "What tattoo I'm getting."

"Oh yeah? What are you thinking?"

He leans back into the chair and shrugs. He makes sure the tattoo is finished and the gun is off her before he tells her his answer. "A heart on my ass."

Angelica laughs like a hyena. Good thing the artist is finished—her laughter would've transformed her heart into an abstract tattoo.

Chapter 23

"I can't believe you actually got a heart on your ass like me. Too soon for matching tattoos, huh?" Angelica giggles as they walk back outside into the crisp autumn air. She thought Damon was bluffing when he said he'd get a heart on his ass—nope. Now he has one exactly like hers.

Damon paid for both of their tattoos—and even tipped graciously. Angelica swooned since he remembered their training.

"Well, I thought it was a good commemoration," he says and then laughs.

"What are all your friends going to say?"

He winks at her mischievously. "Well, I don't know what it's like around your friends, but I never usually parade my naked ass around them."

She laughs and sticks her tongue out at him. "Okay, smartass."

Damon wants this night to go on forever. He dreads going back to his grubby apartment alone. He is getting used to the warmth that Angelica emits when they are together, and so, when he is alone, he feels extra dead and cold. "So ... when will I see you again, little angel?"

They aren't too far away from each other—maybe two feet at most. Angelica looks into his charcoal eyes and bats her long lashes. "Well, when do you want to?"

He sneaks his tongue out to wet his lips as he stares at her. Even though she rejected him last time, he has a feeling that she will finally give in and let her lips meet his tonight.

Standing there in the moonlight, Damon sheds his demon shell and smiles at her widely and genuinely. His tone of voice changes to match the warm tones she always gives off. "Honestly, the sooner the better."

Angelica notices his change immediately and her heart skips a beat. "Well, I have work the next few days ... so how about we plan for next weekend? We can text and work something out."

Damon takes a step closer to her and closes the gap between them. Their bodies are barely grazing against each other, teasing their electricity. "That's too long."

She blushes under his burning gaze. "Well, I could cancel a few plans, and we can do something this weekend ..." The wind causes her hair to shuffle around her face, and Damon reaches out to tuck a strand behind her ear.

"Meet me tomorrow at Gaia's again?" he suggests, trailing his finger down her face and resting it under her chin.

Her eyes—a shade of deep ocean blue at the moment—sparkle. She doesn't answer right away because she is totally under his spell.

"Say yes?" he asks. Not only is he asking about the date request ... but the kiss he is yearning to finally give her.

Angelica's eyes dart away from his and rest on his lips for a few seconds before meeting his gaze once more. "Yes ... and Damon?"

"Hmm?"

"I finally figured out my answer ... to that question."

He doesn't need her to clarify. "What is it?"

With the last bit of courage she has left, she gently reaches up and twists one hand into Damon's long hair and the other on his neck. She slowly pulls him close to her, stopping when their lips are so close they could feel each other's breath. She brushes hers against his slightly before whispering, "Yes."

Warm fire burns through their bodies as soon as she finally closes the gap, and their lips meet. Damon wraps his arms around her waist and crushes his body to hers. The slight buzzing that they usually felt when they touched is nothing compared to the intense sparks they are feeling now. Their lips softly caress until Angelica allows his tongue to meet hers, and their kissing intensifies. Their tongues twist together in a soft, velvety, sensual dance.

They back into a nearby alley, their lips never straying far from each other. All the tension they felt with each other the past month is finally released, and they are addicted to it. Neither one of them felt anything like this before. Damon pushes her against the wall, pressing his groin into her. His hand sneaks under her shirt and rests on her naked hip, not going anywhere else. He loves the softness of her skin, and Angelica melts at his touch.

Damon bites down on her lip, and a soft moan escapes Angelica's mouth.

He then trails kisses below her ear and down her neck.

"Damon," she whispers as he nibbles on her.

"Hmm?" he asks, grabbing her face and pulling their lips back together. With each kiss, he feels more and more alive as if Angelica's internal sunshine is being breathed into him. All the human women he's been with, other demonesses, even Chloe could never compete with the feelings she is giving him. This is definitely something more than their opposite atoms reacting.

Angelica finally forces them to slow down. She kisses him gently on the lips twice before finally leaning her head back on the building. "Wow," she says, letting go of his hair and touching her lips with her fingers. She giggles.

"Yeah," he agrees as he slows his heart rate down.

"I have never felt something like that before," Angelica whispers. "Is that what it's like between angels and demons? No wonder they try to keep us apart."

"I wouldn't know." Damon chuckles. "You're the first angel I've ever kissed."

"And … was it … good?"

He leans down to kiss her once more—softly. "The best."

Angelica maneuvers out from between the wall and Damon and straightens her sweater. She instantly feels ten degrees cooler when she isn't touching him. "Well … I should probably get going."

"Are you sure? Are you up for one more drink tonight?" He asks, not ready to say goodbye.

She looks at her watch. "I would, but I have to be up early due to work … but I'll see you tomorrow night."

"Sounds perfect. I'll have a glass of Moscato waiting for you." Damon smiles.

"You got it." She giggles. "Bye, Damon."

He kisses her forehead softly before pulling away again. "Bye, my angel."

Angelica's heart bursts when he changes her pet name for her, and she quickly teleports home. She runs up to her bedroom and falls on her bedspread, giggling and squealing like a schoolgirl.

Chapter 24

Damon flicks a cigarette on the ground as he leans against a tall brick building. William is standing to his left, his eyes glued on the crowd in front of them. Ben is on the other side of William, bouncing in place. Even though this isn't his assignment, The Devil wanted him to tag along and help them with this big gang fight.

The October meeting went a lot smoother than the September one. Damon relayed the information about Missy and, begrudgingly, Angelica. The Devil nodded and was pleased, and Damon left without a new burn. Thankfully, the current one is finally done peeling and on its way back to a normal color.

The three demons are leaning against an abandoned grocery store in The Middle while two rival gangs argue in front of them. Streetlights turn on as the sky darkens around them.

He tries to keep his focus on the mission at hand, but his mind wanders to Angelica. Not that it went far from her ever since their kiss two weeks ago. Since that night, he has become himself around her. Not entirely—he still has some reserve about his human life—but more with each time he sees her. They text almost every night, hang out when they can—both of them are super busy with work—and when they have only a few minutes to spare, they meet up to kiss and talk for a few minutes like infatuated high school students.

Don't get it twisted ... this is all for the sake of the mission, his Hyde reminds him.

Are we still going through with this? His Jekyll counters. He has been debating going to The Devil and getting out of the mission all week. But each time he was ready, the fear of completely dying again would stop him.

"How much longer are we going to be here?" Damon asks the men.

"You got a hot date?" Ben jokes.

"No. We've just been standing here for hours."

"Well, we will stand here for as long as we need to."

William turns to Damon. "As soon as someone dies, we grab their souls as they leave Earth. We are escorts, if you will."

Damon scoffs, "This ain't my first rodeo."

They watch as the gang presidents yell at each other. Another man runs up and stands in between them, trying to deescalate the situation. The other eight men around them straighten up, watching and waiting.

"So, how's the lovely bride-to-be doing?" William asks.

"Fine," Damon says, popping a piece of cinnamon gum

into his mouth. "I think she is going to go through with it. Which is good, considering it's only two weeks away."

"Good, good."

Damon can hear the sarcasm in his voice. They both think the whole idea is stupid. He remembers a previous conversation they had about it, and William laughed about how *symbolic* it was since it's happening on Halloween.

"He doesn't need another damn wife. He has forty. I have none!" he drunkenly proclaimed with a cackle.

Back in the present, William nudges him. "How's your *other* mission going?"

"Have you got in her pants yet?" Ben snickers.

"Fuck off, both of you."

"I'll take that as a no," Ben retorts, popping his knuckles.

Damon glares at him.

"Easy, mate. We're just messin' with ya," William says.

Damon chews on his gum, the spicy flavor filling his mouth. He thinks back to a few nights ago when Angelica and he met up for dinner. It was Damon's turn to ask a question, so he asked her what her favorite candle scent was. She immediately responded with cinnamon, blushed bright pink, and fumbled with her words. She didn't explain why, quickly changing the subject after, but he knew it had to be because he was always chewing cinnamon gum.

"Regardless, you seem to be in a better mood than usual," William comments, noting Damon's slight smile.

His face slips back into its usual emotionless grimace. "Not really."

"That's one thing that's cool about hanging with those angels. They sure do make you feel better."

"In more ways than one," Ben interjects.

William and Damon ignore him.

"What is she like? She must be pretty amazing if Boss wants her on our team."

"She …" Damon hesitates, not wanting to say too much. William he can trust, but Ben is a snitch. He would say anything to get higher in ranks or on The Devil's good side. As if fate wanted him to talk about her, Ben gets a call on his phone and walks away to answer it.

"She is really amazing, honestly. Besides her good looks, she is kind, sweet, funny, and warm. She has the most infectious laugh. And she actually likes me for me, as crazy as that may seem." He smiles and shakes his head. "I know it's just a job, but it makes it easier that she doesn't hate me."

William nods. "She sounds awesome. And it's good that she likes you. The more she does, the easier it'll be to get her to become one of us."

Damon's smile falls. "Right."

"How is Chloe taking all this?"

"Oh, you know her. She's very happy for me."

William bursts out laughing.

In front of them, the two head men pull out their guns and point them directly at each other. The arguing turns to screaming, and the people behind them are shouting as well, some egging them on while others are pleading for them to stop.

Ben returns, putting his phone away. "Get ready. The one on the left is trigger-happy."

William and Damon stand up straight.

Right on cue, shots come from the crowd. People scatter, and a few slump over. Ben sprints to the first dead body and grabs the soul now slipping out of it. Damon follows and runs to the next body, grabbing the soul, which is a copy of the dead man's body, just a glowing version.

He notices Damon and gapes at him with terrified eyes. "What happened?" He looks down at his lifeless carcass, blood seeping out of the bullet wound in his chest. "Is that me? Am I ... am I dead?"

Damon sighs, his hand wrapped around the soul's arm. "Afraid so, buddy."

"Now what? Where are you taking me?"

In this moment, looking at the terrified dead man, Damon knows he cannot go through with the Angelica mission. He cannot damn her to Hell and make her do the jobs like he is doing now. It would crush her entire soul, and she would hate him for the rest of eternity.

He has to let her go. He has to do the right thing.

Damon looks at the man with sad eyes. "We are going to Hell."

Damon, William, and Ben drop off the three new souls at the check-in portion of Hell before dispersing. It is Friday night, so they are all heading to the bar. Damon hangs back, hoping to catch The Boss before he leaves his office. He takes a deep breath and starts his trek.

His mind keeps finalizing what he will say. This is a very touchy thing to do.

One wrong word and he is dead.

As he walks down the dark street, he knows that if death would save Angelica's life, it would be worth it, as much as the end of his life terrified him.

He kicks a rock and pauses. In the past month, he has changed from a dickhead, selfish demon to a wannabe angel with a conscience. A part of him wishes he never went to that Ouija call and got assigned to this mission because it is really fucking him over.

If he never went, he would've focused on Missy and getting drunk and sleeping with random women and Chloe. He wouldn't have started feeling bad, or being fake better, or walking to his possible death.

But then he never would've met Angelica.

Damon picks up his pace, keeping her in his mind. As much as he wants to tell her how he truly feels about her, he can't bring himself to text her. Yeah, they have been hanging out, flirting, and texting nonstop, but he has never admitted that he is falling in love with her. Now, there is no point—especially if he may be dead in a few minutes. It would just haunt her for the rest of her life.

Or if he survived … he would promise himself that he wouldn't put her in danger anymore. If they somehow started dating, Chloe would be the least of their problems. The world was created this way for a reason—if they upset it, bad things would happen. What if The Devil caught wind and killed her to spite him? The possibilities were endless. He couldn't do that to Angelica.

But you could pass your angel tests...

Damon wants to believe his thoughts, but he shakes his head. He knows he will never pass those damn tests. He doesn't even deserve to. He isn't fooling anyone, and he isn't about to fail regardless and end up nonexistent because The Boss found out that he even tried.

All of his options lead to his death.

So, he doesn't care anymore. At least he will die doing the right thing.

As he climbs the building steps, he pauses to shoot Honey a text. **Honey. If you don't hear from me in thirty minutes ... I'm dead. I'm doing the right thing. I love you. Tell Angelica that I really liked her. Tell her I'm sorry things couldn't be different.**

Before he forgets, he shoots her one last text. **Oh, and please go on a date with William. He's in love with you.**

He takes a deep breath before stepping onto the top floor. Drake is guarding the door, per usual, and when he sees Damon, his eyes narrow. "What are you doing here?"

"Is he in?"

Drake nods sternly.

"Can I talk to him? It's about ... work," Damon says, shifting on his feet. Sweat beads on the back of his neck.

The gigantic, soulless being knocks on the door he guards. The Devil's voice says something that only Drake can hear, and then he opens the door and steps back, motioning for Damon to walk through.

The Devil's back is to Damon. He is staring out his glass windows, marveling at the flames shooting into the sky. The red dress shirt he is wearing is strikingly similar to the bright red of the fires.

Damon's palms sweat as he stands in the position of attention, waiting for The Devil to acknowledge him.

"What brings you to my office, Jones? It's a Friday; you're officially off for the weekend," The Devil finally says, not turning around. He raises the cigar in his left hand to his lips.

Damon takes a deep breath and bows. *Here we go.* "Sir, I'd like to ask you to change missions."

The Devil's head angles ever so slightly. "Change missions?"

"Yes, sir. I feel like I cannot fully focus on Missy while convincing the angel to become a demon." He tries to sound as sincere as possible. "I don't want to disappoint you or hurt your marital sacrifice. I know how important Missy is to you, and I want to make sure I can be fully invested and get her prepared to be yours on Halloween."

"Do you think the angel becoming a demon would be worth it? You've been in contact with her. Do you think she would serve us well?"

Damon hesitates. He doesn't want to bad-mouth Angelica, but it may help his case. "I don't think she is a good fit for us at all, honestly. She would do nothing but disappoint you."

The Devil doesn't respond.

"Plus ... what's one more demon?" Damon chuckles.

The Devil ponders what he said.

Time stands still. Has it been minutes? Hours? Damon can't tell. Finally, The Devil speaks, "Ah, I guess you're right. What's one more demon?"

Damon exhales, a slow smile creeping onto his face. Maybe he will live to see another day.

The Devil finally turns around, a sad look on his face. "Pity ... I never would've guessed you for a man who forfeits."

Damon's eyes widen in shock. "No, that's—"

He holds up a hand, and Damon's mouth is forced shut. Damon cannot move as The Devil approaches.

"Ah, Damon. You were one of my favorites."

And with a flick of his wrist, Damon's body engulfs in flames.

Chapter 25

As per usual, Angelica waits for Cora to appear at her place so they can finish getting ready and head to the bar. Cora is happy that Angelica is going out with her more even though it is mainly to see Damon.

After the kiss, Angelica called Cora and spilled all the juicy details. Cora was so happy that she brought her a commemorative Starbucks to work the next day. Angelica called her ridiculous but didn't turn down the free coffee.

Tonight, Angelica surveys herself in the mirror, lightly coating her lips with her favorite pink lip gloss. She is wearing one of her favorite pink dresses—tight in the bodice with a flared skirt and tulle ruffles. The skirt ends a few inches above her knee and is styled with navy heels.

Her phone buzzes, and she rushes to pick it up. It is only a game notification. She sighs and sags onto her bed. Damon hasn't responded to her last message that she sent three hours ago. She knows he is busy with work, but he should've been off at least two hours ago. Maybe he went to the bar early and got wrapped into a conversation, or his phone died?

Ever since their first otherworldly kiss, they have talked every day. Damon has become his true self with her. Now gone were the days where he would be cold or rude to her. Now, he is always charming and kind, sweet, and eager to talk to her. They meet up for drinks at Gaia's or for dinner at the diner. Or even just to kiss for a few minutes in between work breaks.

Angelica reaches up to graze her lips with her fingers, remembering the many kisses they shared since that night at the tattoo shop.

The only problem is that he still hasn't told her exactly how he feels. Sure, they have been talking, hanging out more, and kissing, but she needs to know for sure. To her, he is her soulmate, and she is falling in love with him more by the minute. Does he feel the same?

She feels ridiculous when thinking that—it is obvious that he likes her, and she isn't just a booty call … right?

Hearing a knock on the front door, Angelica glides down her grand staircase, impressed that Cora is ten minutes early tonight.

Except when she opens it, it isn't Cora waiting.

Garrett is smiling wide, holding a big bouquet of red roses. "Hey, Angelica. Is this a bad time?"

Despite the confusion she feels, she forces herself to smile. "Uh, no! I'm just waiting on Cora, but I have a few minutes if … you'd like to come in."

"Great!" Garrett hands her the flowers. "I saw these and

remembered that roses were your favorite, so I had to grab them for you."

She takes them gratefully even though he was wrong. "Thank you."

Garrett follows her through her house. They arrive in the kitchen, and Angelica hurries to grab a vase and a pair of scissors.

"So, how have you been?" He asks, sitting at the kitchen island.

"Good! Busy with work, you know …" She snips off the bottom of the flower stems and prays that Cora will get to her house early for once. "What about you?"

"Same. I've been on a big case—there's this plan for a sacrifice on Halloween that a few of the other angels and I are working on stopping. It's a lot of work." He chuckles, picking at his cuticles.

"That sounds busy." Angelica tries to sound interested, but she was caught off guard by his sudden appearance. And the romantic gesture. To be frank, she hasn't thought about Garrett since the morning after his party. And she'd figured he felt the same because he never reached out to her about their date … and it's been over a month.

Yet, here they are.

Garrett clears his throat. "Look, Angelica. I didn't come by just to give you flowers and shoot the shit. I wanted to apologize for not reaching out after my birthday."

She slides the flowers into the vase and places them on her kitchen table. "Oh, don't apologize! Like we've said, it's been really busy for both of us."

He nods. "Well, I'm still sorry. I said I'd take you out and never did. So that's why I'm here ..." He smooths down his cobalt blue V-neck T-shirt. "Would you like to go to dinner next week? There's this restaurant in Amsterdam that I've been dying to try."

Angelica's face reddens, and her smile turns awkward. "Oh, Garrett ... that's so sweet ..."

He deflates. "That doesn't sound like a yes."

A month ago, Angelica would've jumped up and down and screamed yes from the rooftops. But now ... she doesn't want him anymore. She looks at his handsome, good angel and feels nothing. Her heart is strictly reserved for another.

Giving the warmest smile she can muster out, she says, "I'm sorry. I've realized that my feelings are more platonic than anything. You are an amazing friend, and I don't want to mess that up."

He presses his lips together, his face resembling that of a kicked puppy, and stands. "I gotcha. Not a problem."

"Plus, I'm not really looking for a relationship right now." She lies and blurts out, trying to lesson the pain on his face.

Thankfully, Cora bursts into the room. "Who's ready to driii—oh, hi, Garrett."

"Cora." He smiles and nods toward her. "I was just heading out."

Cora looks between Angelica and Garrett, sensing their tension.

"Well, thanks for stopping by!" Angelica says, a little

too cheerily. "And thank you for the beautiful roses. I'll see you at work?"

"See you then. Have a good night, ladies," Garrett says and walks swiftly out of the room. The front door opens and shuts moments later.

Cora's head whips around to Angelica with eyebrows hidden beneath her bangs. "Uh, care to explain to me why Garrett was here? And why he brought you roses?"

Angelica groans and relays the awkward situation that she just missed.

"Look at you, *rompecorazones*," Cora teases.

"What did you just call me?"

"Heartbreaker."

"I am not a heartbreaker." Angelica giggles as she turns off the house lights. "But isn't it annoying how he just assumed I'd wait for him to ask me out?"

"Oh, for sure," Cora says.

They grab their purses and teleport to the bar. When they get up to the rail and Angelica doesn't see Honey, an uneasy feeling creeps into her. Honey always works on Friday nights. And Damon is nowhere to be seen either ... something is definitely up.

Sunshine greets the girls and asks for their order. Cora orders two vodka cranberry drinks while Angelica asks where Honey is.

She nods to the back room, her face becoming somber. "You might want to check on her."

Becoming even more alarmed, Angelica slips through the crowd of people to the room Sunshine nodded towards.

Inside, she finds crates of beer, kegs, fruit for the bar, and Honey sitting on a stepstool, crying into her hands.

"Honey? What's wrong?"

Honey jerks up, her eyes bloodshot and mascara smeared under them. "Oh! Angelica."

Angelica immediately sits on the crate next to her and wraps her arms around her. Honey sobs into her shoulder.

"Angelica ... I'm sorry. Damon really liked you."

The hairs on Angelica's neck stand up. She pauses, thinking over that statement, her stomach in knots. "What do you mean *liked?* Honey, what's going on?"

Honey buries her head in Angelica's shoulder as more tears flood down her face. *I should've saved him...* she thinks. *I had the power to, but I didn't think it was my place... and now my best friend is gone.*

Angelica doesn't interrupt her tears to ask for an answer, but with each new sob from Honey, her anxiety worsens. What could possibly be so bad that Honey is this upset? What happened to Damon? Her mind immediately switches to the worst possible scenario.

"Honey ... is Damon okay?" she whispers.

A new batch of sobs racks through Honey. Nausea rises in Angelica's throat.

Finally, Honey hiccups and then leans back. She grabs Angelica's shoulders and looks at her fiercely. "Angelica, there is no easy way to tell you this, but ..."

Suddenly, the door behind them swings open. "Honey, I need a tall fucking drink."

Both girls whip around at the sound of his deep voice.

Damon stands there in his usual black T-shirt and jeans, but something seems ... off. Dirt and blisters cover his face and hands, and the ends of his long black hair are singed. His face displays no emotion, although his eyes are cold as he takes them in.

Honey gasps and flings her petite body to his, sobbing even harder. "Damon Joshua Jones, I thought you were dead!"

Damon hugs her, resting his cheek on the top of her hair—she is quite a bit shorter than him—and closes his eyes.

Angelica stares at them in confusion. The horrible scenario she thought of isn't as bad as the word Honey just said. "Dead?"

Damon opens his eyes and takes in Angelica with the same cold eyes. They are just as cold as they were when they first met. "Yeah," he says. "Boss was pissed at me and burned me. I thought he was going to toss me in the chasm with the humans, but after a few hours, he decided against it and let me go."

Angelica's eyes widen, and her breath hitches in her throat. "So ... you were engulfed in flames the past few hours?" Now, she realizes the dirt is actually soot.

He winces. "Yeah, I was."

Honey steps back and wipes her face, giving Angelica a chance to hug him now. But as she walks up to him, Damon steps back and avoids her arms. "Why won't you let me hug you?" she asks.

"Because I don't want you to," he says dryly.

Ouch. "What?"

Honey scrunches her eyebrows as her mouth falls agape.

"I said I didn't want you to touch me."

"Why?" Angelica asks again.

"Because," Damon says, running his hand through his hair, "teachers don't hug their students."

Angelica's eyes narrow. "What? First, yes, they do. Second, why are you acting like this?"

He shrugs, looking at her with disgust.

Angelica's confused demeanor changes to anger. "Oh, so I can't hug you, but you can French kiss me anytime you want?"

Damon snorts and rolls his eyes. "French kiss? What are we, twelve?"

Honey smacks his arm. "Damon, don't be rude."

He glares at her. "Honey, stay out of this."

Her peridot eyes glow. "There is no reason for this behavior. I understand you may be upset about almost dying, but don't be a dick to your girlfriend. It's not her fault."

Damon laughs. "Girlfriend? Yeah, right." He pulls a cigarette out of his jacket pocket and sticks it between his lips. "Look, angel. We can't be doing this shit anymore. We promised strictly business, and we need to keep it that way. I'm not interested in anything more."

And with that, he turns and walks swiftly out of the room, through the bar, and out the front door. He internally curses himself for hurting her even though he knows it's what's best.

Honey reaches out to comfort Angelica, but she shakes her off and bolts after him. He is getting ready to teleport when she catches up to him outside. "Damon! What the hell is going on?"

He signs and turns to her. His cigarette is lit between his lips, and he lets out smoke with his exhale. "I just told you. I'm not interested in anything else besides the angel tests. Unless you're here to train me—leave me the hell alone."

"Bullshit!" she says, placing her hands on her hips. "Even when we were training, there was always something more, and you know it. And then the kiss, and everything after? Dinner twice a week? Remember when I was gone last weekend for work, and you drunk called me every night just to talk? You don't do those things with just anyone. I know you like me, and I know you feel something between us, even if you haven't admitted it yet."

He throws the cigarette on the ground angrily. "It doesn't matter what I feel, Angelica!"

"Why not? What about the weird feeling that happens when we touch? You must think that it means something more than just our opposite atoms reacting."

"Of course it means something." Damon growls. "It means everything! But it doesn't matter. I am a demon, Angelica. I'm a fucking piece of shit. You are perfect. I could never allow myself to be with you. You deserve so much better than me. I shouldn't've let this go on for as long as it did. I'm sorry. I promise you; I will just end up hurting you." He knows he can't explain almost dying for her without blowing the whole mission. The mission The

Devil made him promise to follow through after he snuffed out the flames eating his flesh.

So why is he pushing her away?

She throws her hands in the air. "What have you been doing? Studying to become an angel! If you can pass those tests, prove that you are really good and can be an angel, then it wouldn't matter!"

"I'm not good, and I'm not good for you."

"How cliché," she scoffs. "Yeah, so what? Good girls and bad guys always end up together."

"Like when?"

Angelica's face reddens. "In romance movies. But it happens in real life, too. I'm trying to be romantic."

"Angelica, we aren't in a fucking romance movie," Damon snaps, angrily shoving a piece of gum into his mouth.

"I *know* that. But it's still true. Why are you being such a coward right now?"

"A coward?"

"Yeah. You are so scared to admit your true feelings."

He turns away from her. "Because I'm not used to having anything good in my life. I'm in Hell for a reason, Angelica. I'm a bad person who did something bad on Earth to end up in a bad place. Someday, you won't want me anymore because of who I truly am, I promise you that."

Angelica marches up to him. "Damon. You aren't just a bad person. Sure, you may have done something bad, but that isn't who you truly are. I know there is good in you.

I've seen it in you since I met you ... well, the third time." She gives him a small smile and cups his cheek in her hand. "You just have to believe in yourself. I promise you ... I'm not going anywhere."

She pulls his face to his, and when their lips meet, Damon really wants to believe her. That he can be the good person he was before everything went to shit and he died. That he could really become an angel and be with her in paradise for eternity.

But he can't. He knows it's just a dream.

Even if he did somehow become an angel, he knows The Boss wouldn't just let it go. He would get revenge.

As he argues with her, he sees his death looming in his future. The Devil told him that he still had to get her to become a demon. Today was just a little taste of the pain he would endure if he were to fail. But he didn't care ... he still needed to save Angelica.

Damon pulls away from her. "Angelica. I have to go."

"Don't you dare leave," she commands. "Do not push me away."

He shakes his head. "I'll talk to you later about ... training. Please, no more funny business. Just work."

Angelica grabs his arms before he can turn away from her. "It's a little late for that. I wouldn't call this funny business. There is definitely a higher power at work around us, and if you can't see that, then you are just blatantly ignoring it."

He disappears without another word.

Angelica stands there with her arm outstretched,

holding on to nothing. A mix of anger, disappointment, and hurt floods her. *Why is he acting as if he doesn't care? Six hours ago, he was telling me how excited he was to see me tonight. What happened?*

She remembers his appearance and what he said. *Does it have something to do with him being ... burned? What could be the reason for that?*

I understand that becoming an angel is scary for him, but what about the kiss, the flirting, the dinner dates, everything? He's opened up to me. I've seen his good slowly breaking through his darkness ...

Is this because he doesn't think he can pass?

He said he was a bad person who did something terrible on Earth ... Angelica shudders when she realizes she has no idea what he did to end up in Hell. What if he was a serial killer? A psychopath? A cannibal? Or something worse?

I don't care. He was judged; it's not my place to. That was the past, but he's working toward a better future.

A future as an angel. A future with me.

She wraps her arms around herself as tears blur her vision. *What can I do to prove to him that I want to be with him ... no matter what?*

Chapter 26

Damon appears in Missy's driveway, sighing in relief when he sees the empty garage. He isn't in the mood to talk to her—he just needs an escape. He walks through her house and into her kitchen, sitting at her kitchen table. Bills, schoolbooks, and an open notebook are strewn on the wooden surface. He leans down to inspect the notebook. A grocery list, notes about geography class, and a few doodles are scribbled on the page. And then one eerie sentence at the bottom:

Am I ready to die?

He shivers at her question.

Leaning back in the chair, he thinks about the poor girl. Wrong place at the wrong time. Well, sorta. She was just out at a bar one night, and The Devil was there. Damon doesn't know the details, but he knows that she went home with him—at one of his many Earth houses—and then the next day Damon was instructed to find her …

It was a normal monthly meeting. Summer was halfway over, and August had finally arrived. All the demons were standing at attention while The Devil passed out their assignments for that month. Everyone but Damon received an envelope, which was odd, and right before they were let go, The Boss called him out personally.

"Damon! Why don't you hang back after the meeting? I have a special job for you."

Damon nodded sharply; fear mixed with curiosity making him sweat.

After everyone left, The Devil motioned for him to stand at ease and then come closer. Jeremy was the only one in the room with them.

"Yes, my lord?" Damon asked.

"Ah, Damon. I have found her!" The Devil said. He dramatically gripped his chest and squeezed his eyes tight.

"Her, sir?"

His eyes snapped open in annoyance. "Her! My next wife. The love of my life."

Damon resisted the urge to roll his eyes. The Devil had many wives and seemed to find the next love of his life at least once a year.

"Congratulations."

"Thank you. Now I need you to get her prepared to come be my wife."

Fuck, Damon thought. He then smiled. "Of course, sir. Does she know who you are? And what she needs to do?"

He shook his head and grinned innocently. "No. We didn't get to talk so much yesterday." He laughed. "So, I need you to break the news to her."

Damon didn't let his annoyance show. Breaking the news

to a human woman that The Devil was to be her husband and she would kill herself for him never went over well.

While the role came with powers, they never suspected that it came with an expiration date. Once The Devil got bored with a wife, he dumped her into the flames and didn't blink twice.

"It'll be an honor, sir. Do you have a certain date in mind?"

"It must be on Halloween night ..."

Damon sighs as the memory ends. He wishes he could've said no. He hated the mission. He could kill people and take them to Hell with no problem. He could possess cult leaders and mess with Ouija board users any day. But convincing a woman to become The Devil's wife? The literal worst possible being in the entire universe? That struck a chord with him.

Especially as he got to know Missy. She didn't deserve that life.

Maybe she'd be one of the lucky ones who got to stay with him for hundreds of years ... Damon thinks to make himself feel better.

His breathing stops as he realizes something.

He never cared about this job and how shitty it was until Angelica.

Sure, he thought the whole thing was stupid from the get-go, but now it just feels wrong.

The good part of him, his conscience ... actually cares about Missy.

"Fuck me." Damon groans, letting his head fall into his hands. He rubs his temples. *This whole fake becoming an angel thing is becoming too much. I cannot see Angelica again. I have to get out now.*

He straightens up and pulls his phone out of his pocket to text Honey. She responds after a few minutes, and then he teleports to the back parking lot of the bar. It was almost always empty, except for people who smoked or wanted to sneak away and make out. Luckily, he is alone until Honey walks out the back door in a jacket a few minutes later. The loud music in the bar muffles as the door shuts behind her. Her eyes are no longer red or splotchy, and her makeup is perfect as if she never even cried.

"Come back to apologize for being an ass?" she jokes.

All the twisted emotions he's been feeling over the past month come flooding out. Tears spring to his eyes, and his breath hitches in his throat. "Honey, I'm fucking everything up."

Her eyes widen in concern. "Hey, it's okay—"

Damon cuts her off by storming to a nearby tree and punching it. It crackles and bark and dust fall to the ground. "No, it's not! I'm fucking everything up! I'm supposed to be convincing this angel to become a demon so that I don't die, and now I have feelings for her! After telling her I didn't want to be with her—even though it was a lie—I went to check on Missy, and suddenly, I feel horrible for doing my job!" he screams, the tears falling down his cheeks. "I have no choice on the Missy matter. What's done is done. She's accepted her fate, and now, all we have to do is wait. But Angelica? I can't do it anymore. I can't pretend to not care about her when I do. I can't make her become a demon and be miserable for the rest of her eternity. I can't make her hate me because of that. But when I think about being without her now, I feel even fucking worse!"

He pauses, taking a deep breath and wiping his nose with his sleeve. "I just pushed her away. I can't hurt her anymore, Honey. I can't fuck over the rest of her afterlife and let her believe I'm a good person. So, I've accepted that I will just die. Even though I don't want to fucking die!" He chokes up, unable to continue, and sits down on a parking block, sobbing into his hands.

Honey stares at him in shock, processing all his shouting. She's seen him cry before—when he first became a demon, he cried to her multiple times a week—but this time it is different. The gravel crunches beneath her feet as she walks to where he sits. Wrapping her arms around him, she holds him as he cries. "Let it out, babe."

Damon doesn't hesitate. He leans into her warm arms and weeps. He cries out the pain of becoming a demon, all the awful things The Devil makes him do to stay alive, the wishing he did things differently when he was alive, everything. He cries more than he thought he ever could.

When his sobs finally turn to sniffles, Honey rubs his back. "Feel better?"

"Not fucking really," he says, wiping his face and keeping his hands over his eyes.

"Are you ready for me to talk?"

He nods.

"Do you know why we are friends?" Honey asks. "Because I can see who you truly are. I know you aren't some scummy demon like the rest of them. I can see into your heart. I've watched you growing up; I know the reason you are in the Underworld, and even though what you did was bad, it also saved many people. I promise you that." She squeezes his shoulders. "I'm sorry you are hurting so bad; I know this isn't easy for you. I wish I could change the course of your afterlife, but I can't … only you can."

Damon turns to her, an eyebrow raised. "What do you mean, 'only I can?'"

She smiles at him as if the answer were obvious. "Damon, what have you been doing over the past month? Specifically."

"Trying to get an angel to become a demon? Convincing a woman to marry The Devil? Drinking a lot?"

She shakes her head. "Go back to the angel part. How are you trying to convince her?"

"By …" His eyes widen when he realizes what she's saying. "… pretending to want to become an angel?"

"Bingo." Honey nods. "Why don't you stop pretending and actually try to pass these tests?"

"I've thought about it …" says Damon. "But it can't be that easy. Even if I do magically pass, you know that The Devil won't just let that go. He would get revenge." He surveys his burn—the shadow of The Boss's handprint still etched into his skin.

Honey shrugs. "You wouldn't be his property anymore. Let's cross that bridge when we get there."

"But do I even deserve it? After what I did …"

"The system is flawed," she says, rubbing his shoulder. "Someone should do something about it," she mutters to herself. "But think of the other possibilities. The Devil may be pissed off, but you'd be able to be with the woman you love forever."

Damon's head whips around. "Love!?"

Honey raises one ashy blonde brow and leans her head to the side in a motherly way.

He hesitates before answering. *Could I really love her? Already?*

But as he stares at Honey and her all-knowing face, he knows it's true.

He's in love with Angelica.

"Can I say something really cheesy?" Damon asks, his face pinking.

"Always."

"I think she might be my soulmate."

Honey grins, and her peridot eyes glimmer in the moonlight. "Then what are you waiting for? Study your ass off and pass those angel tests to be with her forever. I know you can do it. I believe in you wholeheartedly."

Damon reaches around to hug her tight. "Thanks, Honey. You truly are the best friend anyone could ever have."

She nods and kisses him on the cheek.

Damon's smile falters. "But what if I end up failing the tests regardless? And what if Angelica doesn't want me anymore after I pushed her away?"

"Oh, babe. You won't fail. Trust me." She lifts his chin up and winks. "And I would just apologize. Be honest with her—except for the whole *it's my job to get you to become a demon*. Tell her your fears. She will love your honesty and vulnerability, and if she really is your soulmate, she will forgive you."

He squeezes her once more. She smiles and stands, brushing dirt off her dress and waving goodbye as she walks back inside the bar.

Damon sits on the parking block, thinking about how he is going to change his afterlife around. He has been showing Angelica parts of the real him slowly, but now he will open up to her completely. No dickhead Damon trying to be cool and getting her to come to Hell. Now she will see the real him, the one who genuinely wants to be an angel and be with her forever.

The one who is completely in love with her.

Riding the high of his newfound love, he whips his phone out of his pocket, scrolls to Angelica's messages quickly, and takes a deep breath.

Hey. Can I call?

Chapter 27

Angelica, who is lying in bed stuffing chocolate into her face, rolls over to check her phone. After the argument with Damon, she went home. She wasn't really in the mood to drink, anyway, and since he didn't want to see her, there was no point in being there. It took some convincing, but Cora followed her back to her place with the promise of wine, snacks, chocolate, and cheesy romantic movies.

When she sees who texted her, she tells Cora she will be right back, leaves the bedroom, and walks down the hall before pressing the call button.

Damon answers on the first ring. "Hey!" he says excitedly, a complete 180 to how he sounded when they last spoke.

Angelica walks into her home library and sits on a topaz-colored chaise. "Hello."

"I wanted to apologize for earlier. I am sorry for getting upset and just leaving like that."

"Okay," she says, picking at her pink fingernails.

"And ... you're right. I'm scared of my feelings. I've

never had something this good, and I'm terrified to fuck it up," Damon says, sucking in a deep breath to find the courage to pour his heart out to her. "But I really, really like you, Angelica. I'm tired of pretending that I don't. I'm sorry I'm an idiot and that it's taken me this long to admit it. I've felt something since I first bought you that drink at Gaia's. No—wait—before that. When you stole my house." He chuckles. "I know I've said some mean things. I know I've been a jerk. But I will prove to you that I can be the good guy you believe I can. Starting now, I will be open and honest and vulnerable with you. I don't want to lose you … I can't."

Angelica is speechless, her cheeks and ears warm from his sweet words. "I … oh," she stutters.

"Oh?" Damon's spirit falls.

"No! I, um." She clears her throat. "That was extremely sweet, Damon. I just am speechless, that's all. I … really like you, too."

On his side of the phone, Damon grins ear-to-ear. "Good. Can you forgive me? I promise I'll make it up to you."

She smiles to herself. "I forgive you. Just don't push me away again."

He lets out a relieved sigh. "I won't. Good. Thank you. With that … what are you doing tomorrow night?"

Angelica racks her brain. Cora and she are shopping in the morning, but nothing set in stone for the evening. "Nothing as of right now. Why?"

"I want to take you on a proper date."

"A proper date?" she repeats.

"Yes. Like a man should. No more sneaking around at Gaia's or casually getting dinner here and there. Meet me at my family's cabin at seven. Wear the prettiest dress you have. I will text you the address later." Anxiety and excitement tickle his stomach at the thought of her all dressed up in his family's home. Seeing a part of his life that no one else in his afterlife has.

Angelica has to calm her frantically beating heart before she can respond. "Okay."

"I can't wait to see you, little angel."

The phone clicks as they hang up. Angelica stares at the phone in her hand with a wide smile.

Damon heads back into the bar and tells Honey the good news. They celebrate with a toast.

Neither Damon nor Angelica can deny the chemistry—and more—that they have. They are both finally ready to go all-in for each other ... no matter the consequences.

Angelica hurries back to her bedroom, and Cora is waiting for her.

"I'm going on a fancy date with Damon tomorrow," she quickly blurts out.

Cora's eyes double in size. "What!?"

"Yes! He just called and apologized for being a total jerk, told me he really, really likes me, and then said he was taking me on a date and to wear the prettiest dress I have!"

The girls both scream and giggle and jump on Angelica's bed. Angelica feels ridiculous doing so, but she also feels like it is the right way to celebrate. She hasn't been on a fancy date ... well, ever.

Cora instructs her to relay the entire conversation, and Angelica obliges happily. When she is finished, Cora fist pumps the air. "This is so exciting! Oh my god, Ang! He is so hot, he is so sweet, *and* he is going to become an angel. Meaning that you guys are totally meant to be." She sighs dreamily.

Angelica giggles, twisting her pajama top in her hands. "Maybe ... maybe he really is my soulmate."

"Bitch! He totally is!"

Angelica dreams about the possibility of Damon and her being together forever. Him moving into her mansion, them saving the world together, and then coming home to cook dinner and make love all night ...

"Hey Cora ..." she says, blushing again. "What if ... things happen ..."

Cora tilts her head and swallows the chocolate she is eating. "Things happen?"

"You know ..."

Cora shakes her head, still confused.

Angelica can feel her face burning hot. "Like ... if I wanna do more than just kiss him."

"Ooooh." Cora wiggles her eyebrows.

"Don't make a big deal about it!" she says, slapping her arm. "I just feel like I'm finally ready to move to the next step. I'm obviously not a prude—I've done other things, just never gone all the way. But the way we kiss and the feelings I get when we touch … I've never craved a man so much before. His soul or his body."

"I am so proud of you," Cora says and wipes away a fake tear. "Ask me any and all questions and I will fill you in, oh pure one."

Cora proceeds to tell Angelica all about the ways of being intimate, and even though she is comfortable with Cora, she still feels a bit awkward and juvenile during the whole thing. She is a twenty-three-year-old virgin—well, technically nineteen plus afterlife years. Cora is very experienced and gives her a multitude of tips that Angelica tucks away in her brain. Obviously, she knows how it works, but now that sex is definitely on the table for her, it makes her nervous.

They finish their sex talk then resume the movie. Angelica tries to focus on the romance, but she is too swept up in her own romantic love story to pay attention. She lies on her back and rests her hands over her upper stomach—where the feelings that Damon gives her flutter. The sweetness of his confession to her, the excitement of their date tomorrow, the possibility of her finally losing her virginity, and the passionate idea of them being soulmates and spending the rest of eternity together makes her whole body tingle.

Is it too fast for her to give herself to him, entirely? Maybe. But she doesn't believe that. She feels like she has been waiting for this moment for her whole life. She has been waiting for Damon.

Like he told her how he started falling for her when

they first met at that Ouija call. She knows she's felt the same way since then. Gradually falling in love with him …

When Angelica is with him, everything in her life seems dull. Which sounds completely ridiculous considering she literally lives in Heaven. He brings a whole new feeling into her life that she has never known before. She always watched romantic movies and read books about love and how people get a feeling that no one else can explain.

Damon gives her that feeling times one million.

The next morning Angelica and Cora wake and spring out of bed. They can't wait to shop and spend time in sunny Los Angeles. Cora claims the bathroom first, so Angelica starts a pot of coffee. While she pours sugar into her hot ceramic mug, her phone buzzes in her back pocket.

Good morning, beautiful. Have fun shopping, I can't wait to see you tonight!

Angelica swoons when she reads Damon's text. She has a feeling that she will never get used to that.

Cora appears downstairs in a bath towel and swipes a cup of coffee before heading back upstairs. Angelica takes her time showering—making sure her legs are silky smooth, just in case—and then they both dress comfortably and plan their morning.

Neither of them is hungry for breakfast since they drank coffee, so they start the morning straight off with shopping.

They head to Hollywood and Highland and immediately get wrapped into their favorite stores.

While they do have the extra cash, angels don't technically have to buy anything. If they wanted something, then it would appear on their doorstep back home. Living in Heaven and having everything beyond their wildest dreams is definitely a perk, but sometimes they spend real money when they don't want Father knowing what they buy or, like in Damon's training, when they want to generously tip someone or give money to help others.

The girls get new makeup from Sephora, grab more coffee from Starbucks, and pause to walk through the Hollywood Walk of Fame. After, they head to another mall to peek inside a bookstore. Angelica picks up some new poetry books—a poetry book all about love, titled *His Green Eyes*, really caught her eye—while Cora skims some steamier romance novels.

"Here," Cora says, pushing a book in Angelica's hands.

She looks down to read the cover and then laughs loudly, causing an older woman down the aisle to shoot her a stern look. "*Fifty Shades of Grey?*"

"Hey, you don't know what Damon is into," Cora says mischievously. "It's best to be prepared."

Angelica sets it back on the shelf and shakes her head. "I think I'll pass."

They spend the next few hours shopping till they figuratively drop. Angelica knows that when she arrives back home, there will be a mess of boxes and shopping bags on her front porch, waiting to be folded and put away.

On their way to a restaurant for lunch, they pass by a

store, and Angelica hesitates near the entrance. "Uh … do you think we could go in here?"

Cora reads the store sign. "Ooh, are you sure?" She purrs.

"No, maybe not." Angelica squeaks as her cheeks color.

Cora drags her into the lingerie store without another word. Angelica tries to avoid her nerves as she inspects the different types of lingerie. She picks out a few girly baby-doll lace numbers—all different shades of pink, of course—and then Cora helps her decide on a lacey bra and panty set that she can wear underneath her clothes. Angelica quickly pays and stuffs the bag down in the bottom of her purse.

"What, don't want Father to see those being delivered?" Cora teases her.

They finally appear at the restaurant and are quickly sat, given that it is two p.m. and past the lunch rush. They order small salads and waters. While they crunch on their lettuce, Cora chats about the finishing decorating touches she has decided to do for the Halloween party. She extends an invitation to Damon, and Angelica promises to invite him at the date tonight.

"Do you know what you're wearing?" Cora asks.

"I have a few dresses in mind. That pink one I wore to Polly's wedding a few years ago? Or maybe the one I wore when I went to that fancy governor's ball with you?" Angelica giggles. "I forgot you dated his son for a while."

"Oh, I miss Marco sometimes." Cora sighs. "Anyway, no! Neither of those dresses will do. We need to pick out a new one. I know just the place to go when we are finished eating."

"Yes ma'am."

"Are you nervous for tonight? You've got four and a half hours."

"Of course I'm nervous!" Angelica says, tightening her ponytail. "This is the first actual date we are going on. I have no idea where he's taking me, but it has to be nice since I have to look so fancy."

"Don't be nervous," Cora reassures her. "It's going to be amazing; I promise you. You'll go to the date, eat some good food, and then hopefully get some good dick."

"Cora Victoria," Angelica scolds with a smile on her face. "You are crazy. But I love you."

"I love you, too, babe." She winks and shoves her last bite of lettuce into her mouth.

Angelica thinks about all the possibilities tonight may bring. Nothing is set in stone, but she knows that no matter what will happen, it will be a night to remember.

Chapter 28

Angelica nervously smooths down the dress that took her hours to pick out. The dress shop had so many different kinds of dresses in an array of colors, and she had so much fun trying them all on. Until, finally, she laid eyes on the satin cobalt blue dress and knew that it was the one. It was even more set-in-stone when she walked out of the dressing room to Cora's cheering and gushing about how *amazing* she looked.

The girls hurried back to Angelica's place to get her ready. Cora curled her hair into a half-updo with a bun on the top of her head and curls cascading down her back. Angelica touched up her makeup and brushed her teeth twice before slipping on the dress, kissing Cora goodbye, and teleporting to the cabin.

Angelica walks into the cabin and breathes a sigh of relief when she notices he isn't there yet. She tries to calm her beating heart and sweaty hands. To combat her nervousness, she tours the cabin on her own while she waits for him.

The fact that Damon described the cabin as small made her laugh. It may not be a huge house, but it is big enough for a family of four to live there comfortably. Two bathrooms, three bedrooms, a spacious living room, and a vast kitchen. Angelica is happy to see that the kitchen is fully stocked. She steals a piece of bread to nibble on and calm her queasy stomach.

She ends up back in the living room and runs her hand over a fuzzy blanket on the edge of the suede couch. Pulling her phone out of her clutch, she checks the time again. Damon is ten minutes late.

As if on cue, his voice comes from behind her. "Hello, beautiful."

She turns around and almost faints at the sight of him.

Gone are his dark t-shirts and jeans. Instead, he wears a perfectly fitted black suit with a cream-colored shirt. A classic black bowtie decorates his neck. His beard looks freshly trimmed, and his hair is brushed and tucked behind his ears. A bright grin stretches across his face, completing his look perfectly.

"Wow, Damon, you look amazing," Angelica says breathlessly.

His eyes widen as he takes her in. She blushes and adjusts the spaghetti straps under his intense gaze. He trails his eyes down her body, and they pause when they connect with the long slit up her thigh. "Angelica, you look …" He swallows and chuckles while shaking his head. "There isn't even a word to describe how beautiful and stunning you look."

"Thank you," she says. "I never thought I'd see you look so nice."

Damon's awestruck smile turns nervous, and he tugs at his collar. "I had to go buy a suit. Are you sure it looks okay?"

Angelica runs her eyes over his body again. He looks way more than just *okay*. "I promise, you look great. More than great. Very handsome."

He sighs in relief and strolls to her, gently caressing her hip and leaning down to kiss her softly on the lips. "Are you ready to eat?"

"Always. Where are we going?" she asks, the buzz of his kiss reverberating through her body.

"I don't want to give too much away, but we are going to Sarasota. My parents used to vacation there once a year, and there is a fine-dining restaurant they always loved."

"Sounds great!" she says, loving his opening up about his family. She glances down at her floor-length dress. "Although, I don't know if sand and satin mix."

"It won't be sandy in the restaurant," Damon teases. "But if it is, I'll carry you." He winks before lacing his fingers through hers. "Let's go!"

Together they teleport to Florida and in front of Luciano's. Angelica suddenly feels like she is in a scene in a romance movie. Damon rests his hand on the small of her back and gently ushers her up the steps. She holds her dress in her hand as they walk, her silver flats peeking out with each movement. To the right of them, the ocean softly roars, the waves a deep blue in the evening sunset.

"Your dress matches the ocean," Damon comments, rubbing her bare back under her hair. "Beautiful."

Goosebumps speckle her arms.

A young hostess waits as they walk through the stained-glass front doors. She peers at them over her red-rimmed glasses. "Reservation name?"

"Joshua White," Damon says. "We have the private rooftop."

Angelica's heart skips a beat. *Private rooftop?*

The hostess nods before grabbing two menus and motioning for them to follow her. She takes them through the restaurant and up a flight of stairs. Angelica nods at a few tables as they pass, and the guests' eyes widen as they spot her angelic face. Damon grabs her hand, claiming her as his date. She giggles. The hostess leads them up another staircase until they finally step onto the roof. It juts out over the restaurant below, overlooking the water. Lights are strewn around the beams, twinkling in the slow-setting sun. One table sits in the middle, decorated with a bouquet of pink and orange dahlias.

Angelica turns to Damon. "You remembered!"

"Of course," he says, leaning over to kiss her forehead.

The hostess drops off the menus and smiles before leaving. Damon walks to the table and pulls out one chair, motioning for Angelica to sit. She does happily.

Once he sits across from her, she giggles. "You've really outdone yourself, Damon."

He picks up the water pitcher and pours them both a

glass. "I have been to a few fancy places growing up, and I always enjoyed it. I've never been on a date to one though."

"Well, I'm honored to be your first. I've never been on a fancy date either."

He holds up his water in a toast. "To us, then."

Angelica clinks her glass against his. "To us." As she sips her water, she looks out over the ocean. The setting sun is absolutely gorgeous, and the sky overhead is turning a purplish-blue. All the anxiety from earlier erases from her, and she feels completely at peace.

The server appears with a smile that seems forced. "Good evening. My name is Drake, and I have the pleasure of taking care of you tonight. What can I get you to drink?"

Damon grimaces when he thinks of the only Drake he knows but quickly replaces it with a small smile. "Can we please get a bottle of the Verdicchio?"

The server nods and leaves without a word.

"Don't worry, you'll like it. It's sweet," Damon reassures her.

She nods. "What was that weird look?"

He grimaces again. "You saw that, huh? I tried not to make a face." He turns to the ocean. "I just know of a not-so-fun guy named Drake."

"Is he a demon, too?"

"No. He's The Devil's bodyguard who oversees keeping us in line." Damon grabs a roll from the breadbasket on the table. "If one of us screws up, he teaches us a lesson." He shudders as he spreads butter across the bread.

"That doesn't sound fun. Have you been ... taught a

lesson by him?" Angelica asks. She remembers when they first met and the burn on his arm. It's a lot better now, but she could still see the outline when his sleeves were rolled up. She takes his silence for an answer and doesn't press the conversation more, instead reaching for her own roll. Damon intercepts her and hands her the roll he just prepared. "Aw, so sweet."

Crunchy bread and warm butter fill her mouth as she bites down. "This bread is amazing." She moans, taking another bite. The roll quickly disappears down her throat, and she grabs another from the basket.

Drake returns with their bottle of wine and two glasses, popping the cork and filling each glass before handing them to Damon and Angelica. "Have you two decided on dinner?"

Damon and Angelica exchange a wide-eyed glance.

"I am so sorry, Drake," Angelica says. "We haven't even looked yet! Your beautiful views and delicious rolls distracted me."

Drake smiles at her. "No problem at all, miss. I will give you two more time."

After he disappears down the stairs, they both burst into laughter.

"He hates us." Damon chuckles.

"Most likely," Angelica agrees, opening the menu and scanning its contents, feeling overwhelmed at all the mouthwatering options.

"What are you feeling?"

"I honestly don't know. There are so many choices!" she

says, sipping her wine. The savory taste of peaches excites her tastebuds. "My top choices are probably the pan-seared salmon or risotto," she says confidently before noticing his frown. "What?"

"Both sound gross," he admits, giving her a lopsided grin. "I'm definitely getting the filet mignon."

Angelica sticks her tongue out at him playfully. "Well, good for you."

"I would say get both entrees, but then you wouldn't have any room for dessert."

"Oh, dessert!" Angelica swoons before flipping to the dessert part of the menu.

Damon laughs again, and her ears ring with the magical sound.

When Drake returns, she confidently orders the salmon, way more excited to get to the dessert portion of the evening. They both enjoy the wine, Angelica finishing her glass off a little too quickly, hiccupping as Damon refills it. They joke and laugh and talk as if they were old friends and had known each other for years, not weeks.

"I know I've already said it, but, damn, you just look so beautiful tonight," Damon says. "So exquisite, like the opals of your eyes."

She blushes and moves her eyes away from his gaze, imagining how her face now matches the reddish hues of the sunset. "How are you so good with words?"

He shrugs. "My dad raised me to be a gentleman. My parents were famous, so we always had eyes on our family. They taught me from a young age how to treat a lady.

Obviously, when I got to Hell, I threw all manners out the window, but it's nice to act like my old self again. All of my parents' friends used to compliment them on how polite and sweet I was."

"Well, I like this Damon much better." She smiles. "Although, your attitude is endearing in its own way as well," she teases. Before she can revisit the "famous parents" comment, Drake returns with their entrees. They hungrily dig in without another word.

"The salmon was an excellent choice!" Angelica says as she chews on the delicious fish.

Damon stares at her with a small smile on his face.

"What?"

"Just … I can't believe I was about to walk away from you. And this."

"Yeah, that would've been pretty stupid." She laughs.

"I'm sorry for waiting so long to tell you how I felt."

"It's okay. I understand why you did."

He takes a big bite of steak. "So, no more shy questions. Ask me anything you want, and I'll answer."

She raises her eyebrows. "Anything at all?"

"I'm officially an open book. I want you to know everything about me, the more the better. No more silly things like my favorite movie or color. Ask me something deep," Damon says. Ever since he told her he wanted to be with her, a weight has been lifted off his shoulders. The only small fear that lies in the back of his mind is The Devil finding out his plan and his punishment …

He pushes the thought away.

Angelica thinks for a moment while eating, visibly excited and up for the challenge. "Hmm ... what was your family like?"

Damon looks down at his hands, a lump forming in his throat. He mentioned them casually, but telling Angelica about them is entirely different. He takes a deep breath. "My mom is a retired singer. She is one of the most amazing women I've ever met. Strong. Caring. Hardworking. She is so nice to everyone that she meets and adores her fans. She was a great mother." He leans back and observes the ocean. "She always believed in me and my art and helped me hone my craft. I remember when I got picked to be in the art gallery, she celebrated me for weeks after."

"Who is your mom?" Angelica asks.

"Miranda Russo."

"No way! That's your mom? My grandma loved listening to her—she was big in the 70s, right? Didn't she sing 'Train 'Round California'?"

He smiles. "Yeah, that's her."

"That's so cool. That explains the hair." Angelica examines his dark locks. "She has the prettiest dark hair. So that means your Italian?"

"On my mother's side, yes. My grandmother came to the states and had my mother and uncles here. I've been to Italy a few times to see extended family."

"Your life was so much cooler than mine." She giggles.

Damon winks before taking another bite.

"My dad is her agent. James Jones. That's how they met. He had just got hired by a big agency, and she was the first singer he signed. They fell in love almost instantly. They toured together and everything, and once my mom got off the road, they had me and my twin sister."

"You have a twin sister? Wow, that's amazing!"

Damon slowly frowns. "Yeah. Demi. She was my best friend growing up. Literally my partner in crime. She was the wilder one of the two of us—always dragging me with her to crazy parties and adventures. I miss her the most." His heart falls even more when he thinks about his family finding him dead, then watching him at his funeral. Demi was the most heartbroken out of all of them. Her teammate, closest friend, and twin died.

He hasn't visited them since. He doesn't even know if they ever forgave him for killing himself, or for the reason why he did kill himself …

Angelica can tell that he is done talking about his family. She reaches over the table to rub his hand. "Thank you for sharing your family with me."

Damon meets her sparkling green eyes. "Of course. It's nice to talk about them after all this time."

Drake interrupts by setting a huge molten lava cake on the table. The warm fudge oozes onto the ice cream, and both of their stomachs somehow growl for more. Damon and Angelica stuff heaping bites into their mouths, not wasting a single drop of chocolate. While Angelica rubs her bloated and happy stomach, Damon quickly pays for dinner. Drake's mood instantly lifts when he sees the tip Damon left on the bill. He thanks them over and over and bids them a good night.

Angelica wipes her mouth with her napkin and reapplies her lipstick, staring into her hand mirror.

Damon shrugs back into his suit jacket. "Care for a stroll on the beach?"

Angelica closes her lipstick with a *snap*. "Don't forget, I'm wearing satin."

"Oh, you'll be fine, angel," he says, extending his hand.

Angelica knows she cannot say no to that smile, so she intertwines her fingers through his and they stroll down a back staircase that ends at the edge of the white sand. Angelica slides off her flats and hands them to Damon so she can hold her dress.

They walk down to the water, and Angelica shivers as it hits her toes. The sun fully disappeared, and the moon is rising in her place. Angelica leans her head on Damon's shoulder. "I believe it's your turn for a question."

He laughs, letting go of her hand to wrap his arm around her waist and pull her closer to him. "Are we still playing?"

"Of course. There's still so much I want to know about you. And so much you don't know about me."

"Okay … what's your least favorite ice cream flavor?"

So much for getting personal, she sighs internally. "Sherbert." A ghost crab scurries past her foot. "Scary movies or funny movies?"

"It depends. Some scary movies *are* funny. Especially now that I'm a demon—have you seen some of those demon movies? They are ridiculous." He laughs.

After they walk down the beach for a while, they run

into a long pier extending deep into the water. Benches and standing binoculars are scattered on the illuminated dock. They step on to it and head for the very edge.

"And that's why I will never feed a stray bird again." Angelica laughs. She sits on the last bench on the pier, stretching out her toes.

Damon sits next to her, setting her shoes down under them and chuckling. "Good to know."

She leans onto Damon. Since the temperature is cooling down and her dress doesn't retain her warmth, his body heat is nice. "Your turn."

Damon shifts his shoulders, thinking about what to ask next. The dark waves roll under them, loud and pounding against the dock.

He decides he is ready to tell her about his life, entirely. He showed her a glimpse of his family at dinner, but she deserves to know the real reason why he killed himself, why he ended up in Hell as a demon. Was it pretty? No. But he is confident that she will not run away screaming ...

He hopes.

Angelica playfully elbows him. "Hello, earth to Damon?"

"Sorry, I just ..." He sits up and pulls his hair back into a low ponytail. "I think I'm ready to tell you about my life. If you are ready to hear it ... the ending isn't pretty ... but I feel like it's finally time you know. So ... do you want to know?"

Chapter 29

"Oh!" Angelica says, sitting up in surprise and facing him. "Of course. I'd love to hear all about it."

"Okay, good. Just promise me you won't run away screaming," Damon says. He tried to make it sound like a playful joke, but it came out a little too seriously.

She hesitates. She is about to find out why Damon is in Hell ... and what if it's as scary as her brain has worried about? What if she finds out he did something awful and really deserves to be there?

No. You see him. He's good. It can't be that bad ...

"I promise."

Damon nods and then leans forward, taking deep breaths and trying to calm his frantic, nervous heart. He gathers the courage to tell her his story, watching the ocean quietly.

After a few minutes of nothing, Angelica leans over to rub his shoulder. Sensing more of his hesitation, she trails her hand to his cheek and turns herself toward him. "Hey.

Why don't I tell you my story first? Will that help you open up to me?"

He relaxes and slowly nods, grabbing her hand and bringing it to his lips to kiss her fingers. "Thank you."

"But now it's your turn to promise me that you won't get upset or sad, okay?"

His black eyes search hers for a sign of what's coming, but he finds nothing. "Okay. I promise."

Angelica takes a deep breath and stands, stepping a few paces in front of them to lean on the railing.

"I died when I was nineteen. Time means nothing to us, but it was about four years ago on Earth. Which is why I say I'm twenty-three now."

"But you became an angel?" Damon interrupts.

She swivels her neck around to glare at him. "Yes. I was grieving my death in Heaven. It took me a while to get over the fact that I died young and would never accomplish the dreams I had planned. Then I met some friends and started enjoying my new life—learning new things, gardening, writing, and relaxing. Last January, I studied and took the angel tests. Don't interrupt again."

He is embarrassed by her scolding. "Sorry. Continue."

Angelica turns back to stare at the waves. "I had a normal life, I guess you would say. I lived in a small town in West Virginia, not too far from Virginia Beach. I played volleyball, as you know, and was in the writing club—although I didn't really get into poetry until after I died. I was an only child, just me and my mom and dad. Gosh, I love them so much ... they're still alive. I visit them sometimes, but it's too painful. We aren't allowed to mingle with family ..." The last time she visited them was so hard. She was happy because they were finally starting to move on from her death, but she wished she could appear to them. Tell them she was okay, that she loved them so much, and that she was counting down the days till they were together again. But if she did, she would lose her wings forever.

"My major focus was on school. I was taught from a young age to take care of myself first before anything else—get a good job and be able to support myself entirely before looking for a husband or wife. I really wanted to become a doctor and help people, so I had to make sure I studied hard and got good grades to get into a good college.

"I was the only girl on the volleyball team who wasn't into dating. I didn't have a date to prom or worry about boyfriends and girlfriends. I just honestly wasn't interested in any of it—I had plenty of time to date later.

"Fast forward, and I was accepted into Georgetown studying pre-med. My parents were so proud of me even though they were sad I was moving out of state. I definitely didn't have time for love, as I had at least another eight years of school ahead of me. But then, fall of freshman year, I met who I thought was the love of my life."

Her stomach clenches up at the thought of him.

"My sister went to Georgetown."

She turns, not angry this time. "No way? Small world. Did you?"

"No, I stayed in California." He nods, letting her finish her story.

"That man was everything I wanted in a husband. He

was going to school to be an engineer. He was a dog lover and wanted to have a big family. We met through a mutual class and started dating shortly after. We were *the* couple on campus, and everyone said we were Ken and Barbie. Perfect in every way." She snorts. "Yeah right."

Damon's eyebrows knit together, not liking where the story is heading.

"We dated the whole year. He told me he loved me and wanted to marry me someday. I really believed him. The night before summer break, we were hanging out one last time in his dorm. He lived across the country, so he was flying home the next day. We ended up at a frat party, and it was all fun until, suddenly, I felt super dizzy and close to blacking out. I couldn't walk, and I could barely keep my eyes open.

"Before I knew it, he was pulling my pants down in a stranger's bedroom. Luckily, before he could rape me, my roommate found us, and her boyfriend beat him up."

She shudders. "He had drugged my drink. The man who told me he loved me. Turns out that he and his friend made a bet that he would get my virginity before the year was up, and that was the last night to do it, so he had to improvise. I am so happy Deb caught him, because if she didn't ... I don't even want to think about it. Now looking back, I can see how much of a jerk he was. He always pressured me for sex, and now that I know about the bet, I don't believe he ever really cared about me at all."

She turns around to see Damon clutching his stomach. "Are you okay?"

He feels like he was punched in the gut. He wants to

kill the man who did this to her. But at the same time, the story strikes a chord. "What did you say his name was?"

"I didn't."

"What was it?"

"Does it matter?" she asks.

His eyes meet hers. "Yes."

Angelica's palms start sweating at the anger in his eyes. She wipes away a fallen tear and purses her lips. "His name was Ryder Wilson."

Damon's body goes rigid, and his face twists into pure rage. He lets out a low, animalistic growl. All he can see is red. He stands and turns away from her, hands balled into fists.

Angelica watches his reaction and—for the first time—is genuinely terrified of him. "Why are you acting like that? It's not like he actually raped me. Please calm down."

He punches the bench they were previously sitting on.

"Damon, what the hell?"

"Angelica, you don't understand."

"Then make me understand!" she pleads.

Damon turns to her, and the next sentence makes her blood freeze.

"Ryder Wilson is the reason why I'm in Hell."

Chapter 30

Angelica is sure that she didn't hear him correctly. "What?"

Damon tries to calm down, but his hands continue shaking. "Ryder Wilson raped my sister."

"What?!" she repeats, her stomach lurching.

He braces his hands against the pier and stares at his feet. "My sister also went to Georgetown, remember? The night of her graduation two years ago, there was a big party on campus. She went there and met some guy who brought her a drink. It was laced. She woke up naked in his bed the next morning. It was him."

"Oh my god, Damon, I'm so sorry …"

"She got a rape kit done, and they found his DNA—Ryder Wilson. Except the cops and school did nothing. They said that there was no hard evidence that it was a sexual assault—even with bruises and the drugs still in her system. I guess his dad was a huge donor to the school, so they dismissed the case."

Angelica holds her stomach. The delicious dinner they just ate is threatening to come back up.

"Damon. I don't know what to say. I'm so sorry for your sister."

He pulls a cigarette out from nowhere and lights it. "Yeah, well, he got what he deserved."

She doesn't like the sound of that. She waits until his cigarette is halfway smoked before speaking again. "How … how is he the reason you're in Hell?"

Damon sighs. This is *not* how he wanted to tell her. "After everything went down, I went out to see her. I was there when the cops called and dismissed her case and held her when she cried. Once I realized the justice system wasn't going to help, my buddies and I decided to teach him a lesson. The cops wouldn't handle it, so I had to."

Angelica doesn't know if she should ask him to elaborate or not … she isn't sure that she even wants to know.

"How did you handle it?"

He finishes his cigarette and throws it on the ground. "I murdered him."

Angelica's core freezes. She stares at her hands, speechless.

"I didn't mean to. It got out of hand. I was so mad, and I let that pent-up rage dictate my decisions. As soon as I realized what had happened, I felt so guilty. I killed myself a few days later."

Angelica already knows that he killed himself, but it is still a shocking reminder. She closes her eyes and breathes through her nose, thinking over his words.

Damon watches her carefully. "I know that you may not want to see me anymore ... and I understand completely if dating a murderer is way out of your comfort zone."

Angelica sits back down on the bench, wrapping her arms around herself. Her head is spinning madly. She doesn't know what to think. She didn't expect this to be the reason he was in Hell, or for his story to be so closely intertwined with hers ...

I'm in love with a murderer.

Even as she thinks that statement, whether it is right or wrong, her anxiety lessens. He didn't murder someone just because. He didn't even mean to kill him. He was trying to get justice for his sister. It got out of hand, and then he ended up killing himself because of it.

She thinks about one of the main things angels believe. *It's not my place to judge ...*

Angelica stands and smooths down her dress. "Damon ... I'm not going anywhere."

Damon's eyes widen. "You aren't? I just told you I murdered some guy and then killed myself."

"I know." She clears her throat. "And that is not okay, and I don't want you to think that I think it's okay. It was very wrong of you to do. But ... you know that. You felt guilty for doing it, which is why you ended your own life shortly after. But you were judged, and you are where you are because of it. What have I told you? It's not my place to judge you." She walks over to him and puts her arms on his chest. "I'm not condoning what you did, but you may have done more good than harm in the long run. If he tried raping me and then succeeded in raping your sister, who knows how many other women he could've hurt."

Damon looks away from her. *Damn. Is she really okay with this?*

Angelica caresses his cheek and turns him back to face her. "Damon. I'm not going anywhere. Would my parents approve of me being in love with a murderer? Probably not. But good thing I don't need their approval. Because I want to be with you."

Despite the shame he is feeling, a smile creeps onto his face. "Did you just say that you were in love with me?"

Her hands fly up to her mouth. "Shoot—I—uh—"

He moves her hands away from her mouth so that he can kiss her. Their bond ignites between them as he holds her. Damon leaves her lips and kisses both of her cheeks before resting his forehead against hers. "Angelica. I love you."

They are so close her eyes can't focus on his, but she stares into them anyway. "Really?"

"Yes, really." He smiles. "I know we haven't known each other long, but we have a connection that neither one of us can explain. It's as if my soul has been waiting for you all this time, as if I have loved you forever and just needed to meet you for it to ignite. I know without a doubt in this world that I absolutely love you. I mean ... when you know, you know, right?"

Tears spring to Angelica's eyes. *Margaret was right.* "Yes. And I know. I love you, too, Damon."

They kiss again under the crescent moon before they

decide to head back to the cabin. As they leave the beach, Damon looks up to curse the huge reminder that Halloween is only two weeks away.

Chapter 31

Back at the cabin, Angelica and Damon sit on the back deck with their arms wrapped around each other. They changed out of their fancy attire and are now comfily dressed—she in leggings and a crewneck while he in sweatpants and a T-shirt. A firepit provides heat against the chilly autumn night.

"How are we so connected?" Angelica asks.

"Coincidence, maybe?"

"I don't believe in that. There are too many instances. The touching is weird. Then the feeling of us knowing each other forever is different. And now the connection with our lives? I think the universe is trying to tell us something."

"Like you're my soulmate?" Damon chuckles.

Angelica doesn't. She blushes against him, thankful he can't see. "I mean …"

He rests his cheek on the top of her head, snuggling closer. "I mean … it makes sense."

"You think so?"

"I know so."

Angelica's heart sighs happily. A nearby creek burbles in the night, and the wind breezes through the trees.

"What color were your eyes before you died?" she asks.

"Hey, you skipped me," Damon teases.

"Fine, ask a question then."

"I'll let it slide this time. Instead of me telling, why don't I show you?"

Intrigued, she follows him back into the cabin, through the house, and into a bedroom. He stops in front of a hanging picture frame and nods to it, a grin on his face. She steps up and examines the memory frozen in time.

It is a family—Damon's family—standing in front of the cabin. All of them are dressed in hiking gear. Angelica's eyes instantly fall on his mother, Miranda, because she recognizes her from the many CDs her grandmother had. She is just as gorgeous with her long black hair and bright smile. Her arm is around a small girl—presumably Damon's sister, Demi. She looks to be in high school and is just as gorgeous as her mother. On Miranda's left is a man in a baseball cap, mid-laughter. Even though he isn't looking at the camera, Angelica knows it is James and can identify the distinct features that he passed down to his son.

And last, but definitely not least, she looks to the young man on the far left. Damon. He can't be older than seventeen or eighteen. His dark hair is the same long length that it is now and still falling into his eyes. He is holding up a big water bottle and wearing a smile that stretches the entire length of his cheeks. Angelica zooms in closer to find the answer she is looking for …

"Hazel," she says triumphantly. "Your eyes were hazel."

He nods. "This was the day we got the cabin. Demi begged us to go hiking, so we did, and Mom had the idea to take a picture first. We leaned our camera up against a tree, and literally seconds before it went off, my dad farted super loud. He blamed the hot dogs and beans we had for lunch." Damon laughs. "He laughed so hard once the camera went off. It was a great day and an even better memory now."

Angelica laughs with him, imagining the scene.

"So, what about you?"

"Guess," she says, fluttering her eyelashes.

He thinks for only a moment. "Green."

"How did you know?" she asks, crossing her arms.

"When your eyes are green for a day, they just match you in the most perfect way. I can't even explain it."

She swoons and sits on the bed that is behind them. "You are a real softie, you know that?"

"My turn for a question?" he asks, sitting next to her.

Angelica nods and lays back onto the fluffy comforter, sighing into its luxury.

He lies down next to her and holds her hand. "Not to bring back up your trauma ... but you never explained how you actually died. How did it happen?"

She shrugs nonchalantly as if it were something unimportant. "Oh, that. Car accident. I went home for summer break and got hit by a drunk driver."

Damon's lips turn down. "I'm so sorry."

"Don't be! It is what it is."

He rubs his thumb against hers. "And you waited a few years to become an angel, right? Why is that? Did you not want to at first?"

"I honestly didn't know if it was the path I wanted to take. I was enjoying my time in Heaven while also grieving my death. It's weird—grieving your own death. Every time I feared dying as I grew up, I never thought about how I would feel *after* it happened. Anyway, after a while, I wanted to do something more. I knew that I would never be a doctor and save lives that way, so I thought saving lives as an angel would bring more meaning into my afterlife. Plus, Cora really wanted me to hang out with her on Earth, so I signed up and passed the first time I took the tests."

"Is that uncommon?"

"Meh. Some people take two to three times to pass."

Damon must've shown his worry on his face because she rolls onto her side to face him. "Hey, you will be okay! I promise. Even if you take a few times to pass, you will make it."

He doesn't have the heart to tell her that he may not even get the first chance, let alone survive a second or third. Instead, he smiles. "Thank you, love. Are you ready to call it a night, or do you want to watch a movie before you go?"

Angelica is not even close to being ready to leave. "I'd love to watch a movie!"

Damon grabs the TV remote and flips through the channels until they come across a rom-com that looks fun. They crawl under the covers and watch together, snuggling and sneaking the occasional kiss.

When the two main characters start a love scene on screen, both of their hearts quicken.

Angelica's baby pink lingerie hidden under her baggy sweatshirt feels like weights against her body. She knows she wants to be with Damon—especially after he said he loved her—but she can't bring herself to just woman up and *do it*. She remembers Cora telling her to be confident and take control, but she is feeling the total opposite. When she notices him admiring her while biting his lip, she lets go of her fears and leans over to crush her lips against his.

Damon kisses her back with the same intensity. They wrap their arms around each other and pull themselves closer together. He traces his tongue over her soft lips, asking for permission. She opens her mouth, and their tongues collide.

Angelica's confidence builds as they kiss longer. She pushes him up and against the headboard and straddles him. She leans over him with one hand in his hair and the other on his neck. He grabs her sides and grinds her on top of him. When she feels him harden under her, a new wave of fire rushes over.

Damon's hands move to the bottom of her shirt. He traces circles against her naked skin, asking for permission again.

She responds by eagerly raising her arms.

He swiftly lifts the crewneck up and off her. When his eyes connect with her pink, lacey bra, he makes a low groaning sound.

"Do you like it?" Angelica says breathlessly.

His answer is a bite on her neck.

She giggles and leans back to take off his shirt. Once it's thrown to the floor, she gawks at his chiseled chest. She rubs her hands down his abs, and he shivers, leaning back down to kiss her.

He nibbles her ear and starts working down her neck and onto her chest. Angelica leans back and twists both of her hands through his hair, closing her eyes and getting lost in the feeling of his lips all over her. A soft moan escapes her lips as he kisses her breasts, only a few kisses away from meeting her bare nipple.

When his hands reach back to unclip her bra, she freezes.

"Damon."

"Hmm?" He murmurs against her skin, the vibration giving her goosebumps.

"There's something I have to tell you."

His hands pause, waiting for her confession.

"I'm a virgin."

Damon stops kissing her and looks up into her shy eyes. He knew that earlier she said she didn't have time for boys, but he assumed that she at least had sex before …

He isn't used to stopping or taking things slow, but he knows that the first time should be special. This isn't a drunken fuck like what he did with Chloe. This is important, monumental. He reaches his hand up to cup her cheek. "That's okay, my love. Do you … do you want me to keep going?"

She doesn't hesitate. "Yes. I want you. I love you, and I want you to make love to me."

A cheeky grin appears on his face. "Good. Let me get on top."

He flips her over and kisses her again. Once she is comfortable, he leans down to kiss in between her breasts before finally unbuckling the bra and flinging it across the room. When his mouth meets her naked bosom, she arches her back and moans again. This time, it is louder.

Damon, visibly turned on by her reaction, runs his fingers down her body and slides it right underneath her waistband.

Suddenly Angelica is transported back into her college dorm. Her eyes snap open. "Damon. I'm not ready."

He pauses.

She sits up and pushes him away. "Please stop."

Damon moves off her and lays by her side while their breathing slows. Angelica awkwardly covers her nakedness with her arms.

After a while, Damon clears his throat. "I'm sorry, Angelica. I got carried away."

She lets out a breath. Reliving her trauma only hours ago definitely affected her more than she originally thought. "No, no. It's not you. I wanted to until … I just got scared."

He leans over and rubs his thumb on her cheek. "Baby, you never have to be scared with me. I'm not that jackass, I promise." Neither one of them needs him to clarify who he is referring to. "I love you. Meaning that I won't pressure you. Whenever you're ready, I'll be ready."

Angelica falls in love all over again after he said that. She knows she wants to be with him physically, but not tonight. And she is so lucky that he is so good to her and turned out to be a good guy and not the asshole demon she originally thought he was. "I love you, too, Damon."

He gets off the bed, grabs her bra and sweatshirt, and hands it back to her. She gratefully accepts and redresses. They finish the movie—Angelica wiping away a few tears after the uber-romantic ending—and then she still isn't ready to leave, so they head to the kitchen for some snacks.

Damon grabs a bag of chips and a can of soda. Angelica scrounges through the cabinets until she finds some Cheez-Its.

"What are you thinking about?" Damon asks, noticing her scrunched-up brows.

She sighs, sticking her hand in the cracker box. "This is going to sound ridiculous, but… what if I'm bad at it?"

He shakes his head and chuckles. "Trust me. You can't be bad at it." He gives her a warm smile. "Especially when it's filled with love."

That is exactly the answer she needs.

He rubs his hand over his beard and clears his throat. "So, I was wondering … would you like to spend the night? I'm sure my sister has some pajamas here, and there are extra toiletries and stuff in the guest bathroom."

Angelica smiles so wide her cheeks ache. "I would love to."

Damon leans over to give her a Dorito-crumbed kiss.

After they finish snacking, Angelica looks in the guest bedroom for a change of clothes. She would sweat if she slept in her heavy sweatshirt …

She pauses with her hands around an old T-shirt. *Am I sleeping in here ... or with him?*

Once she changes into the T-shirt and a pair of shorts—a little baggy but comfortable—she brushes her teeth with a brand-new toothbrush. She combs through her curls and braids her hair back, then walks back to Damon, who is lying in bed without a shirt on. She bites her lip at the sight of his sculpted chest—even more attractive in the light.

"You look so cute," he says.

She curtsies. "Thanks. I was wondering ... where would you like me to sleep?"

"Wherever you'd like. Although I'd prefer if you'd sleep with me tonight."

She doesn't hesitate and giggles all the way to the bed, jumping under the covers and snuggling up to him.

"Good choice," he says and kisses her forehead.

The next morning, Damon is surprised to wake with Angelica in his arms. A part of him believes that he dreamed the previous night. Dreamed about the date and the kissing and the way she said she loved him. But as he gazes into her peaceful, sleeping face, he knows that it all really happened. He grins and leans down to kiss her head.

He gently eases out of bed to go to the bathroom, and when he returns, she is sitting up and stretching.

"Good morning," he says, leaning against the doorframe and smirking.

"Good morning! How did you sleep?"

"Better than I have ever since dying," Damon admits happily. "Care for some breakfast?"

"Definitely! I can help cook!" Angelica says and then hops out of bed, kissing him on his cheek as she passes him.

I definitely can get used to that, Damon thinks as he follows her to the kitchen.

Angelica bangs around the kitchen, looking through cabinets and drawers for the utensils she needs. After finding a frying pan and skillet, she douses them both in butter and heats the stove.

"What are you making, chef?"

"How about omelets? And some bacon?"

Damon clutches his heart and sits at the island. "Oh, you really love me, huh?"

She giggles as she grabs the ingredients from the fridge. Whisking together milk and a few eggs, she makes a proposition. "I was thinking last night … I want you to meet my friends."

"Oh yeah?"

"Yeah."

"Do you think they'd be up for it?" he asks nervously.

"Oh, totally! As long as they know you are planning to become an angel and not just a douchebag demon who wants to get in my pants."

Damon laughs, more to himself than anything. It's crazy how he used to be like that. "Well, as long as they're okay with it, I would love to. When do you want to?"

Angelica pours the eggs onto the sizzling pan. "Well ... we kind of already have a date planned."

He raises his eyebrows. "Oh?"

"Cora has this annual party that is the celebration of the year. It's always so fun and crazy, and she's invited you—well us—to it."

"That sounds fun, but slight problem. I can't get into Heaven, remember?"

She laughs. "That isn't a problem. We don't have the party in Heaven. She rents out an Airbnb every year in different places. This year, it's on the Gold Coast in Australia. Such a beautiful beach!"

Damon is nervous to ask the next question because he fears the answer. "When is the party?"

"It's a costume party on Halloween!" Angelica exclaims, sprinkling ham, cheese, and chopped green onions in the pan. "Cora is so happy that it lands on a Saturday this year, so we can celebrate the actual day."

His excitement falls at his horrible luck. He can't go to the Halloween party—it's the biggest day of the year for him. He has to make sure his mission with Missy is carried out and finally finished. Damon thinks about a way to get out of it without disappointing her or explaining why he can't.

She sets his breakfast in front of him. "So, is that a yes? Will you be my date to the party?"

Damon looks at her bright, smiling face. It is makeup-free and breathtakingly beautiful. He knows he can't say no to her. "Oh, why not?" he says before leaning over the island to kiss her.

Now, all he needs to figure out is how to be in two places at once.

Chapter 32

Once again, Damon is standing in front of the small townhouse, knocking on the door.

It's finally the day that Damon gets an answer from Missy.

The door swings open this time, and Missy peers up at him with her wide chocolate eyes. "Hey, Damon."

"Hey, Missy."

She steps back to let him inside. "Thanks for coming."

"Thanks for inviting me," he says.

Missy stands in the foyer, her hands in her pockets.

Damon can feel the awkward tension. "So ... how was your week? I'm sorry I haven't checked in much; you've seemed busy."

She glares at him. "Oh, cut the crap. You know why you're here, and it's not to ask me how my week has been."

He swallows. "Fair enough. So?"

Missy ponders with downcast eyes. She shifts her weight between her feet.

Damon waits. He looks around the room and notices a hanging coat rack with a few coats and sweatshirts, a side table with a bouquet of dead flowers, and a candle next to the door. A sign reads *Welcome, please stay a while!*

"No," she finally says.

He snaps his head toward her. "I'm sorry?"

"My answer is no," Missy says again, looking at him fiercely. "I am not going to become his wife. I will not commit suicide on Halloween."

She storms away from him and into the living room, plopping down on the couch and sighing angrily. If she expects him to leave, she is sadly mistaken.

He tries not to let his building anger surface as he calmly follows her and stands next to the couch. "Are you sure?"

"Yes, I'm fucking sure."

"Why do you say no?"

Missy's face twists up in disgust as she looks at him. "Why do you think? Did you really think I would jump at the opportunity to marry *The Devil?* I figured since we'd talked and hung out that you would've realized that I'm not a fucking psychopath. I would never do something like that."

"Did you ever even consider it?"

She lets out a breath. "I did in the beginning. But like I said, the whole suicide thing got me. And all I could see were my parent's heartbroken faces, my sisters crying over me for the rest of their lives and wondering why I did it. I can't tell them the reason. Plus, I have so much to live for.

I have to finish college and finally become an accountant and open my own firm. Travel the world. Adopt a dog. Eventually have kids. I can't just give all that up for a man I barely know. A man who is literally the ruler of the underworld."

Damon closes his eyes and brings his hands to his lips. "Missy. I think it would be in your best interest to reconsider."

She stands, rushes to him, and shoves him back. "I think it would be in your best interest to get out of my house and never speak to me again."

He straightens up against her push, his anger leaking onto his face. "I hope you know that you're being a total moron right now."

Missy points to the door. "Leave. Now."

Damon runs his hands through his hair and screams, not moving a muscle. *Fuck. Fuck!*

"Damon, why can't you just accept my answer and leave?" she asks, her voice wavering from the fear towards his yelling.

"Because you don't really have a fucking choice!"

She freezes. "What are you talking about?"

He turns away from her, his hand covering his eyes. "Do you really think The Devil would let you say no? He knows it's always the possibility that he won't get his way. Or he lets you think that. If you don't end up killing yourself on Halloween and marrying him, he will kill you regardless."

Her face is blank. "No, that can't be true. You said I was the one to make the call—"

"And you believed me? You believed him? You really thought he'd give you the choice? If you really say no, he will pretend to be okay with it. He will let you be for a while—a few months, a year, maybe even a few years. But he will *not* let you go or out of his sight. He will kill me and the other demons who have been watching you, and eventually, he will kill you, too. He will make it seem like an accident, but it won't be. And once you get to Hell, he will not want you anymore and will make you suffer more than the rest of them for rejecting him."

Missy's expression is still flat.

"I'm sorry you are in this mess. I really am. But I can't get you out of it. You are marked for life."

Missy sits back on the brown couch, staring at nothing. "How ... how do you know that's the case?"

"I've seen it happen before. The last woman he tried to marry said no, and three months later, he made one of his demons possess a robber to kill her in her sleep. She is now burning in the flames right outside of his home so she can see what she missed out on," Damon says gravely.

Missy clutches her stomach in agony. A few seconds later, she sprints to the kitchen and throws up in her sink.

Damon hears her sobbing. He really wishes he can save her. Maybe he can ask Angelica to do something? Could the angels interfere and protect her?

But he can't do that. If the angels saved her, he'd be a dead man for failing.

Whenever he tries to be better, the path ends up leading toward his death.

Damon looks down at his feet and prays to the Father Angelica always talks about that he will pass those tests and get out of this hell.

He slowly approaches Missy, but she cowers away from him with mascara running down her cheeks. "Missy, I'm so sorry."

She doesn't answer and cries harder. After a few minutes, she finally lets him put his hand on her back to comfort her. "Fine. I'll do it. I'll go through with it because I'd rather do it on my own terms than be murdered later."

Damon nods silently.

Missy wipes her nose and then looks at him with a splotchy face. "I know you'll take care of everything, right? So, I should just expect to see you here on Saturday? On Halloween?"

"Yes," he says.

"Okay," she says, a little calmer. "I will talk to you soon. Please go … I need to be alone."

He hesitates.

"I won't do anything stupid," she snaps. "Okay?"

"Okay." Damon leans over to kiss her forehead. "I will talk to you later."

When he walks outside, one sad tear slips down his face. Missy is such a young, fiery woman who doesn't deserve this. Seeing her give up and let The Devil get his way really pisses him off. He wipes away the tear as his sadness turns to anger and hatred towards The Boss.

He sits down on the stoop of her house and then texts the group chat. **Mission is a go.**

Jeremy quickly texts back with instructions to meet in the office for one last run-through of the situation.

Damon sighs and then teleports.

Chloe, Jeremy, and Ben are all sitting in the conference room on the third floor. He sits in the last empty chair.

"Nice of you to show up." Chloe sneers, pumping up her curly black afro. "Wasn't sure if you'd be too busy with your *angel friend* to even do this mission anymore."

Although he really wants to flip her off, he ignores her.

Jeremy clears his throat and calls them to attention. "Okay. Here's the plan …"

Chapter 33

"Maybe this was a dumb idea." Damon groans as he looks at himself in the mirror.

Angelica bursts out laughing.

They are standing in the Joneses' family cabin. The cabin that has become their makeshift home. Their own beds haven't been slept in for ten days.

She came to him with the tongue-in-cheek idea for them to dress up as themselves for Halloween—he an angel and she a devil (because there was no distinct way for her to look like a demon). He agreed only because she looked so happy when she voiced the clever idea.

Angelica looks hotter than literal hell in her tight red dress, long feather boa, and small devil horns poking out of her straightened hair. Damon looks goofy in his white T-shirt and halo headband.

"I think you look adorable," she says, leaning up to kiss his cheek.

"You'll be the only one."

"Good thing no one else matters!"

He smirks at her and pulls her close to him. "Good thing."

Before he can lean down, she dances out of his arms. "No distractions! We have to get going. Cora will murder us both if we are even later than we already are!"

"Fine." He sighs but leans down close to her ear. "But later, I want to rip that dress off ... with my teeth."

Goosebumps form on her arms as she giggles and walks to the bathroom. They still haven't done the full deed ... but they have explored more of their bodies. She found out that he was very skilled with his hands, and he's been teasing her with promises of using his tongue next time. "Give me ten minutes and then we are leaving!"

Damon sits on the couch and pops open a beer. This is his third of the night—he is nervous to meet Angelica's friends and thinks loosening up will help. Cora seems awesome from the few times they've talked at the bar, but he isn't sure if the other angels will be as welcoming.

And then, he needs the alcohol to calm his anxiousness about the mission he will finally finish tonight.

He has been in a constant state of crippling anxiety about Halloween since he agreed to come to the party. Damon thought out all the ways the night could go wrong ... and then the only way it could go right. Missy finally agreeing helped the situation, but Angelica could never find out what he was doing. Even though she still loves him, surprisingly, after what he told her about his life, he has a bad feeling about this job. She knows that he still has his own work, but ... would this be too far? Especially for someone who has been pretending—or not?—to study to become an angel?

He has to carry it out without Angelica knowing. That's the only way the night can end up perfect. He knows she plans to get drunk, so once she is and it's time for the mission, he will pass her over to Cora and disappear for the twenty to thirty minutes it will take to finish the job. When he gets back, and if they ask where he was, he will explain that he had to get William out of a bar fight or something.

Then they can have a good time the rest of the night and end up back at the cabin where they can drunkenly cuddle and kiss until morning.

Damon shakes his head at his thoughts. *This woman is really turning you into a sap, huh?*

Angelica emerges from the bathroom with a few more sparkles on her body and grabs his hand. "Are you ready?"

"Ready."

Next thing they know, they're arriving in the land down under. A huge two-story beach house is towering in front of them. They stand in the back of the house that is directly on the beach, and it is almost entirely covered in windows. On the first floor, a bunch of angels take shots in the kitchen; on the second floor, a DJ commands a room of dancing angels, who spill out onto the balcony. A few notice Angelica and wave down to her.

She waves back and then grins at Damon. "Let's go!"

They walk up the concrete path to the back door. Damon hesitates, but she squeezes his hand before strutting inside. They look around the spacious room and admire the orange, purple, and black decorations. A few women scream and then run up to Angelica with their arms outstretched for a hug. Damon stands awkwardly to the side.

"You look so hot!"

"Damn, mama!"

"Ow owww!"

Angelica giggles and then motions to Damon. "Holly, Priscilla, Isla … this is my boyfriend, Damon."

The three angels turn to him and give genuine smiles, even after noticing his black irises. "Welcome, Damon! We hope you have so much fun tonight," they gush.

He clears his throat and nods. "Nice to meet you, ladies."

Angelica wraps her arms around him and kisses his cheek. Holly, Priscilla, and Isla all swoon at their cuteness.

"Alright, move along, bitches! The best friend is here!" Cora says, appearing behind them.

The three girls giggle and depart for a group of men.

"Angelica and Damon. It's about damn time you showed up!" she says sternly.

"Sorry, we are so late!" Angelica apologizes and hugs her, then steps back to inspect Cora's costume. She is wearing a beige leotard with a pouch in front and similarly colored tights and boots. "Uh … what are you supposed to be?"

She sighs and turns around, shaking her butt and the long tail that is attached to her leotard. "*Por favor*! I'm a sexy kangaroo. Duh."

Damon and Angelica nod and say, "Ahhh."

Cora shakes her head in disbelief and then looks them up and down. "Okay. I like the theme we have here." She laughs. "Hilarious!" She meets Damon's gaze without a hint of judgment, like the three girls did. "Damon, thank you so much for coming! I'm so happy you're here." She catches him off guard by hugging him, smushing her gigantic breasts across his lower abdomen, but he hugs her back happily.

She points up to him. "If anyone tries to start shit with you, let me know and I will take care of it. You are the guest of honor tonight, and I will treat you accordingly. Got it?"

Damon smiles and fist bumps her. "Okay, got it. Thank you, Cora."

Angelica watches their whole encounter, and it makes her feel all warm and fuzzy inside. She is so thankful that Cora is protecting him since she knew how much he means to her.

"Okay, lads, let's get you two some drinks!" Cora says with a horrible Australian accent.

They follow Cora through the house, stopping by the kitchen to grab a few drinks—Damon a beer and Angelica cup of jungle juice—before going to say hello to the other party guests. Angelica recognizes most of the angels but is introduced to a few sprites and spirits she doesn't know. Even a few random humans are there, blabbering about how they met Cora at a bar a few weeks ago.

Everyone that Damon meets seems taken aback at first, but only for a moment before they smile warmly and shake his hand eagerly. It makes him happy that they accept him, and his anxiety subsides.

The only person who doesn't greet Damon warmly is Garrett.

"Why was he being like that?" Damon asks Angelica once he is out of earshot.

She grins awkwardly. "Oh, yeah, that … he asked me out a few weeks ago and I friend-zoned him. Then I told him that I wasn't interested in dating anyone right now … and I brought you here tonight, and I'm sure Cora told everyone we've been seeing each other for two months now. Oops."

"Yeah, oops." Damon chuckles, kissing her cheek.

After they say hello to everyone, Angelica pulls him back to the kitchen for a refill before they dance. Feeling overly confident in her sexy red dress and with her new boyfriend—that she can proudly now show off—Angelica slurps down two Jell-O shots before Damon even finishes pouring his next beer.

"Easy, little angel." He purrs.

"They're just so tasty!" She giggles, flicking her tongue into another small cup.

He presses his lips together and shakes his head.

Cora appears again. "Jell-O shots? Wimp. Let's get you some real shots."

Before they can object, she hands them both a shot of a clear alcohol that is sitting on a tray.

"Let's get drunk!" she exclaims.

They all shoot back their shots and cringe.

"EW!" Angelica gags.

"What did you get?" Cora asks with a sour face. "They're all supposed to be mystery."

"Vodka," Damon says. "Super sweet, too—maybe cake?"

"Lucky." Angelica is sucking down her jungle juice to get the flavor out of her mouth. "I had Rumplemintz!"

"I had tequila. Yay me!" Cora laughs and then flits away to her hosting duties. *"Hasta luego!"*

Angelica and Damon are about to head upstairs to dance, but they hear shouts and cheers coming from the garage. Intrigued, they follow the excitement and get wrapped up in a game of beer pong. Angelica is surprisingly good, thanks to the alcohol in her system. Damon and she take the lead right off the bat, but it is she who ends up sinking the last cup and winning the game. She jumps in excitement and pulls his face down to give him a huge smooch on his lips, the alcohol hitting her hard.

"Nice shot, Ang!" calls the curvy strawberry blonde with a huge diamond ring on her finger. The man with her, presumably her fiancé, kisses her cheek before pulling out a pack of cigars.

Damon is pleasantly surprised when he comes over and offers him one. "Want to go outside and smoke?"

He glances at Angelica, who is nodding and pushing him out the door. "Go! Have fun! Stay out of trouble, Connor."

Connor laughs and salutes her. "Always am, ma'am."

The men walk out the garage door and then turn to the beach. A group of guys is already standing outside in a circle, a beer in hand and a lit cigar in the other. Damon would've been nervous if it wasn't for the shot and five beers in his system.

They don't talk about much. A stocky angel comments that the party is smaller than last year, but another guy points out that it is only ten and more people show up later. Connor jokes about how much a pain in the ass wedding planning is and the men all tease him.

"Are you planning to be around long? I'd love to have you come to the wedding," Connor asks Damon.

He lets out a puff of smoke and grins. "That's the plan. Thank you for the invite."

Connor nods and then calls out Jacob about whether he was taking a certain girl home, and the group hoots and hollers.

Damon is happy to feel included, and extra happy when no one brings up his job or his life, even if they were all curious. He is happy that Connor is being so nice to him; he seems like a really cool dude. Someone he would be friends with.

His senses pick up on someone staring at him, and he looks to his left to see Garrett shooting him a glare. Damon raises his eyebrows tentatively.

Garrett stands next to him and whispers so that no one but them can hear. "Don't do anything stupid or hurt Angelica. She is one million times better than you ever will be. Don't take her for granted."

Damon nods. "I know that. I won't. Thank you for your concern, though," he says dismissively.

Garrett narrows his eyes at Damon but doesn't respond, turning back to the group and drinking his beer with a grin on his face.

Damon observes Garrett from the corner of his eye. He has the slight feeling that he recognizes Garrett from somewhere …

His breathing stops when he realizes how he knows him. Garrett was the angel that Jeremy and he saw outside of Cora's house. The one who was watching them. That means that Garrett must know about the mission. Which is why he warned Damon.

Unless he is just jealous that he is with Angelica and not himself. Maybe he didn't recognize him from that night?

An uneasy feeling mixes with the alcohol in his stomach.

The cigars are finally finished, and the men head back inside. Damon searches the house until he finds Angelica talking to the strawberry blonde in the living room. He remembers Connor saying her name is Lily.

Her eyes are glassy when she notices him, and a huge smile appears on her face. "You're back!" She wobbles up and throws herself into his arms, giggling all the way.

"And you're drunk."

"Maybe just a little." Angelica waves her hand and then her face twists. "Oh, I have to go to the bathroom. I'll be right back!" She kisses him and then scurries away.

He walks back to the drink stand, looking for some water.

"Hey, Damon," Cora says, finding him alone. "How are you doing?"

"Fine, thanks."

"Has everyone been nice? I invited Honey so you would know someone, but of course, she was working."

He smiles. "Yes, very. Everyone has been so welcoming. Thank you for inviting me. It's … nice."

She nods, pushing her brown hair behind her ears. "Good. Look, I don't want to be that person, but it's time for our heart-to-heart. I can see that you genuinely care about Angelica, but I need you to promise me this isn't some game. She really, really loves you. I've never seen her this happy. And I want to believe that you are really becoming an angel to be with her, but I know how demons can be. They like to play these kinds of games and destroy people without a second thought."

"It's not," Damon says definitively. "I promise. I love her, Cora."

"You better. Because if I find out you don't, you know I'll fuck you up."

He chuckles but knows she totally would. "I know."

She punches his arm and then smiles.

Angelica appears, straightening her dress. "Uh, oh. What did I miss?"

"Oh, I was just challenging Damon to a serious game of flippy cup. Are you two in?"

"Totally!" Angelica answers for them and then drunkenly pulls them both to the garage.

After three intense and exciting games of flippy cup, Damon's phone buzzes in his back pocket.

Missy's. 10 minutes. It's time.

He gulps and looks to his right, where Angelica is dancing with Cora and Lily. They are all heavily intoxicated, and their dancing is not very graceful. As he looks at Angelica, his heart swells.

This is the last thing I have to do before being with you forever, he thinks.

Making sure she doesn't see, he slips back into the house, weaving through the rooms until he finds the front door. He sets his cup and his pack of cinnamon gum on the table, just in case she comes looking for him, so she knows he will be back.

Right before he can step out the door, a throat is cleared behind him. Damon looks over his shoulder to see Garrett with his arms crossed and eyes narrowed.

"Going somewhere?"

"Uh, yeah," Damon says, pulling a cigarette out of his pocket. "Time for a smoke."

"Hmph."

"If Angelica asks, will you let her know I'll be back in a second?" Damon smiles weakly.

Garrett looks him up and down and then gives him a fake smile. "Sure."

Damon doesn't have time to think about if Garrett is going to rat him out or not. He flees outside and teleports to Missy's house, meeting Chloe, Jeremy, and Ben in the driveway.

Chapter 34

Damon is confused about why they all start laughing until they point to his headband.

"What the hell are you wearing?" Chloe sneers.

He quickly slides off the headband and throws it in a nearby bush. "Nothing. What's the status?"

"She hasn't invited us in. You need to ask her."

"You couldn't go in by yourself?"

Chloe glares at him. "We didn't think just appearing in her house would be a good idea, given the sensitivity of this situation."

He glares back at her, not in the mood to deal with her attitude. He looks to Jeremy and Ben, who are watching their encounter. "Give me a minute."

Damon appears in the house and searches for Missy until he finds her upstairs in her bedroom. She is sitting on the floor in front of her bed in a satin slip. Her arms are slack at her side, her face emotionless.

"Hey, Missy," he says.

Her head whips up. "Damon."

Damon crouches in front of her. "How are you?"

"Are you really asking me that?" she asks with narrowed eyes.

He gives her a small grin. "Well, I thought it'd be a good conversation starter." His voice turns serious. "How are you, really?"

Missy looks down at her hands. "I don't know if I'm ready, honestly." Her voice cracks, and she takes a deep breath. "But I know I don't have a choice."

He nods. He increases the pitch in his voice. "Well, we are ready for you. We are so excited to have you come join us."

"We?"

"Yes. Me and my friends. The ones who have been watching you for the past few months with me. Taking care of you. Preparing for you." He smiles warmly, although it is completely fake. "Can they come meet you?"

Missy purses her lips together, and Damon can see that she is biting back tears. "That's fine."

Immediately Chloe, Ben, and Jeremy appear in the room. Missy takes them in with wide eyes.

"Hello, Missy," Chloe says. "It's such a pleasure to meet you finally!" Even though she looks mid-twenties, she warms the room like a loving mother.

Damn, she is good, Damon thinks. Disgust floods him when he thinks about all the times they've spent together. Especially now that he's been with Angelica. Warm, sweet, loving Angelica. Chloe is cold and selfish and enjoys sending innocents to their death. The difference is astonishing. How could he have ever been with her?

Missy doesn't respond, her eyes transfixed on the bundle in Jeremy's hands. The blade is wrapped in the finest silk, but the holt is peeking out. Metal as black as night with a fiery orange stone is glinting in the light of the room.

"If it's okay, my Queen," Chloe says and bows, "may I help you get ready?"

Missy's eyes dart to Chloe and size her up. "Yes, servant. Help me up and get me ready to meet my eternal death."

Damon presses his lips together, trying not to laugh. *Even in the eyes of death, she is a fighter.*

Chloe gives her a sweet smile, although Damon can see the anger hiding behind it. "Wonderful." Chloe turns to the boys. "You guys get the room ready. I'll get her dressed and prepared."

The men nod, and Ben grabs the candles that are in the backpack on his shoulder. Ben and Jeremy set them around the room while Damon lights them with a tight stomach. Jeremy lays the dagger on the bed and turns off the bedroom lights, and then they wait in the hallway while Missy gets dressed.

"Dude. You look sick," Jeremy says to Damon, his voice low.

Damon reaches a shaking hand into his back pocket. "I've been drinking. The alcohol is making me woozy."

"I don't believe that. You look like you feel guilty."

Damon sticks the cigarette between his teeth. "And you don't?"

Jeremy exhales slowly. "I do," he admits. "But we don't have a choice, now do we?"

"Maybe not with this. But we have a say on if we decide to stay in Hell."

"What are you talking about?"

Damon can see Jeremy giving him a look of concern out of his peripheral vision. "Did you know that it is possible for us to take the tests that humans do to become angels?"

Jeremy is taken aback. "What?"

"Yeah. Pretty shitty how he kept that a secret from us, huh? I get it, though; he doesn't want his pets running off." Damon snorts, exhaling a long breath of smoke.

Jeremy doesn't answer. Ben is in his own world, rummaging through the upstairs house and stealing jewelry and other valuables.

"Does this have something to do with the angel you've been working with?"

Damon doesn't answer and extinguishes his cigarette on the bottom of his sole.

Before he can react, Jeremy grabs his shoulders and turns him to face him. His black eyes bear into him, staring down into his soul. "Look, Damon," he says quietly. "I'm not going to tell you what to do or what not to do. I just want you to know that you have the choice, and it's up to you to make the call. Do what you need to … I will not stop you or get in your way."

Tears spring to Damon's eyes. Damn the alcohol making him extra emotional. He hasn't ever talked to Jeremy like this—he's always been his boss—but getting his permission warms his heart even though he can hear the warning in his words. He may not stop him, but that doesn't mean others won't try to if they find out. "Thanks, man."

Jeremy nods once and lets go, turning to smoke his own cigarette.

Suddenly, the bedroom door opens, and Chloe motions them to enter. Damon, Jeremy, and Ben usher inside and look at Missy with wide eyes.

She is standing next to the bed wearing a long, black, iridescent ball gown. The halter neck has real diamonds and precious gems woven into the fabric, twinkling and sparkling every time she breathes. Her copper hair is twisted and curled onto her head around a black tiara with gems that match the ones on the dress.

Missy will no longer be Missy. She will soon be Queen of Hell.

Well, one of them.

The three men bow in front of her.

"You look beautiful." Damon smiles.

Missy smiles back, but it doesn't reach her eyes.

"Okay, baby, it's time to lie on the bed," Chloe commands.

The strong, spirited Missy that Damon has come to know finally breaks as she glides toward the bed with tears falling down her face. The demons help her into position, smoothing her dress down.

Damon holds the dagger out to her. The gems on the hilt sparkle menacingly. He takes a deep breath to give her the next instructions, but the bedroom door swings open with a *bang!*

"Stop it right there!"

All the demons and Missy look to the door where a gaggle of angels stand. Damon almost vomits from recognizing some of the faces.

Garrett is first—his opal eyes flashing with different colors—the one who yelled. To his left is an angel he just met but can't name. Behind him is someone he's never seen.

But to Garrett's right, standing with her eyes fixed on the blade that Damon holds in his hand, outstretched to Missy, is the woman that Damon is in love with.

Angelica.

Chloe snatches the dagger out of Damon's hand as he staggers back.

The angels barrel into the room, all grabbing onto a demon. Garrett rushes to Damon and puts him in a chokehold, clearly enjoying himself. Ben growls at the two angels who are holding his arms before they force him to the ground. Jeremy doesn't fight the angel around him, while Chloe shoots daggers at the scrawny angel that is holding her.

Angelica runs over to Missy—or tries to. She is clearly still intoxicated and putting extra effort into moving. "Missy, darling, you don't have to do this."

Missy, who covered her face with her hands at the encounter, peeks at Angelica through her fingers. "I don't?"

"No, there is another way," Angelica says in her softest voice.

"Don't listen to her!" Chloe spits, fighting out of the scrawny angel's arms and shoving Angelica back. "She's lying. She just doesn't want you to be happy."

Missy starts sobbing, visibly frightened.

"Damon." Chloe turns and glares at him. "*Tell her.*"

Damon opens his mouth to speak, but when Angelica looks at him with a look of pure hatred, he freezes. His heart splits open. He knows that now any future he imagined with her would never come true. His worst nightmare has come to life. She doesn't want him anymore.

A sharp gasp echoes through the room, and the smell of blood fills the air. Everyone looks to the bed, and their eyes widen when they see Missy's neck slashed open and blood seeping out. The dagger slips out of her hand and clangs to the floor.

Chloe, very obviously the one to guide Missy with her final decision, as she is leaning over her, straightens up. "Oops," she says.

"No!" Angelica screams in agony, and her hands cover Missy's throat to stop the blood, but it's too late. She can't heal her.

Garrett lets go of Damon in defeat, and Damon rushes over to her, tears falling down his face as he clutches her hand. "I'm so sorry, Missy. The pain will be over soon. And then you will be okay."

Missy coughs as the blood gurgles in her throat.

Angelica steps back and leans on the closet door, blood on her hands and tears in her eyes.

One by one the angels leave, heartbroken for the poor

girl lying on the bed. The only one who stays is Angelica, whose gaze flickers between the dying woman and the man she thought she loved. Her heart breaks as she realizes that, all along, he was playing her. She was a ploy to distract them from this mission. Or something worse, she doesn't know. All she knows is that she believed that he was really good, he was really willing to change, and he wasn't the demon that everyone said he was.

She was wrong.

The sounds of Missy's struggle finally stop as she exhales one final time.

Angelica wipes away her tears with her blood-stained hands and forces a glare at Damon. "You disgust me," she says, hate dripping off every word.

"Angelica," Damon pleads, but she disappears.

Missy's new body appears as she sits up and coughs. She isn't a floating soul like the dead humans but appears like the angels and demons do. Her eyes widen when she sees Damon. "Am I dead? Is it done?"

"It's done," he whispers, finally letting go of her old body's hand.

He helps her up. Chloe tries to grab her, but Missy cringes away. Chloe's lips turn up in a slight grin in response to her fear.

Jeremy walks over to them and bows again. "Come, my Lady. It's time to go to your new home and join your betrothed."

Missy looks at Damon reluctantly, but he nods. "We will meet again, my Queen."

She gives him a slight smile before taking Jeremy's arm and disappearing with him.

Damon is finally alone in the room. He sits on the bed, next to the dead body. His stomach is in knots while trying to decide if he should explain himself to Angelica or not. Will she even listen?

He must get her to understand.

He stands to go, but none other than The Devil himself appears in the bedroom. Damon quickly bows. "My lord, they already left."

The Devil motions for him to rise. "Ah, I know. I just saw her, and, wow, isn't she the most beautiful Queen there ever has been? But that's not why I'm here. I wanted to personally thank you for handling this mission and completing it perfectly. I knew you could do it."

Damon forces a smile. "My pleasure, sir."

The Devil walks to the body and runs his finger through the pool of blood. "I also wanted to tell you that you can stop trying to get the angel to join us now."

Damon freezes. "What?"

"Oh, yeah, that was never my goal." He laughs, sending a chill down Damon's spine. "I thought that she was the main angel who was trying to stop us from getting Missy, so I needed her to be distracted. And when I heard she stole your house and met you already, I knew that you were the perfect man to keep her away from this." He rubs the blood between his fingers. "Turns out that she wasn't even the main one—it was that man, Garrett, or whomever. Oh, well. We succeeded nonetheless."

"Why didn't you just tell me that was the case?"

He grins at Damon. "I didn't think you'd take it as seriously, my boy. Plus, I felt like you were getting too big for your britches and needed to be knocked down a few steps. I'm sure the looming fear of me killing you for failing was enough to do that—especially since it was double the fear if you failed Missy and Angelica. I figured the pain you felt those three hours really set it in stone."

Hearing Angelica's perfect name come out of his mouth angers Damon. *This whole time it was a game to him, to teach me a lesson?!* He tries to find his voice, but he can't speak.

"Anywho, I should get going. I have a wedding to attend, ha-ha!" The Devil turns and pats Damon on the shoulder with the bloodless hand. "Next month I won't give you such a dire mission. Something easy – like Ouija Duty or Cult Watch to let you relax a little."

Damon nods once, his stead still spinning from The Devil's confession.

"However," he says, his tone changing. "I have been told what you have been planning with this angel. A joke or not, I hope you know that you are sadly mistaken if you think you can get out of Hell, get out of my army." He leans close to Damon's ear. "If I find out you are continuing this plan, I will murder you and her faster than you can say the word 'angel.' Are we clear?"

Damon swallows the bile rising in his throat. "Crystal."

"Good boy." He laughs and then disappears.

Damon takes a few deep breaths before collapsing in a heap on the floor.

Everything he told Jeremy doesn't matter now. Angelica hates him—he saw the look in her eyes, the look that is seared in his brain. And The Devil knows about the plan … and is planning to kill them both.

Damon knows what he has to do.

The love he has for Angelica means nothing now. All the fantasy he had about actually becoming an angel and being with her was just that—a fantasy. He knows that he can never get out of Hell and out of The Boss's fiery hands. If he would even try, they both would end up dead. He has to protect her and let her go—for real this time. He has to break her heart more than he has already.

Even if it will destroy him.

Chapter 35

Damon appears back at the beach house and finds Angelica sobbing on the front steps, her hands still stained with Missy's blood. Garrett is sitting next to her, rubbing circles on her back. When he sees Damon, he shoots to his feet.

"You need to leave!"

Damon's nostrils flare in anger. "Why did you bring her there? It wasn't her mission, and you know that!"

"She deserved a right to know who she was really dating," Garret scoffs, striding toward Damon.

He hates that Garrett is much taller than him. Damon glares up at him and says, "She doesn't fucking want you. Why can't you understand that? Leave her alone."

Garrett growls and raises his fist, but Angelica's voice stops him.

"Garrett. Please give us a minute alone." She sniffles, sounding utterly heartbroken.

He glowers at Damon but listens to her, pointing at Damon before walking inside.

"Angelica ..." Damon tries to say, but she holds up a hand to stop him.

"Why did you do it?"

"You know I had no choice."

"No, I didn't know that. Couldn't the other demons take care of it? You left me at my best friend's party to sacrifice a human. You know how stupid that makes me look? After me telling everyone that you've changed and you wanted to be better?" She doesn't look at him as she speaks.

He feels physically sick to see her in so much pain. "Sorry," he spits.

"Please tell me that I'm hallucinating because of the alcohol. You promised me that you really were good and wanted to become an angel. Why does this make me feel like you lied to me, that this has all been a game?" Angelica says, finally meeting his gaze with her tear-stained eyes. "Please tell me that I'm hallucinating," she repeats.

He looks away and quickly lights a cigarette. "I can't. I lied, Angelica."

She blinks through her tears at his proclamation. "What?"

"I lied!" he says again. "I've never wanted to become an angel. It was a game. Congratulations, you figured it out."

Shock spreads across her face, and her tears dry up. *So, I was right*, she thinks. When she made that conclusion earlier, she still wanted to believe that she was being irrational, that he was just playing the part, or she was so drunk it wasn't really him. But he just admitted what she had suspected. "You haven't?"

Damon's word is final. "No." He is glad that he is looking away from her because he cannot imagine seeing the pain on her face. "I used you to get insight into your world. I have been reporting back to my boss the whole time. My job was to distract you so that you and your friends couldn't fuck up the mission with Missy."

He forces a cold laugh. "Did you really think that you could convince me to become an angel? You know what I am. You know what I do."

"Yeah, but all that work. New York and the shelter. The bar. Our tattoos. Our kissing, our date … you saying you loved me. That was all a lie? That all meant nothing to you?"

"Correct."

"But you said you loved me."

"I lied. I really said that so you'd sleep with me. You hadn't put out yet, so I figured that'd do the trick. But it didn't work. Such a shame," he snaps, exhaling cigarette smoke.

Of all the cruel things he has been saying to her, that one hits her the hardest. Angelica clutches her stomach as the feeling of vomiting rushes over her. She feels so ridiculous in her devil costume—it all being a poor joke to her now. She closes her eyes and tries to breathe through her nausea, not wanting to believe him. After everything they've been through? He opened up to her; he was so kind, so sweet, so excited to stop being a demon and be with her. It doesn't make sense.

It doesn't make sense, she repeats.

She stands up and straightens her dress before strutting over to him and stabbing a finger into his chest. "No. I don't believe you."

He raises his eyebrows before dropping his cigarette onto the grass. "You don't believe me?"

"No!" Angelica proclaims. "You can't just do a complete 180 like that. The past two months we have become friends. I have learned so much about you. When we talked about you getting out of Hell, your eyes lit up brighter than I've ever seen, and I could tell that you genuinely wanted to. When you said you loved me, I knew you really meant it."

Damon tries to interrupt, but she puts a finger to his mouth, buzzing where their skin meets. "I don't know why you are doing this, but I don't care that you left. I can forgive you because of that—I know you have your own job. I wish you would've told me, but it's okay. We can move past it, and I know you can be the angel you want to be." Her kaleidoscopic eyes are brighter than Damon has ever seen. "But please don't lie to me and act like I have meant nothing to you."

He wants so badly to tell her that she is right. That he wants to be with her … but he can't. He can't put her in danger. He sneers and cringes away from her. "Oh, fuck off about that. You think you know me? After two months? News flash, you dumb bitch, you don't." He leans down close to her face angrily, like he did in the basement the first time they met. "You meant nothing to me from the start. You were just a mission. I manipulated you; I used you."

He swallows before putting the icing on the cake. "I don't love you, nor do I want you—now or ever."

The feeling of being punched in the gut racks Angelica. She stumbles back from him and his hateful words. She was wrong. She was so, so wrong.

Anger quickly replaces the hurt in her, and she pushes him over so hard that he falls on the ground. "How dare you!" she screams. "I trusted you! I'm in love with you, Damon!"

He scoots up on his elbows. "That's not my problem."

Cora appears behind them, alarmed by Angelica's yelling. "What the hell is going on here?"

Angelica turns to Cora, her voice shaking. "He lied, Cora."

"Lied about what?" she asks, noticing Damon on the sand.

"About everything!" Angelica shouts. "He never wanted to become an angel. He used me." Her voice breaks on the next sentence. "He never loved me." She turns away from both of them and storms toward the water before spinning on her heel and shooting him a defeated look, tears pouring down her face. "Don't you ever come near me again. I hate you!"

"Angelica, wait!" Cora calls, but she disappears. Cora turns back to Damon, confused. "What the fuck just happened?"

Damon stands and brushes the sand off him, letting his hurt show. "I know that I'm not good for her. The Devil cornered me and threatened mine and Angelica's life if I would continue studying to become an angel. I don't know how he knows, but I can't put her in danger. I had to let her go."

Cora tilts her head to the side. "Why didn't you just tell her that?"

"You think she'd just accept that and never talk to me again? We both know that she wouldn't care. I had to break her in order to save her."

Cora puts her hand on her shoulder. "Well, you accomplished that well. I know you were trying to do the right thing, but she won't ever want to be with you again."

"I know," Damon says in a low tone, wiping tears from his eyes.

"It's time for you to go now."

He nods and leans down to give her one last hug. When they let go, Cora steps back to slap him across his face. He nurses his cheek and nods. "I deserve that."

"You deserve a lot worse, but I know you are hurting way more inside," Cora says frankly, walking back towards the house. "Goodbye, Damon."

He quickly teleports back to his shitty apartment. He screams and cries and punches walls and breaks glass in anger. After the glass and dish shards cover his kitchen floor, he slides to the ground, buries his head in his hands, and sobs.

Chapter 36

The following days, Damon doesn't leave the bar except to go home and to bed. He's been consistently drunk out of his mind since Halloween, the need to erase the entire memory of Angelica more important than anything else. The only time he was barely sober was the November work meeting, but he went to the bar straight after. Honey brings him beer after beer, and once that doesn't help, Damon switches to hard liquor.

During his drunken stupor, he has concluded that he's an asshole, a fuck-up, a murderer who deserves to be exactly where he ended up. No more trying to be better when that will never happen for him. This is his life, and there's no changing that. So, it's time to be the worst kind of demon that he can be.

On his fifth straight day of being drunk, William joins him. He doesn't say much but the occasional chit-chat, knowing that Damon isn't in the mood to talk. He can barely form a coherent sentence anyway.

Damon overhears him talking to Honey about their

concern for him, but he doesn't even care, downing another whiskey.

"He's heartbroken, Honey. Let him be."

"I know that, but this isn't healthy."

"Fuck off, both of you," Damon utters.

After too many drinks to count, Chloe appears and wraps her arms around Damon. "Hey, lovey. Why don't we go home?"

He isn't drunk enough to go home with Chloe. Not after all the shit she pulled. "No," he slurs.

She clings to him like white on rice, sliding her hand down his back and nuzzling into his neck. "You've had a lot of drinks. Let me go home and make you feel good. It's been too long."

Damon can see Honey in his peripherals giving him a worried look. He knows he needs to say no, especially when he remembers Chloe and how happy she was to kill Missy, but remembering Missy brings up the one person he is trying so hard to forget.

"Just tonight." He stands and staggers into her. She wraps her copper hands around him and carries him towards the exit.

William stops them right before the door. "Let me take him home."

"No. He wants me," Chloe fights.

"Chloe, he is totally drunk. He doesn't need you trying to sleep with him. He needs to go to bed."

She rolls her eyes and brushes past him, Damon in tow. Damon hears the whole conversation but doesn't care enough to contribute. He looks back at William to see him shaking his head. Chloe takes them to her place, and Damon collapses on her bed.

Chloe sits on top of him, raising his shirt to kiss his chest.

Damon tries to get in the moment, but he is way too drunk. Her spindly fingers move over him as she rises to kiss his neck. It is familiar, but not in a good way. It feels off. Wrong. Like she is trying to claim him even though he's made it clear to her more than once that she will never be his. He snaps out of his stupor enough to remember that he still doesn't want her and never will. Plus, he is way too gone to give consent. "Chloe. Stop."

"What, now that you've been with an angel, am I not good enough for you?" She laughs, although her voice clipped with every word. Her hands find his belt buckle.

With concentration, he forces himself to roll over onto his stomach, away from her roaming hands.

She is forced to slide off him, and she props herself up on her knees, glaring down at him. "Don't be a baby. We've had sex when you've been drunker."

"I don't care," he mumbles against her blood-red bedsheets. They're too bold and commanding, like Chloe. He misses the sweet and sassy pink of Angelica. "I don't want you, Chloe."

"Why not? Because of that angel bitch?"

Damon groans, his head starting to throb. "Leave her out of this."

She huffs and gets off the bed, straightening her mini

skirt. "You are pathetic. It's your own fault for falling for a stupid angel. I don't know why you ever thought you could be with her, or even tried to be. We aren't meant to be with them. You are meant to be with someone like me."

He sits up agonizingly slow and leans against her headboard. Damon meets her gaze. "I will never want to be with you."

Chloe's eyes narrow, and her lips curl up in a sneer. "You know what? Get the fuck out of my house," she yells, her voice wavering from the pain his words caused her.

He heaves himself off the bed and shuffles to the front door. The second his hand curves around the doorknob, a delayed lightbulb goes off in his head. "Hold on … how did you know so much about me and Angelica?"

Her name kicks him in the stomach.

She crosses her arms. "Come on, how stupid do you think I am? After our fallout, I wanted to see what your angel mission was all about. I found you in NYC one day, thanks to my awesome detective skills, and you two were sitting in the back of a coffee shop, laughing over breakfast. You even reached out to touch her chin … the way you looked at her … it was the way I always wanted you to look at me."

She rolls her eyes and reclaims her attitude. "So, I put two and two together. I asked a few of my sprite friends to monitor you. You two were *so cute* together. Then they told me about your plan to become an angel, and I assumed it was to get her to become a demon until I heard you cry to Honey like a little bitch outside the bar. '*I'm supposed to be convincing this angel to become a demon so that I don't die, and now I have feelings for her!'"* she quotes perfectly, then laughs.

Her words sting and disgust him at the same time. He knows Chloe is an evil bitch, but not a conniving stalker. "That means you are the one who tipped off The Devil."

Chloe shrugs, a sickly-sweet smile on her lips.

"You know, you're a real bitter bitch, Chloe."

"I'll take that as a compliment."

"Never ever come near me again. We are through. Friendship and everything else." He wobbles out the door.

Before it can slam shut, she leans out. "You are fooling yourself if you ever thought you could be anything more than a demon! Don't call me when you are lonely. I won't be here waiting for you!" Her words and the slamming door echo down the hall.

Damon ignores her and climbs the stairs to his apartment. He misses a step and falls, lying on the steps pathetically. *Is this rock bottom?*

After a few minutes, he forces himself up and finishes the walk to his apartment, flinging himself through the door. Once inside, he lies on his couch, too intoxicated to find his way to the bedroom.

The room spins. *Am I going to vomit?*

He closes his eyes and pinches the top of his nose, breathing in and out deeply. *Stupid alcohol.*

Damon fumbles for his phone to check the time, and when he sees his background picture, he throws the phone across the room, the screen shattering when it hits the kitchen floor, which is still covered in glass. He keeps meaning to change that stupid picture.

Angelica's beautiful smiling face staring at him from across the dinner table at Luciano's is now all that he can think about. The thoughts that have been pestering him since that night have resurfaced again.

Should I just have told her the truth?

No. If anything would happen to her because of me, I could never forgive myself.

He tries to stand but falls to the ground. An angry scream erupts from his mouth before he cries. *Fuck me.*

Her smiling face twists into a new memory, the look of pure hatred that she gave him at Missy's. That look will haunt him for the rest of his existence. He thought that if he could be good for her, everything would turn out okay. He could become an angel and be who he truly wanted to be, with her by his side.

Not in the slightest.

Now she hates him, and there's no going back. Why did life get worse when he tried to do the right thing? He was trying to save her from him, from the possibility of death, from The Devil's burning hands. What if he captured her and tortured her forever? Too many bad things could happen to her because of him.

You could still choose to be good, though … the tiny remaining good, hopeful part of him thinks.

"And what? She won't just forgive me. She thinks I never loved her. I ruined everything," he whispers aloud.

Prove to her that you were lying about lying to save her.

Show her you can become an angel. Be the person you want to be.

"*Crush those tests and be with her forever. I believe in you wholeheartedly.*" Honey's voice rings through his mind.

Damon cries for hours. If the sun appeared in Hell, it would've definitely been rising by the time his sobs turned to sniffles. His drunkenness is fading, and he stands, shaking his head and staggering to the kitchen sink, avoiding the mines of broken glass. After chugging a glass of water and refilling it, he heads to the bedroom and finally flops onto his bed.

Option one—forget about Angelica. Move on. Continue living my life in Hell, get drunk at the bar, fuck random women, and try to forget how she made me feel until I retire as a demon and never leave this horrible place again.

Or option two—become an angel. Fulfill my demon duties while working my ass off to study and pass the tests. I could prove to Angelica that I love her and really want to be with her ... and prove to myself that I can have a better life. No matter what.

But if The Devil finds out, I'm dead. And possibly her.

But would she even forgive me? I wouldn't.

But if I told her the truth, maybe ...

But at this point, I will end up killing myself again if I have to live like this for the rest of eternity...

Damon shakes his head and screams again, letting his anger and fear out with the blood-curdling sound. He opens his eyes and stares at the popcorn ceiling. All options end up with him dead.

Death would be better than being without Angelica for the rest of his eternity.

He finally passes out. When he wakes again, he knows what he has to do.

Chapter 37

Angelica slides her pink headband through her freshly dyed hair. Gone were her long, platinum locks, and in their place is a rich, beautiful shade of mahogany.

Change is good.

That's what people do after a breakup, right? Get a tattoo, move to a new city, change their hair. She couldn't move to a new city and the only tattooing experience she had was already tainted with memories of … him … so dying her hair it was.

After a shoddy box-dye job and a panicked call to Cora, Angelica went to an actual hairdresser to fix it up. Cora pointed out how she could've just magically changed it with the flick of her wrist, but Angelica wanted the whole experience. After the hairdresser fixed the damage, added a few highlights, and shampooed and styled it, Angelica stared at the mirror in awe. She was a completely different angel … at least on the outside.

An angel who would not let a manipulative, lying demon ruin her afterlife.

That horrible night still seems like yesterday to her, but it has been three weeks. Fall is in full swing, and some places are already putting up Christmas trees. Angelica is usually an early decorator, but she has no energy to get into the Christmas spirit, instead holing up in her house like the hermit she longs to be.

She took a week off work after that night and wanted to take more time, but Cora forced her to return to work and continue on with her life. So, Angelica would busy herself with work during the day and then come home and busy herself even more with hobbies at night. Writing, watching movies with no romance, and teaching herself how to knit. Knitting was fun and relaxing, and she completed sixteen projects in the last two weeks: scarves, beanies, socks, and a blanket.

Angelica made herself forget about Damon. Every time her brain would wander to his dark eyes, bright smile, or laugh, she would shake all the thoughts of him away. She purposely stayed away from the bar, and anywhere on Earth for that matter, to make sure she wouldn't accidentally run into him. The Monday after Halloween, she deleted all their text messages and donated all the clothes she wore when she was with him. A few tears slipped down her face when they took away the blue satin dress, but she knew it was for the best.

Still, every night, she fell asleep staring at a selfie they had taken down by the beach. She would cry when she looked at his smiling face staring at her instead of the camera. The way that he looked at her made her question everything. How could someone who was pretending to love her look at her with such love on his face? She was sabotaging herself and knew it, but she couldn't help it. Their short-lived romance was an electrifying whirlwind ... even if it was all a lie.

Her phone sits next to her, and the temptation to look again pops in her mind ... but she decides against it. She has to get to work ... no time for tears.

Angelica throws on a blush sweater, jeans, boots, and gold hoop earrings before teleporting to work. She doesn't even care enough to put on makeup.

Gabriel is his usual cheery self when she walks up to grab her assignments. He compliments her hair again, and she nods once and smiles softly before bolting to her cubicle, not saying hello to anyone who passes her. A lot of people heard of her and ... his ... fight on Halloween, so a lot of pitying glances and smiles are thrown her way. Angelica hates each one.

As soon as she reaches her chair, she plops the manilla envelope down and opens it. A few kids need check-ins, watching for a few people who are ready to pass over, yada yada, same old ...

The last point on her list makes her stomach lurch.

Ouija duty.

Angelica groans, her head falling into her hands. She thinks briefly about asking Gabriel to switch jobs, but she knows it won't be helpful. Ouija duty is her assignment for the week, and there is nothing she can do about it. The words bring back an unwanted memory about the last time she was given this assignment ... when she first met the handsome demon she is trying so hard to forget about.

Damon.

She takes a deep breath, keeping the tears at bay. As much as she can stop thinking about Damon, she can't deny the empty feeling in her soul. She believed they were soulmates, and now, with him gone, it is exactly as if her heart were missing a vital piece.

Her brain keeps going back and forth about the whole situation. He said that he was faking. He helped murder that innocent woman. He said he didn't love her. So, she needed to believe him … but it still felt off.

He couldn't have faked *everything*. The warm kisses and the sparks, the wanting to be an angel, and the heartfelt way he said her name. It wasn't all a lie … was it?

What do I know?

"What are you doing?"

Angelica sits up and dries her eyes with the back of her sleeves. "Nothing."

Cora leans against the cubicle divider, popping a piece of gum. "Whatcha got for work today?"

"See for yourself," Angelica says, handing her the piece of paper.

Cora scans its contents. "Not bad! Seems like a pretty chill day for you."

"I don't want a chill day. I want to save lives and be crazy busy."

"So you don't have to think about …" Cora stops talking when Angelica's eyes shoot daggers. She raises her hands. "*Lo seinto*."

"Did you need something?" Angelica snaps.

"I just wanted to see what you were doing tonight."

"Nothing. I'm hoping to finish the sweater I've been knitting. Maybe find a seven-season TV show to dig into."

Cora *tsks*. "You're not seventy."

Angelica starts braiding her dark hair. "I feel like we've had this conversation before."

"I know you're hurting because of Damon, and I'm sorry. I get it. You loved him … but you can't waste away in that big mansion of yours. You have to keep moving forward." Cora tries to sound sincere and warm, but Angelica doesn't take it that way.

"I am," she says angrily. "But I don't need you to rush me. I am taking the time to grieve my breakup, and only I can decide when it's time for me to *keep moving forward*."

"Ang, I—"

"Save it. I'll talk to you later." Angelica grabs her documents and struts out of her cubicle, teleporting back home to wait for a call. The second she walks through her front doors, she bursts into tears. It is only 9:47 a.m., and she is already crying about Damon.

Not long after she finishes crying, her phone alerts her of her first Ouija assignment. She cools down her face with cold water and grounds herself with a few breaths before teleporting to a small home on the edge of Rhodes Town, Greece. The glassy, blue ocean is only a few short yards away from where she is standing. The smell of sea salt fills her nostrils, and the waves crash against the sand before retreating, beckoning her to come closer.

She forces herself to turn away from the water and squints up at the home. The white, textured brick is illuminated by the sun, and the ocean-blue shutters accent the house perfectly. She spies the door, the same blue as the shutters, and heads to it, lazily walking up the steps instead of teleporting inside.

Angelica enters an empty kitchen. She doesn't hear anyone in the house, so she closes her eyes and feels for the buzzing of the board, finally recognizing the presence upstairs. She walks to the bottom of the staircase but then pauses.

She can feel the presence of the person there. But it isn't a human. The feeling is too familiar to her …

Her heart quickens. "Damon?"

Shadows move from a room upstairs. Suddenly, Damon is standing at the top of the stairs, wearing a nice pink button-down shirt and unstained jeans with his hair brushed back. His eyes are apologetic. "Angelica."

Angelica's heart stops when she realizes that it really is him, but her face hardens. "What are you doing here? Are you the one who called me?"

Damon walks down a step. "You changed your hair …"

"Don't come near me!" she shouts. "I can't believe you jumped me at work!"

He puts his hand up in innocence. "Yes. I called you. I need to talk to you." Dark circles are under his eyes, matching the ones on Angelica's face.

"I have no interest in listening to anything you have to say," she says, turning on her heel towards the direction of the door.

"I know, but—"

"Plus, how can I believe anything that comes out of your mouth!?"

"Angelica. Please," Damon pleads. "I want to make things right."

She scoffs, turning to glare at him with her hand on the doorknob. "Fuck you, Damon. There is nothing you can do."

"I know. I'm not here to win you back. I only want to tell you the truth. No lies. I promise. You can listen, and if you don't want to see me again, I will leave you alone for the rest of eternity," he says.

She opens the door and lets the cool ocean breeze hug her skin, calming her down and clearing her head.

Damon watches her as she quietly debates his offer. On one hand, she does not have any interest. She is trying to heal—and she can't do that if she is around his intoxicating eyes and touch. But when she turns around and searches him, all she sees is sadness ... and he seems to be telling her the truth.

How would you know if he is lying to you? He did it so smoothly before ...

On the other hand, she misses him dearly and genuinely wants to hear him out. *Why would he come here just to lie some more?*

Angelica shuts the door. She walks into the living room and sits in a lounge chair.

He follows her and sits in the chair opposite hers. He runs his hands through his hair, and his onyx eyes watch her wearily.

She motions for him to talk, her lips in a tight line.

Damon takes a deep breath and begins. "Look. Before I met you, I was a mess. Even though I was good at my job, and one of The Devil's top workers, I hated everything about what I had become. I hated being a demon and every part of my new life, but I had to do it to survive. I would spend my nights getting drunk at the bar and sleeping with random women to ease the pain.

"Right before we met, The Devil gave me the mission of Missy's sacrifice. That was the only thing on my mind for weeks. Then I had to do Ouija duty a few nights for punishment, and that's when I met you. That night changed my world forever.

"I'd seen angels before, but you were different. I know how cliché that sounds, but I mean it. You didn't just look at me like I was scum, but like I was a person, even if you did give me some sass. Then, when you confronted me at the bar, I thought it was cute but nothing more, until we touched, and my body felt like it was on the best kind of drug. I was addicted ... I couldn't think about anyone else. You were stuck in my head. Always in the background, waiting to be focused on. Even when I was with other women, you were all I wanted."

Angelica doesn't comment.

He sighs. "Like the dick I was, I really wanted to get

into your pants. Then The Boss gave me the impossible mission for me to get you to become a demon, and then you just became a job to me."

"He did what?!" Angelica screeches.

"I didn't tell you because in the end, that wasn't even his plan for you. Can I continue?"

She huffs but nods.

"I had no choice in the matter. If I couldn't do it, he would've killed me. So, I met you in the bar that next night, and I had no idea how I was going to get close to you until you said you'd date me if I became an angel … and I found my way into your life. But when I actually spent time with you, everything changed. I got to know you. You aren't a bitchy, uptight angel like I figured you were. You are kind, wonderful, literal sunshine … I could go on forever. I started falling for you. I wanted to open up and get you to fall for me too, knowing it would help me condemn you later, because that was still my main goal."

He pauses, and his eyes study the floor. "However, I started liking you more and more, and I decided that I couldn't go through with it. I couldn't damn you to Hell, to an afterlife filled with misery like mine. I knew it would crush you. So, I went to The Devil to ask him to end the mission. I wanted to do the right thing, and he almost killed me. That's the night I tried ending things with you, after I survived and freaked out. Honey convinced me to really try to pass the tests. To get out of Hell, and to be with you … I decided then that I would. I was going to turn my afterlife around, even with The Boss looming in the background, ready to end my existence at any given moment.

"Then we had our date, you said you loved me, everything. It was the greatest day of my afterlife. I wanted to leave everything behind and be with you forever starting then. But life didn't stop. I still had to do my demon duties. I couldn't say no to you about Halloween, but I couldn't abandon the mission that I'd been working on for months—another death threat if I failed. When you caught me and looked at me in disgust for what I was doing, I felt utterly ashamed. I knew in that moment that I really was a bad guy who didn't deserve you.

"To top it all off, The Devil threatened your life if I ever saw you again. That's why I ended things. I knew I had to protect you and that you wouldn't go down without a fight."

He looks up from the floor with tears in his eyes. "Angelica. I am so, so, so sorry for what I said to you. I didn't mean any of it. I just couldn't imagine you dying because of me. I thought I was doing the right thing."

Her eyebrows knit together as she processes what he said. *He left to save you ... but he still lied from the beginning and ripped your heart apart.* "Well, I appreciate your apology."

"I'm not finished," Damon says, wrapping a hair tie around his hair. "I didn't just call you to apologize. I wanted to show you I have changed ... and that I want to be with you. I want to crush these tests and become an angel. For real this time."

Angelica opens her mouth to object, but he raises a hand.

"Since a few nights after the breakup, I have been in

contact with an angel who has been helping me continue on with my studies. I have been volunteering at the same shelter we did together." He pulls a folded piece of paper out of his pants pocket and places it into her hands. "I even had Karla give me a service hours sheet in case you needed proof."

Angelica reads the document. He's right—Karla wrote down the exact date and times he's been there the past few weeks. Her heart starts to soften.

"I have also been trying to help as many random people as possible that I can. Just last week, I went to NYC again and helped make meals for the homeless. I've been going to restaurants and tipping people twice the percentage. Oh, you'd like this; I stopped to say hi to Brandon, and he finally got his big break in a Broadway play!"

She meets his eyes.

"But even though I'm trying, I can understand if you still don't want to forgive me. I was a complete ass, I know. Plus, you are in literal danger if you decide to, so …" He sighs but then straightens up. "Regardless, I will take the angel tests, and I will love you the rest of my eternity—no matter if The Devil kills me again or if I become an angel and spend forever in Heaven."

After Damon finishes confessing his undying adoration for her, he waits. He wants to give her time to process and really think about what he said—and hopefully realize how much he cares for her. If she takes him back, he will spend the rest of his afterlife proving to her every day how much he loves her.

A tear slips down Angelica's face, and she swipes it

away. "Damon ... I don't know if I can just forgive you right now."

"That's okay. You don't have to today. I know I hurt you, and I know it will take time. But I will wait for you no matter how many days it takes." He gives her a crooked smile. "I'm not going anywhere, little angel."

She raises an eyebrow. "I thought you said you'd leave me alone forever if I said I wanted you to?"

"Yeah, well, that was a lie. I can't stay away from you. I love you too much ... you're my soulmate."

Angelica touches her braided hair. "Is that so? How can you be so sure that I really am your soulmate?"

Damon leans over to her, only inches away from her face. "Remember when I hugged Cora at the Halloween party?"

"Yeah?"

"I felt nothing. No electric buzz. No warm fire."

Angelica's eyes widen, and she clutches the bottom of her sweater. "Nothing out of the ordinary?"

He shakes his head. "No."

"So ... that means ..."

"It isn't an angel and demon thing." His lips part in a ginormous smile. "It's a you and me thing."

"We really are soulmates," Angelica says, her heart bursting in her chest. She sniffles once before the gates holding back her tears break and tears flow down her face. She throws herself into Damon's awaiting arms and buries her face in his shirt.

"You ... douchebag ..." she cries. "How could you

have just let me go? Say all those horrible things? I know you want to protect me, but you should've just told me the truth."

"I know, sweetie, I know. I'm sorry," he says, kissing her forehead.

"Don't ever leave me again."

"I won't," Damon promises.

Angelica sobs harder, pulling him closer, enclosing herself within his arms. "I love you so much, Damon."

He kisses her hair, her forehead, and her cheeks before pressing his lips to hers softly. "As I love you, Angelica."

Chapter 38

Damon and Angelica hold each other in the recliner while Angelica cries. "I never thought I'd see you in pink." She giggles through her tears.

"I knew it was your favorite," he says, kissing her forehead again.

"Wait, who has been helping you with all the angel stuff?" she asks even though she is pretty certain she knows the answer.

"Cora, of course. She agreed to help me even though it took a little convincing."

Angelica laughs, sitting back to look at Damon in the face. "I'm happy to have her."

"Me, too." He runs his fingers through her dark hair. "I like the hair."

"I don't!" She admits, crying harder. A few seconds later it is blonde again.

He shakes his head and wipes her tears away. "Beautiful either way, but you're right, you do look better blonde."

She sniffles. "One note, though—I'm still technically in danger of being murdered by The Devil, right?"

Damon shrugs. "Not really. Honey said he is mostly all talk, and killing you would start a huge problem with Gaia and your Father, so I wouldn't worry about it."

She wipes her nose with her sweater sleeve. "Okay, good."

He starts grinning madly. "Hey, I have a surprise for you."

"Oh?"

He helps her stand and then walks to the middle of the room, raising his hands and motioning all around them. "Ta-da! I bought this for you!"

Angelica looks around the walls and tables for a present. She doesn't see a wrapped box or bag anywhere. "Uh ... bought what?"

"The house, silly."

Her head whips to him. "You ... bought us the house?"

Damon's grin widens, and he shoots his eyebrows up and back down again.

"Why?"

"Well, until I become an angel, we don't really have a place to meet or be together, and I really didn't want to go to my parents' cabin every time ... so I bought us our own place. Just for you and me." He looks around proudly. "What do you think?"

Angelica observes the room again, this time taking it in with fresh eyes. One wall is just a window looking out to the ocean under a cloudless blue sky. A brick fireplace sits in the middle wall with white shelves built into it on each side. Next to the robin egg blue chairs they were sitting on is a long white couch with a small circular coffee table in front of it. She notices a candle burning bright on it and recognizes the smell of warm vanilla, her favorite scent. Second to cinnamon, of course.

Second to cinnamon, of course.

"It's beautiful." She gapes, thinking about it being theirs. Together.

Damon grabs her hand. "There's so much more to see! Let's go look."

"Why Greece?" Angelica asks as he pulls her through the house.

"I remembered from our question game that it is one of your favorite places to visit. I figured it'd be a good idea—get me some brownie points." He winks.

"It was. Extra points for sure." She giggles, kissing their intertwined hands.

The kitchen is the next room with only a small wall separating it. Angelica surveys the small kitchen and runs her fingers over a wooden table. The cabinets are all white with blue door handles, and a light blue backsplash accents the wall perfectly. Fresh fruits and veggies are tucked away in the corner as well as spices and baking supplies. As she looks through the kitchen, she envisions herself baking warm chocolate chip cookies on a spring day. Damon comes home from work, hugging her from behind before kissing her cheek and stealing a cookie. Angelica giggles as she thinks of all the opportunities they will have in this kitchen.

"Lots of blue," she comments.

"Well, they were out of pink," Damon jokes before pointing. "There's a back porch that overlooks the water that I really like. I can't take credit for the decorating or anything—I had Honey's help. We tried to keep it minimal in case you want to change something. Are you ready to go upstairs?"

He doesn't wait for an answer as he ushers her towards the staircase.

Angelica is still speechless as they step onto the second floor. It is small with only four doors. The first door guards a bathroom with a standing shower and the rest of the essentials. The second is a broom closet.

Damon clears his throat, his face pinking. "This way is our bedroom …"

She opens the door on the left, and her eyebrows raise as she notices the furniture inside. Two bedside tables, an armoire, and a dresser. And then one bed.

They were sleeping together at the cabin, but the enormous four-post canopy bed with tulle curtains falling from the top makes it seem more real here. More meaningful.

Angelica's face pinkens, too. *Our bedroom.* "It's very nice."

"Indeed." He chuckles. "There is one more room …" He motions to the unopened door on the right, smirking.

She narrows her eyes at him but opens it. When she looks inside, she stands speechless.

A white desk with a brand-new laptop—still covered

in plastic film—is the first to catch her eye. Next to the laptop sits four notebooks, pens, sticky notes, and a gold wire basket filled with other writing accessories. A pink fuzzy chair in the corner faces a window, and next to it is a small hutch filled with coffee mugs, a pink single-serve coffee maker sitting on the top.

"An office?"

"Yeah, for your poetry and stuff. Although I will probably use it from time to time to paint," Damon says, motioning to his easels poking out of the closet.

Angelica notices a painting hanging on one wall, and she walks closer to inspect it. It is a close-up of a blonde woman in a pink dress, holding a wine glass. Angelica turns to Damon with a grin. "Did you paint this?"

"Yeah, I finally finished my homework. Although I did cheat a little. This was the first painting I ever created of you—the dress was originally blue, but I repainted it to match the room. I painted this the day we went to the animal shelter."

Cupid's arrow shot into Angelica's heart. "Damon. This is the sweetest thing that anyone has ever done for me. The house, the room, the painting ... all of it."

The pure, indescribably feeling of love courses through their veins as she crosses the room and holds him. She is so happy that she was right about everything—he was lying about not loving her. She knows he was stupid and should've just told her, but now everything is going to be okay.

"Not trying to buy your forgiveness or anything ... but does this make up for me being a complete dick?"

She giggles and pulls back to wink at him. "Mostly."

"So, what do you want to do first?" Damon asks, tilting his head to the side and smiling.

Angelica thinks about his words. They could walk down to the beach, start a movie, eat, anything … but only one thing could complete the perfect happiness that she feels right now.

"I want you to make love to me."

His eyes widen. "You … what?"

Angelica runs her hands up his body, pulls out the ponytail, and curls her fingers into his hair. She leans close to him so that her breath is on his lips when she speaks. "You heard me. I want you to make love to me."

Damon pauses only for a second before leaning down and meeting her awaiting lips. The world fades away as they kiss, Damon wrapping his arm around her waist and the other on the back of her neck. They hold each other as close as they can, sliding their tongues against each other's over and over.

They shuffle into the open bedroom behind them. Angelica giggles as they lay down, Damon getting on top of her. His mouth leaves hers to trail over her body, kissing her neck and nibbling her ear.

She raises her arms, requesting for him to slide off her sweater, and it quickly gets thrown on the floor.

Before he leans back down to her, Damon notices her face. "What?"

"The one day I'm not wearing my cute undies." Angelica laughs, covering her face with her hands.

Damon leans up to grab her wrists and pulls them away, laughing and biting down on her lip. Her hands trail over his shirt, unbuttoning as she went. He sits back to finish sliding it off, and she rubs her hands over his bare, sculpted chest.

He shivers. "I love you, Angelica."

"I love you, too." She smiles, grabbing his neck and bringing his mouth back to hers.

Damon kisses her mouth before moving down to her neck, then chest. Angelica lifts her back so that he can undo her bra, and once it's off, he immediately flicks his tongue and kisses her nipple.

He trails his hand down her body again to slide them under her jeans, but this time she doesn't stop him. Damon leans back up to kiss her, and when his fingers rub against her sweet spot, she moans into his mouth.

"Damon," she pants.

He bites her neck again and then leans back to watch her face contort in pleasure. When she opens her eyes and makes eye contact with his, he licks his lips hungrily and moves down her body.

When he slides off her pants and his mouth meets the spot he was just rubbing, Angelica arches her back and cries out in pleasure. This is nothing like she's ever felt before. He wasn't kidding—he is way more skilled with his tongue. The way it flicks and twists and rubs all over her, each stroke increasing her desire for him. He teases his fingers down her middle thigh before easing them into her.

That does it. She tangles her fingers in his hair, moving against him until she explodes. Ecstasy flows through her and the flames that she feels when she touches him are nothing compared to the fire rushing through her veins at this moment. Damon doesn't stop as she orgasms, going for as long as he can until she sits up and grabs his face to bring him to her. He quickly grabs his shirt and wipes his face before she brings their lips back together.

"How did that feel?" he mumbles.

"Like Heaven."

She reaches for his belt buckle and undoes his jeans, holding onto him and stroking lightly. Now he is the one to groan.

"I need to get inside you," he says gruffly, moving her hand away and shoving off his pants and boxers.

Angelica lies back and spreads her legs eagerly, not at all embarrassed about being completely naked in front of him. She is completely, totally in love. And totally ready to make love with him.

Damon pulls her body close to him, and she giggles in anticipation. "Are you ready?" he asks, positioning himself in between her legs.

She nods.

With a slight push, he is inside her. Both of them intake a sharp breath as he fills her and slowly moves back and forth, in and out. He angles himself so they can still kiss, and their lips don't break apart until his fingers find her again and she is forced to gasp. He leans back to admire her and groans.

That sound makes Angelica feel even better.

All the buzzing, flicking feeling of electricity that they

feel when they touch has been magnified as their bodies connect as one. Both of them are in a state of pure euphoria as Damon pounds into her. Their souls connect as their bodies combine.

"Fuck, baby." Damon groans. "I'm getting close."

His fingers circling Angelica merged with the shaft of him penetrating her make her feel the same. Her hips rise up as she tips over the edge once more, calling out his name. The way she looks under him is his undoing—he cries out with her as he releases.

He leans down, laying on her chest with her legs wrapped around him.

"Damon ... that was ... amazing," she gasps, trying to catch her breath.

He looks up to her and rests his chin on her chest. "I'll say."

They giggle, and he kisses her before standing to clean them both off. Angelica lays there, naked, in complete bliss.

Damon walks to the bathroom, and she hears him turn on the shower. When he comes back, he leans against the doorway, one hand above his head. She admires his gorgeous naked body from top to bottom.

"Would you like to shower with me?" he asks.

Angelica sits up and nods before biting down on her lip. "As long as we can do that again."

Damon's answer is scooping her up off the bed in his arms and carrying her out the room, Angelica laughing all the way.

Chapter 39

The next morning, Damon wakes to the smell of brewing coffee and Angelica's side of their bed empty. He yawns and stretches, his muscles aching from all his exercise with her yesterday. He grins to himself as he throws on a T-shirt and heads to the kitchen. Angelica is mixing sugar in her coffee when he walks in and wearing one of his T-shirts as a mini dress. In this moment, Damon knows that he loves her with his complete heart and soul and can never love another person more.

"Good morning, sleepyhead," she says, giggling when he kisses her cheek.

"Good morning, gorgeous."

"I snooped around the kitchen and found tons of breakfast ideas! I was thinking pancakes, what do you think?"

Damon pours himself a cup of coffee. "Pancakes sound great."

Angelica smiles and starts gathering the supplies. Damon sits at the kitchen table, watching her flit about the room. As he watches her mix pancake batter, he thinks about how perfect yesterday was. The lovemaking was a plus, but seeing her frolicking on the beach, eating pizza with her on the couch, and then sleeping in her arms made it that much more perfect. Being with Angelica is the best feeling ever. She makes him laugh and smile, and his heart aches with adoration. And making love to her wasn't dark and demanding like Chloe. It was soft, meaningful, and filled with pure, true love. If this is a sneak-peek into the rest of his afterlife, he knows it will be nothing short of perfect. He is one lucky son-of-a-bitch, that's for sure.

As he watched her sleeping in his arms last night, the perfect idea popped into his head.

"So, I've been thinking …" he says, his voice wavering.

She pours the pancake batter onto the hot stovetop. "Yes?"

"I want you to promise me something."

Angelica flips the pancake and then raises an eyebrow towards him, hearing the nervousness in his tone. "And what is that?"

"If I pass these angel tests and become an angel, you have to marry me."

Her stomach jumps into her throat. She turns to look at him, and his smile is the biggest, albeit orneriest, smile that she's ever seen yet. "I think you meant to say that you'll *ask me* to marry you."

He laughs and rolls his eyes before correcting himself. "Okay, fine. If I become an angel, I'll *ask you* to marry me."

Angelica squints at him and his wide smile. Damon

becoming an angel and then becoming her husband? She can't think of anything more perfect.

"Would you say yes?" he asks, cocking his head to the side.

She shrugs and turns back to the stove, scooping the pancake onto a plate and setting it in front of Damon. A coy smile is on her face. "I guess you'll have to pass to find out."

Chapter 40

Chloe backs away from the small window, her vision red.

It's your own fault for stalking him. He said he didn't want you!

She reaches for her phone to delete the tracking app she downloaded on her and Damon's phone but decides against it. It may come in handy for future reference. She glares at the couple one last time before teleporting back to her apartment.

Chloe sinks down at her vanity and cries.

No one has ever seen Chloe cry, and she likes keeping it that way. But seeing Damon with Angelica, them laughing and kissing and making breakfast together, after everything she tried to do to stop them, breaks her. When her friend, Cypress—well, more like a person she was manipulating—said he saw Damon buy a house in Greece, she was intrigued. What was he playing at?

When she saw on the app that he was there, she went to scope it out, and low and behold, she saw *that angel* making coffee in one of his T-shirts. For thirty seconds,

Chloe seriously debated murdering her in cold blood, but then Damon walked in the room, and she was transfixed. She watched them giggle and kiss and look at each other with adoration.

Then she heard Damon say he was going to marry that *angel* someday ...

Chloe can't even think about it.

That was all she ever wanted with Damon. Who cares if she slept with their boss? Who cares if she was a huge bitch sometimes? In love, people see the good and the bad. She loved him. But she was never good enough for him.

And now he is going to become an angel and marry her, too. He will get the perfect life, but without her.

Anger replaces the pain in her stomach. She looks at herself in the mirror and wipes away her tears. *No. He will not get away with this.*

Chloe reapplies her favorite shade of lipstick. The blood-red shade accentuates her brown skin perfectly, highlighting the warm tones in her cheeks. She revels in the powerful look that it gives her. She adjusts the black mini dress she is wearing and fluffs her big, curly afro with her fingers.

Remember who the fuck you are, she instructs her reflection.

Without a second thought, she stands and leaves her apartment to walk to The Devil's office. Her red stilettos echo through the void with every step. She knows that he is busy with his new wife, but he would never say no to her. He might be her boss, but he is wrapped around her finger.

Outside of the apartment complex, Jeremy is leaning against the building, smoking a cigarette. He looks up from his phone when she clicks by. "Where are you off to, lady?"

She doesn't even glance at him as she struts off. "I have some pertinent information to share with our boss."

Jeremy tosses his cigarette on the ground. "This isn't about Damon, is it?"

"Nope."

He sighs and jogs to catch up with her. "Babe. Let it go. There are plenty of other guys who are begging to be with you."

She scoffs, "I don't care. He messed with the wrong girl, and now he will pay."

"What is your plan?"

"Oh, nothing too big. I'm just going to tell The Devil that he is continuing on with his little plan to become an angel and leave us. Directly disobeying his commands."

Jeremy stands in front of her, putting his hands on her shoulders and forcing her to stop. "Chloe. Don't. It's not worth it. Let him be. If you truly loved him like you say you do, you will let him go."

Chloe ignores him and glares. "You know who the fuck I am. I will not let him get away with this."

"So you're going to completely fuck up the rest of his life—probably get him murdered—just because he doesn't want to be with you?"

She shrugs out of his grasp, strutting past him. He doesn't follow, shaking his head. After she's a few feet away,

Chloe looks back over her shoulder, her face turning up into an evil, remorseless smile.

"Absolutely."

END OF BOOK 1

Coming Soon

Dark Perfection
Book 2

Acknowledgements

Thank you to my mother, who listened to all the stories I used to tell as a child and help me write them down. Thank you to you and dad for pushing me to keep writing all these years and supporting me every step of the way! I love you so much!

Thank you to my husband who pushed me to actually finish this book! Thank you for holding me each time I cried out my frustrations and listening to my endless ranting and planning of the story. And for making me sit down and work on it when I wanted to give up. Wicked Transcendence would never have been finished without you! I love you forever.

Thank you to my coach, Ramy, at Self-Publishing School for making me love my writing and my abilities! Thank you to Self-Publishing School for teaching me everything I need to know about self-publishing.

Thank you to my BETA Readers, Angela and Elodie. Your feedback made Wicked Transcendence that much better!

Thank you to Jenny, who is the best editor ever! I hope

you know you're stuck with me forever now hehe. Thank you to Les for my beautiful cover art! Like, WOW!

Thank you to my friends who have supported me this whole journey, the writing community on TikTok and Instagram, and everyone else who have rooted for this story.

And thank you to YOU! Thank you for reading my book. This story is ten years in the making and I have loved writing it for you. I truly hope you enjoyed it.

About the Author

Pandora Bluett was born and raised in Springfield, IL. She knew she wanted to be an author when she won her school's Young Author competition in the fifth grade. She has been writing her whole life, and this is her first fiction novel! When she isn't writing, you can find her reading, baking, crafting, napping, and spending time with her family.

Pandora also writes poetry under the name Cheyenne Bluett.

Instagram - @thepandorabluett
www.cheyennebluett.com

Can You Help?

Thank You For Reading My Book!

I really appreciate all of your feedback,
and I love hearing what you have to say.

I need your input to make the next version
of this book and my future books better.

Please leave me a review on Amazon letting
me know what you thought of the book.

Thank you so much!

xoxo,
Pandora